The Darkest Gift

A novel

Len Handeland

authorHOUSE·

AuthorHouse™
1663 Liberty Drive
Bloomington, IN 47403
www.authorhouse.com
Phone: 833-262-8899

Published by AuthorHouse 08/05/2021

ISBN: 978-1-6655-3073-6 (sc)
ISBN: 978-1-6655-3074-3 (e)

Print information available on the last page.

Any people depicted in stock imagery provided by Getty Images are models,
and such images are being used for illustrative purposes only.
Certain stock imagery © Getty Images.

This book is printed on acid-free paper.

Because of the dynamic nature of the Internet, any web addresses or links contained in
this book may have changed since publication and may no longer be valid. The views
expressed in this work are solely those of the author and do not necessarily reflect the
views of the publisher, and the publisher hereby disclaims any responsibility for them.

To my husband and eternal soulmate Byron and to my late parents Leonard and Ursula

"Yes, I now feel that it was then on that evening of sweet dreams, that the very first dawn of human love Burst upon the icy night of my spirit. Since that. I have never seen nor heard your name without a shiver half of delight, half of anxiety"
Edgar Allan Poe

Table of Contents

Acknowledgements

I want to thank my beloved husband Byron Hancock, for his love, support, patience, and encouragement in writing this book. To my late parents Leonard and Ursula, who raised a very complex and imaginative son. They inspired me to always do my very best as I continuously reached for the stars, I'm eternally grateful! Naturally, my gratitude extends to my lifelong obsession with vampires, which I fell in love with as a small boy extending all the way into my adulthood.

CHAPTER 1

Fabien And Stefan (Fabien Narrates)

Some have said there are advantages to being a younger son. The older son got all the land, but the younger son has more freedom. Nothing was more important to me.

My older brother did not understand why I wanted freedom; —I didn't realize it myself at the time.

"Why do you want to go to Paris?" he asked me when, after our father's death, I applied to him for money. Teasingly, he added, "Do you want to see all the fine ladies of the court?"

This was a standing joke with him, my supposed finicky taste in women. I had reached the age of twenty-two without ever having had a sweetheart of any kind. My sisters teased me about an acquaintance of theirs who, (they said,) made eyes at me and whose heart they accused me of breaking. Did I think I was so good-looking I could have any girl I wanted without troubling myself to be polite?

Well: I *was* good-looking; I did not know why I should deny it. Naturally, I did not say that to my sisters, but I did say the girl in question was not exactly the reigning beauty of the Loire Valley. I would not go so far as to say she was ugly, but surely, I could do better than that.

My sisters went into gales of laughter, and from that day onward, my arrogance was added to my being highly selective as a subject for teasing.

How I longed to get away from them! I wanted to leave and needed to get away from country life, with its few neighbors and its dearth of entertainment. By the time I asked my brother for money, I did not know exactly what I wanted, but I had a fairly good idea of what I did not want.

"Here, take this," my brother said to me, handing over a small bag in which coins clinked against each other. "It's not much, I'm afraid. I don't know why you want to live in Paris when you can live here so much better on so much less. Be sure to call on our cousins in the Marais as soon as you can. The Vicomte is said to be easily offended." These cousins were the Vicomte d'Amboise, which consisted of an elderly bachelor, and those of his family who lived with him—his widowed niece Louise and her young son.

My sisters wished me good luck on finding a wife suited to those fastidious tastes of mine; and two days later, I set out with the servant Jacque walking behind me, carrying my things.

Jacque was able to talk with other servants along the road, with the result that, by the time we reached Paris, we had a guide to show us the city. It was summertime, and we were glad to stop at an inn on the edge of the city, where they furnished us with water both to drink and to wash off the dust of the road, and then with a simple meal. The proprietor himself served us. He was full of a place called the Café Alexandre, which he had visited for the first time earlier that day. Apparently, it was the newest place to see and be seen. While I was wondering what the word *café* meant, he asked us if we had ever tasted coffee.

"What is it?" I asked.

"It is the most exquisite drink from the East that tastes like nothing else. It is rich and yet somewhat bitter—but somehow the bitterness adds to rather than detracts from the flavor." He had bought a small amount, ground, from the Café Alexandre, and he insisted on brewing us some. With the enthusiasm of a true aficionado, he said that if he were looking for new quarters—which he wasn't—he would look for rooms near the Café Alexandre, so he could have coffee every day.

Jacque and I and our guide, Luc, laughed at the man's enthusiasm as we walked on into the great city, but in the end, we were so curious that we ended up visiting the Café Alexandre. By the time we got there, night had fallen.

Jacque and Luc soon got into conversation with a waiter. He was clearly giving them directions of some kind.

"He knows of some rooms that might be what you're looking for," Jacque explained.

"Attic rooms," the waiter said apologetically. "But I understand that may be what the gentleman requires."

"Admirable," I said. "But we will have some coffee first."

We were glad to sit down. I looked around at the café and marveled. First, I marveled at the great number of people who managed to crowd themselves in. All of Paris was like that to me, though. Country-bred as I was, I was struck by the density of the population. The café was also remarkable for its mingling of the classes. I had never seen anything like this before. There were bakers with loaves of bread for sale and apprentices who had no money to pay for a drink and were standing round as if waiting for someone to pay. Up the social scale were master craftsmen—printers showing around their latest pamphlets, tailors showing off their latest coats. Then there were lawyers' clerks and such-like, and the lawyers themselves—I guessed that was what they were by their inkpots and pens and long rolls of parchment, and by the arguments going on around them—and then there were gentlemen, the members of the upper class, in silk suits and stockings and long, curly brown wigs.

One of these gentlemen caught my eye with his, which was bluer than any eye I had ever seen before. This blue-eyed man held my gaze for some moments, long enough to signal to me that his glance was not an accident. He was perhaps the finest gentleman there, judging by the white lace that overflowed his bright blue vest. This lace was of a quality I had never seen before, and it was as clean and fresh as if he had just put it on for the first time. What was even more remarkable was that his skin was as white as his lace—a smooth porcelain-like complexion, as beautiful as it was strange. As he held my gaze with his eyes, which grew more intensely blue every moment, I began to feel embarrassed—yet it was a pleasurable sort of embarrassment. I did not look away. I was confused but somehow thrilled as well. These were the sort of looks I had seen men and women exchange. And with that thought I realized what the most remarkable thing of all was: *there were no women in the café*.

Was this the paradise I had come to Paris unknowingly seeking? I suddenly became exhausted. It took too much effort to go on gazing into those unearthly eyes. Jacque and I left the café and crossed the street, and just around the corner we found the sign of a mortar and pestle that marked an apothecary's business. The apothecary was just closing shop, and when he was done, he showed us upstairs to the rooms.

They truly were nothing more than an attic, fairly large but entirely unpainted, and unadorned in every way. There was a bed and a table and two chairs, and aside from a cupboard and a washstand, that was all the furniture. For Jacque there was a minute room that doubled as a broom closet. I stepped across my own room and looked out of a dormer window. All was black in the night, but since there was no trafic abroad at that hour, I could hear people at the café, around the corner. I heard a strange, far-away sound of music and clinking glasses and laughter.

Was I happy I came to live as a poor man in Paris? I could not have expressed how happy I was.

There were no curtains on the windows, so I awoke in the morning with the sun. Leaving Jacque asleep, I went down the stairs and into the street, seeing it for the first time. Few people were abroad at that hour, and the shops were all closed. However, Café Alexandre was open. I went in gladly and asked a waiter what time they had opened. He told me that the café never closed. As soon as the last stragglers of the night had gone home, the first of the men taking their wares to market arrived, wanting coffee and a shot of brandy to go with it. Could he get some brandy for me?

I declined and said I wanted only coffee and rolls. A hungry young man of twenty-two can eat rolls almost without number, so while I ate, I had plenty of time to observe the life of the café. Men came in and discussed the news of the day. I heard "the king" mentioned several times, and the name of his present mistress, and I caught mention of a duel to take place in the Bois de Boulogne, of various tennis matches, and of the latest opera to be put on. I listened to everything with great interest, but what I was really doing there was waiting for my gentleman with the blue eyes and immaculate lace. I sat most of the day waiting in the café for him, getting up to take a stroll round the streets and to see that Jacque was provisioning us properly.

Our guide from yesterday turned up—the one who showed us first the Café Alexandre and then the rooms I was letting. For a few *sous* he showed me some of the sights of Paris. Despite my exhaustion of yesterday, we walked as far as the Ile de la Cité to see the Cathedral of Nôtre Dame, and to climb the bell tower to see the city of Paris laid out before us. It is hard to describe how I, a farm boy who had never seen anything higher than the roof of the parish church, felt when I saw the full magnificence of Paris.

When we got back to the café, I paid and dismissed my guide, and, giving up for today on my gentleman in blue, I was ready to climb the stairs to my attic. The sun had gone down about an hour ago, though, and I thought I would have a brandy before going home. I turned to look for a waiter, and there he was, wearing the same blue breeches and vest, the same lavender coat, the long brown wig, and the lace at his neck that was as white as the first snow. And he was looking at me with those bright blue eyes. Staring, really. Not to be intimidated, I stared back. Finally, he smiled. With one hand, he indicated a table with a chessboard set up upon it. I took a chair and we sat down opposite each other.

"I am a habitué here. You are the guest and must take the white" were the first words he ever said to me.

Since I was young, I thought myself to be an excellent chess player, ready to match my skills with the best the capital had to offer. I had often played against my sisters and my brother and beaten them all. However, my father would never take me on—and that should have told me something.

This gentleman checked me in two moves. He did not actually laugh at me, but he did smile out of the corner of his mouth. We played another game and this time he checked me in three moves.

"Sir, I perceive I am out of my class," I said. "I thought myself a good player at home, but I had only my family to play against me, and I see now that what we called chess was very different from the game you play. I am not worthy to play against you, sir."

It was clear the gentleman had enjoyed dominating me game after game. He was pleased by my tribute, however, and he smiled at me now in a more indulgent way. "I suppose you must learn from me, then". And he proceeded to show me a series of maneuvers. I would have felt foolish except he so obviously enjoyed instructing me.

A waiter stopped at our table and said, "Milord?"

"Two tankards of ale," my gentleman—my lord—answered without raising his eyes from the chessboard.

Now, assuredly, I would learn his name.

"If you buy me ale, you must know my name," I said boldly. "I am Fabien Levesque" I waited.

"Stefan, Baron of Vitré."

There, it was on the table: if he were an aristocrat, he would have heard the name Levesque. Although I was no better dressed than a tradesman and Stefan was clearly a member of the court, we were both members of the aristocracy. Things between us were now put on a new footing. We could associate openly. We might even visit each other without risking suspicion from anyone. It was a great step forward, and I began to hope I would see Stefan again even after this night was over.

When our ale arrived, we drank the health of the king. I drank freely while Stefan sipped. By the time I got to the bottom of my tankard, I could feel my face getting warm — the ale was strong. Notably, however, Stefan's face remained that uncanny white. I wondered if he were ill.

We lingered over the chessboard long into the night. Other men joined us to watch and to learn from Stefan. I gave up my seat to a man who wanted to play, and Stefan finished him off in a matter of minutes. I couldn't help observing that Stefan had given me much more leeway— had allowed me to lose much more slowly—as if he had enjoyed my company and wanted to keep it. He beat several other gentlemen. By then it was quite late.

"Come, let me take you back to your rooms," Stefan said. "Are they far from here?"

"No, just around the corner," I said.

"Nonetheless, it is pitch dark, and you do not know how dangerous Paris can be at night. My carriage is waiting." He made a gesture to a servant who sat on the sidewalk outside of the café.

I did not want to look like some effeminate coward who could not be trusted to walk around the corner by himself, so I protested.

Stefan ignored my protest and repeated, "You do not know Paris. Come." He put down his tankard, and I noticed, with considerable surprise, that it was full. Those sips had been pretend: he had drank nothing.

Stefan brushed the servant cruelly aside and helped me into his carriage himself. He lifted me as easily as if I had been a cat. When he got in, he brushed his knee against mine. An accident, no doubt. However, the carriage was big, and there was no need for him to sit so close to me.

"This is it," I said when we came to the sign of the mortar and pestle. "Did the apothecary give you a key?" Stefan asked, and I had to admit I had not thought to ask.

"Here, give me that lantern," he said to his coachman; by its light, we picked up dirt clods from the street and threw them at every window we could reach. After a time, my landlord, the apothecary, appeared in his dressing gown, rubbing his eyes.

"Good night, my friend," said Stefan, and he tipped his hat to me and was gone.

The apothecary had taken Stefan's measure, so he scolded me little for waking him up. "I will have a key made for your lordship," he said.

"I'm not a lord. But I will be obliged."

I ought to have gone to visit my cousin d'Amboise the next day, but I could not pull myself away from Café Alexandre. I knew I was making an idiot of myself, but there I stayed, as fixed as if I had had a meeting planned. I played chess. I played cards. I listened to men talk politics, which was all new to me; at first the only name I recognized was that of the king, Louis. At last, as the sun waned, I ordered brandy. What a jackass I had been to suppose that that fine gentleman, Baron Vitré, had nothing better to do with his time than to hang around in a café with an infatuated young man! Didn't *I* have more important things to do? I asked myself angrily as I drank another brandy. If he showed up, he would know I had been waiting for him, and the power imbalance between us would weigh even more heavily on his side. I didn't even know if he had these kinds of feelings for other men. What a young jackass I was!

Thus I spoke to myself as I consumed my third large brandy. When it was empty, I sat the glass down and stood up—and the next thing I knew, I was grabbing at the table, and there was a crash as the dishes hit the floor. Everybody looked at me, of course.

"Don't worry; I'll take care of it" said a voice in my ear. Stefan's voice. I turned quickly, and our faces were so close we could have kissed. For a long moment, neither of us moved. I was staring into the depths of his blue eyes and seeing thoughts and images I had only seen before in my own mind.

The proprietor came forward, and Stefan moved his face away from mine, circled my bicep with his hand, and told the proprietor he would pay for everything. He brought out a gold coin that would have paid for everything many times over. The proprietor smiled and took it, and the café swirled back into its customary amusements. Stefan was still holding my arm. I was stock still, afraid if I attempted any move, my knees would buckle.

At last Stefan dropped my arm and moved away. He smiled in a quite ordinary way and said in a quite ordinary voice, "Did you do your duty and visit your cousin today?"

I blushed. "No, I'm afraid Cousin Geoffrey will have to wait one more day."

"And who is this Cousin Geoffrey? Is he a Chaumont?" "No, Geoffrey d'Amboise."

"The vicomte?" Stefan said in surprise. "I know him well. Let us call on him together."

"You mean tomorrow?"

"I mean tonight. He keeps late hours. Lately he has gotten an idea into his head that he dislikes crowds, so now he sits at home for an evening with no more company than his silly niece. He's decided he's going to read all the books in his library—which is an exceptionally dull one—so he's probably nodding into a volume of Euclid right now. He'll be glad to see us."

We got into Stefan's carriage, and he held my hand as if this were the most natural thing in the world to do. It was as cold as milk on a winter morning, but I decided I did not care. There had to be an explanation— some rare malady—and Stefan would explain when the time was right. I laid my head on his broad, strong shoulder.

CHAPTER 2

The Transformation Of Fabien

Stefan was right: Geoffrey was glad to see us. He sent his niece off to her room, put down his book, and asked the servant to bring Cordials. "Stefan never drinks anything, but you—"

"I have come to pay my respects to you, vicomte: I am your cousin Fabien Chaumont, just arrived in Paris."

"Little Fabien? The last time I saw you, you were—well, let us not go into the number of years that have passed. Sufice it to say you have done a good job of growing up. You were always pleasing to the eye, but now, well, you could get into any sort of trouble you liked."

I was shocked by his forthright immorality, but I could hardly say it displeased me.

"Yes, that's what Fabien has come to Paris for—trouble," said Stefan. "We must steer him in the right direction, mustn't we?"

"It seemed to me that if he's met you, he's in suficient trouble already," said the baron.

Stefan laughed hugely. He seemed pleased to be cast as someone who would corrupt youth.

The servant came in with a tray of cordials. The baron poured me a tiny glass of what turned out to be elderberry cordial, the same as we made at home.

"Yes, your dear Mother sends me a bottle every year," the baron said when I remarked on this.

From then on, the conversation dealt with all the new marvels of Paris: the opera, the ballet, the musical gatherings, the public dances, and the galleries where you could see fine paintings. Paris was quickly turning into a center for the arts, and the baron, for one, was glad about it.

"So much of the time, the city has been just like the country, only muddier. You've done well to come in the summer," the baron said as he caught me looking at my boots. "This new Paris will have the world flocking to it. It will be a city like no other."

"There's already the university," Stefan said.

"The university! A bunch of drunken, penniless would-be priests who would duel each other to the death for a bottle of cheap red wine! The university has not brought us any glory, and it never will. I don't hold with priests. I don't hold with the Church."

"And our precious Notre Dame de Paris, said to be the finest cathedral in Europe?" Said Stefan.

"Notre Dame is a thing of beauty in its own right," said the baron, and then he changed his subject to the opera. He planned to go tomorrow night, and would we care to go with him?

I had never heard any music in my life beyond the pipes and guitars that the peasants on our estate played on feast days. Before Stefan could answer, I said, "We would love to go with you!" "They're putting on a new opera by Lully, called *Persée*, at the Palais Royal. The king will be there, which means everyone will be there. Shall I meet you in my carriage at—?"

"Call for us at the Café Alexandre," said Stefan.

As we left, I thought to myself that life in Paris was going to be more magnificent than I imagined. Tomorrow night I would hear an opera for the first time—witness the new art of the ballet— perhaps even see the king. As for tonight, I did not even dare look ahead to what would happen when Stefan and I were alone. I was sure it would be the fulfillment of my dreams.

Stefan handed me into his carriage once again with those enormously powerful arms. I must admit I was growing to like it. His strength made me feel delicate and treasured. I wanted to give in to that strength and see where it would take me.

Stefan got in and called out to the coachman to start, and I heard the sound of the whip cracking at the horses.

The Paris night was so dark that Stefan did not bother to close the curtains before he took me in his arms and kissed me.

"What is wrong? Are my lips too cold for you?" he asked a moment later.

That was, indeed, what had made me draw back, despite all my desire for him.

"I have a rare circulatory disease. The blood does not flow properly. Do you wish me not to kiss you?"

"Oh, no, Stefan, I want nothing more in the world than for you to kiss me again and again."

Which he did, with his strong arms tightening me against him. I have no idea how long the drive was to the apothecary's, but I know I was surprised when we stopped there. Stefan withdrew his lips from mine. I tried to think what to say so that he would come upstairs with me. I wanted him so much I could hardly speak for confusion. He had a word with his coachman, who drove off into the night; and then I let us into the building.

It was just as dark inside as out, and I had to feel my way up to the attic stairs, with Stefan holding onto my coat tails. Just outside my room was a small table where a candle and a tinderbox always stood. I tried to strike a fire, but my usual skill at this had evaporated along with my nerves. Stefan took the flint and steel from me, and in a moment, the candlewick shone a muddy light. I was embarrassed that I had not bought a beeswax candle, being able to afford only tallow.

Stefan asked me if he was invited in. I looked at him with a confused look on my face and said, "Yes," We only needed enough light to show us to the bed. Closing the door, we pulled the curtains closed and then we were alone, as I had wanted to be with Stefan ever since the moment, I first saw him. We stood face to face, with him leaning forward to kiss me, deeply, passionately, our tongues wrestling with one another. He picked me up as if I were light as a feather and carried me over to the bed.

He threw me on the bed and then slowly nuzzled up to me growling a bit as he got closer and closer to me. He undressed himself and stood before me. I could tell he was aroused. His body reminded me of a marble statue, even though Stefan was obviously well to do, his body was not as soft as a woman's. No, every muscle was defined, his veins protruding, and his skin as white as the winter snow. "Undress!" he commanded me. I did as I was told, for I had longed and dreamed about an encounter such as this for as long as I could remember.

At once he was at my neck, licking it, smelling it as I heard myself groan with pleasure. Stefan continued making sexual advances along with licking and smelling my neck, which quickly led to him caressing both of my thighs with his large hands leading higher and higher until they had found their way to my buttocks giving them a slight squeeze. Then using his tongue he licked every inch of my body, returning from time to time, kissing me deep and passionately. At times I experienced various emotions, the feeling of anxiousness, as I had not been intimate with anyone before, man or woman. Feeling such incredible passion, as if I were about to burst out of my own skin, and a fear I could somehow not point my finger on. I had the feeling of being completely under his control, feeling powerless to prevent anything that I might not desire from happening.

I will not try to describe the ecstasy of that night, even though it was all about to change. Stefan took even more pleasure in dominating me than I guessed he would. I became his possession; before the small hours came, I belonged to him completely. As we lay back on the pillows, resting, Stefan stroked my hair away from my forehead and called me tender names.

"You really have made me hungry, Fabien," he said. "It's been a long time since I was with someone of your energy, your passion. However, now I must get up and go out to nourish myself."

"Shall I come with you Stefan?" I asked, feeling confused.

"No, this is something I need to do alone, soon you will join me" he said.

As I thought to myself, there were times when I felt I understood Stefan, and there were many times when his mood would change so quickly from a momentary display of tenderness to outright cruelty, as in this moment.

"But, when will I see you again?" I asked feeling weak and timid and suddenly aware of my nakedness. "We shall meet again at the café. Perhaps in a day or two, I cannot say for sure," he said coldly. "Good night, Fabien," he said.

"Good night, Stefan." I watched him leave, feeling confused and empty. While we were physically exploring each other's bodies, I felt as if I was his and he were mine, then suddenly everything changed? Perhaps the handsome gentleman I met at the café, had suddenly lost interest in me, as if I were merely some sort of conquest? The thought of finally having had a physical encounter with another man, and possibly losing him, or rather, him losing interest in me, left me feeling sad and empty inside. I knew I had to return to the café and win him over once again.

The next morning came and my mind once again became fixated on Stefan. All that mattered was to reignite the passion and tenderness we had shared before his sudden departure the night before. I made my way over to the café, hoping to see him sitting there, perhaps enjoying a breakfast, and perhaps he would be willing to have me join him. Instead, I arrived not seeing him, thinking perhaps he was trying to avoid me?

I ate my breakfast alone, asking myself, would I ever see him again? I decided I would return to the café that evening and perhaps I would see him again and my luck would return to me. Later that evening, I returned to see him seated with another man in the back of the café, engaged in a game of chess.

I walked over to where he was seated and asked if I could pull up a chair to observe the game. He merely glanced at me and returned his attention to the game, easily defeating his opponent. The man got up to leave and offered me his chair, as I nodded my gratitude to the stranger.

"Stefan, I don't understand why you left so abruptly last night," I said as I watched his expression.

He looked at me and glanced away saying, "I told you Fabien, I needed to satisfy my hunger" as he appeared to dismiss my question with a simple answer.

"Stefan, I have spent the entire day thinking of only one thing you. Thinking I must have done something wrong?" I said practically pleading with him. I hated the fact he had such a hold over my emotions and hated myself even more for allowing it. "When can we be together as we were last evening, I long for you?" I asked in a suggestive manner.

"Well, I am feeling a bit tired," he said, indicating he was willing to return to my room at this moment. He looked at me and grinned. I, all at once, felt a tremendous relief. He hadn't lost interest in me, and we were about to become once more intimate, my last night in fact as a mortal. I was about to learn everything about this handsome and cunning creature. We returned to my room above the apothecary, once again, as before, Stefan asking me if he could enter.

I replied "Yes, with pleasure," as we both broke out into laughter. "Will your servant be in?" Stefan asked softly.

"No, I let him go for the evening. He'll be at some whorehouse, no doubt, drinking watered wine by the quart and disporting himself with the ladies. He'll stumble in at dawn."

"Shall we go upstairs, then?" Stefan asked even softer. We made our way and entered my room. As soon as the door closed, we became as one, into a world of ecstasy and passion. Our bodies clinging together tightly, soft caresses, and deep passionate kisses. We walked over to my bed hand in hand, despite his icy cold touch, the flames of passion had ignited once more. We undressed each other and lay on the bed. Just as our first physical encounter had been, exploring each other's bodies yet again when Stefan froze; he stopped talking. He was listening.

Unfortunately, I had heard the same sound. They came from the bottom of the house, from the front door. I realized that in offering myself to Stefan a second time, I had omitted re-locking the door behind us. So, whoever it was had no difficulty gaining access to the house and only the difficulty of darkness in finding the stairs. Whoever it was stumbling and singing bits of a popular song as he climbed. It was my servant Jacque. Near panic, I told Stefan.

Stefan's reaction was one I could not have anticipated. He was not discomfited in the least. "Your servant, eh? Tonight, he'll serve me better than he has ever served you before."

I could not imagine what Stefan meant by this. Surely Jacque was about to provide the most scandalous of interruptions. I racked my brains for solutions to the problem as Jacque's footsteps sounded closer and closer. At the same time, I wondered at Stefan's actions. He had found the tinderbox next to the bed and was kindling a spark and then a fire. A stick from the fireplace smoldered at the end, first red, and then yellow. Did he want Jacque to see us?

No, that was not it at all. It was he who wanted to see Jacque. "Monsieur, monsieur, I am so sorry to be so late," Jacque said through the door. "I found the front door unlocked—maybe you have the key? I will go down and lock it."

With these words, Jacque opened the door to my room. Faced with a tall, powerful, naked stranger who seemed more like an animal about to spring at his prey than a human being, Jacque stopped in his tracks.

"Monsieur?" was all he had time to say before the horror began. I was too afraid to close my eyes to it—I was so afraid of Stefan at this point that I was afraid that I might be his next victim. But I was not the one chosen.

Stefan seized Jacque by the shoulders, pulled him close, and bent over him. No, no, this could not be, not Jacque! But as I watched, Stefan pierced Jacque's neck with those two extraordinarily long incisors, and he began to drink Jacque's blood. Perhaps the greatest horror was that Jacque was still alive—and, still worse, that his terrified eyes caught mine. I read in his gaze the belief that I would do anything to save him, as he would have done anything to save me.

How could I have looked on as Stefan murdered him? How could I have stood there and watched and done nothing to stop the carnage?

I have thought about this many times over the years, and I still do not understand it myself. I was paralyzed by fear, I felt there was nothing I could do, nor anyone on this earth that could have done anything to prevent this attack. I felt as if I had betrayed my servant, who felt more like a member of the family, my Jacque!

At last, after what seemed like a long time, the light in Jacque's eyes dimmed and then went out. My good servant Jacque was dead, and I had watched passively. My lover, Stefan, who had overwhelmed me with pleasure, now overwhelmed me with grief and terror. He turned toward me, and his face was that of an animal still seeking more prey. I shrank into the bedclothes, but that did no good. I had to fight him. His physical dominance, which had appealed to me so much when I was looking forward to being sexually overpowered, now took on a new and threatening aspect. There was no way I could crush this man—who was no ordinary man.

He saw my fear and began to laugh. He was delighted he had terrified me. For a moment, I thought my terror alone would afford him sufficient pleasure, but I might as well have expected a wild boar to lose interest in a newborn lamb. I was at his mercy, and I was nothing more than food to Stefan. His appetite for sex was just that, another appetite. He experienced no tenderness, no passion, nothing that made an encounter human.

I crouched in the corner, waiting for him to do whatever he would do. I could not think of a single way to defend myself.

He threw his massive body on mine, crushing me into the mattress, and he put his hands around my neck. Now no other part of my body interested him.

"Are you going to kill me?" I asked faintly.

"Oh, no, not you," said Stefan. "I have other plans for you."

His hands grabbed me and tightened on my throat. I noticed for the first time, his hands were warm.

"What are you going to do to me?" I insisted.

"I am going to make you one of my kind: a creature of the night, a vampire."

I had never heard the word before and he did not elaborate on the meaning of the word, saying only, "You will learn over time, but for now..." he said menacingly, as he bit into my neck and drew my first blood. He drank for a long time, as I got weaker and weaker. It did not matter much to me whether I died or lived. I thought I found love— the love I had unknowingly longed for all my life—and that love had turned to degradation and horror!

Stefan did not kill me, true to his word, I was about to be transformed into the same creature he was, a vampire. "You are very weak now: you must be strengthened, or you will die," he said as he bit his own wrist till

19

the blood flowed, and then he held his wrist up to my mouth and ordered me to drink. "Our blood combined will make you as I am."

"Go on, drink. It will not seem unnatural to you now," he commanded.

He was right. I was now as thirsty for his blood as he had been for mine, I clutched his wrist ever tighter. Once I had drunk enough, I sat there and thought about what I had done, asking, "What is a vampire?" Stefan said mockingly, "A vampire has the best of life, never needing to work, having nothing to do but go to parties and all these fashionable new amusements, the opera and the ballet, and mixing with the best of society."

Stefan continued to educate me, giving me an even greater clarity. That a vampire could change shapes at will into any number of animals, whether it be bat, wolf, or rodent. That a vampire could turn into mist or fog. That there was no longer a need for food or alcohol, in fact, if consumed by the vampire, it might generate extreme nausea. That the tears we shed are not the salt tears of mortals, but rather made of the same substance we needed to consume to survive, blood. That vampires had the ability to levitate, fly through the sky and move incredibly fast, so fast that a mortal's eye could not detect. That the vampire was free from sickness and death (or rather the traditional death which befell mortals) that the vampire was neither living, nor completely dead, in addition to the word vampire, there were other descriptions such as the undead. And lastly, that vampires were not entirely invincible as immortal beings. That sunlight would disintegrate a vampire. That fire could destroy us, as would a wooden stake through the heart.

"And killing innocent people to stay alive."

"Jacque? He was nothing. He was a mere servant. There are always more servants to replace him," he said cruelly.

"I think he was more than a mere servant to his Mother," I said. "Why are you so sentimental? I expected better of you. You seemed to enjoy the kind of life I lead."

"Jacque was not simply 'a mere servant' to me, either. I knew him all my life," I said.

Feeling enraged, it was at that moment I began to hate and distrust him. I realized he was diabolical, who not only took delight in luring me with his charm and his good looks, but also took great pleasure in destroying me, as well as Jacque or anyone he chose to. "I still feel the hunger," Stefan said, as he told me I would soon experience the thrill of the hunt, Stefan said mysteriously. "Come"

We got dressed and went out into the pitch-black street. I had an idea he would be looking for another victim to satisfy his cravings, however I was under Stefan's spell, and I would do whatever he told me to do.

Remarkably, we encountered someone right outside my building. No sooner had we left than a man approached us from the darkness, carrying a dagger and a lantern. He demanded we hand over all the money we had. Stefan's reaction was not that of any mortal man: he began to laugh uncontrollably, almost doubling over. The thief became enraged and took the dagger and stabbed Stefan in the stomach, and that was when the attacker realized Stefan was no mere mortal. He stopped laughing and removed the dagger from the thief's hand and threw it on the ground; there was no blood coming from where the knife had been thrust. The thief stood quite motionless, undoubtedly shocked.

"Shall we dine, Fabien?" Stefan asked, and with that he took the thief by the neck with his powerful hands and ripped open the thief's shirt, lunging towards his throat. Baring these large incisors, he bit into the man's throat. Blood spurted on the dirt below.

In a muffled voice, Stefan commanded me to join him. "Here, bite into his wrist," he said.

I knew I was powerless to resist, although I did not yet understand why, only that he made me into the same unholy creature as he. I followed his command, for now Stefan was my lover, as well as my maker and master, all my instincts told me to obey. In the time it takes to blink an eye, I took the man's wrist and bit into it. All the while the thief was screaming. In lawless Paris no one cared if you screamed, nor would anyone come to your rescue. We drained every drop of blood from this man, and we left the body propped up against a building as if the corpse were some poor marionette that had had its strings cut.

"How do you feel, Fabien?" Stefan asked. He had hold of the lantern now, and he held it up to my face.

"I feel as if an unquenchable thirst has for the moment been satisfied." I wiped the blood from my lips with my handkerchief, which I then handed to Stefan to use.

Stephan wiped his mouth as if he had finished a long and sumptuous supper. He spoke quietly, as his sensuality returned. "Shall we go back to your room?"

CHAPTER 3

Parting Is Such Sweet Sorrow
(Fabien Narrates)

The next morning, I woke alone. Stefan had left in the night, and mercifully he had taken Jacque's corpse with him. But as soon as I felt gratitude that I would not have to get rid of the body, my heart smote me. How could I think of Jacque, who had always been kind to me and was almost like a family member, as merely "the body"? This was Jacque, who had looked out for me since I was a tiny child with a talent for falling into water butts, finding patches of nettles to get lost in, and angering the ill-tempered ram.

I had a flash of memory now of Jacque throwing me up in the air and laughing as he made me laugh. He passionately loved to fish—particularly when he was supposed to be doing something else—and he taught me all the ways of angling. He loved girls, too. It sometimes seemed to me there was not a girl in the world that Jacque did not think was pretty, and he had winning ways of complimenting them. Someday I would be grown up, and I would admire girls just like he did. It came to me now that my brother had not chosen at random when he sent Jacque with me to Paris. No, indeed. Jacque's family had worked alongside our family since before anyone could remember, and Jacque himself had been looking out for me my whole life.

And now, because of me, Jacque was dead. For a night of

pleasure—my pleasure—Jacque had given his life. Instead of being glad of the removal of the body, I became anxious about what Stefan had done with it. It seemed doubtful Jacque would get the Christian burial he deserved—how would Stefan explain to a priest his possession of a dead body? You didn't walk into a church and say, "Hello, I've murdered this fellow. Would you please begin the requiem mass?"

No, Jacque's body would have been consigned to the Seine hours ago. As I thought of this, I wept; and as my tears fell on the white bed sheet, and I was startled to see that they were red, and in a flash, I remembered Stefan's words about creatures such as us not shedding mere mortal salt tears. And how white my hands were! My whole body was as white as Stefan's. And my heart, which should have been thumping—my heart was silent. I put my hand to my chest: nothing. With this thought I became more frightened than ever, but the worst had yet to happen. As the sun rose higher and the light in the room grew stronger, my skin began to burn as if I were in the Sahara Desert at noonday.

I quickly sought refuge in an empty trunk I had bought to store valuables in. The empty trunk would be used instead to provide me an escape from the blinding and blistering sun, which only a short time ago had provided pleasure and warmth and was now and forever-more my enemy.

I fell into a deep slumber, but I sensed the moment the sun set, and I climbed out of my chest. Stefan was sitting on my bed.

"Why did you leave me?" I asked him in an agitated voice.

"I had every confidence you would put that empty trunk to good use, and I was not mistaken," he said as he laughed. "You will come and live with me and give up this ridiculous room you have called home. Perhaps now you understand why I was a bit secretive with you?" His mood had abruptly changed: he now looked at me tenderly. He seemed to switch from cold and cruel to loving and caring in an instant. I didn't know exactly how I should feel about the man who was now my master.

I stayed with him. For a hundred years. I felt powerless to leave; I felt like his prisoner. Though he continued to be cruel, he also continued to be tender. After each incidence of cruelty, he lured me back with the hope of physical affection and bodily lust. I could see that he enjoyed having power over me: he delighted in controlling me and forcing me to kill uncontrollably, commanding me, cheering me on as I unwillingly stalked my victims alongside him. I felt that I had no choice but to remain with him.

We spent it pillaging the city of Paris as well as the countryside, feasting on the blood of human beings. Nightly we strolled through the parks or the darkened streets of Paris looking for victims. Sometimes we happened upon on a robber. Other times we would simply observe a patron from the café going out into the blackened streets of the city, and we would ambush him as he went around a corner into the darkness, where no one would hear the cry for help. It felt as if Stefan and I were unstoppable, since the police were powerless—they had no idea what was causing this endless list of casualties.

During this time, as was very much in keeping with Stefan's personality, there were also brief enjoyable outings. We attended dances and the opera. And the theater. However, every night invariably ended in slaughter. I recall one instance involving an entire family together, a Father, a Mother, and their children, along with their coachman, who had enjoyed a picnic outside in the Luxembourg gardens.

Stefan and I arrived after sunset as the family began to board their carriage. There were no other onlookers around except for the driver of the coach. Stefan felt it was the perfect opportunity to drain each one of them, including the two small children. I remember hearing the cries from the coachman, and from the husband as well as the wife to take their lives and spare the lives of the children. Stefan merely laughed a deep, diabolical laugh. I shuddered inside, knowing what he and I were about to do.

The first victim was the coachman, who pleaded for his own life, to no avail. He tried to run away but was tackled by Stefan's muscular frame. He was drained of blood in an instant.

Next came the father, who bravely held his screams to himself, eyes fixed on his wife and his children as if offering an unspoken final goodbye. He appeared stoic, finally uttering a sound more like a whimper, until his lifeblood flowed out of his jugular vein like a stream during a heavy rain, with Stefan lapping and sucking until the man was nothing more than a corpse. Next came the Mother, huddled with terror in the carriage, trying desperately to protect her children. She screamed "No, please, for the love of God, spare my children and me!" But it was useless. Stefan and I (under Stefan's command) attacked and killed her within a few short minutes.

All the while, I was heard the screams of the two small children, who appeared to be five or six, and who had wild-looking eyes that spoke of panic and terror. Taking the lives of the children left me feeling hollow inside, as if everything inside of me was empty—as if Stefan had destroyed my innocence and ripped out the last vestige of my soul.

I felt numb, abandoned, and guilty for existing. Just when I would begin to think some normality might be possible in our otherwise damned existence, my hopes would be dashed. So many times, I pleaded with Stefan to spare the lives of our victims. An inhuman and uncaring laughter answered my desperate pleas. Stefan was mocking me, and worse, I was beginning to question my sanity. Because my actions were not freely willed but forced, I felt as if I were a mere witness to them. It was almost an out-of-body experience. I did not want to grasp the horror I was helping Stefan to inflict on so many people; I did not want to look at their faces or see the terror in their eyes; I did not want to hear their cries for help or pleas for their lives. On more than one occasion I broke down and cried my blood tears, cursing Stefan and cursing myself as well.

My actions caused me to loathe more and more what I had become. As Stefan's accomplice, I had become what he was— a bloodthirsty animal. Even though I tried to maintain such human emotions as love and tenderness, I felt that these things were slipping away during the endless nights with their diabolical killing sprees.

Stefan knew my feelings for him were changing. When I met him at the café, believing him to be a man, I had become consumed with visions of passion and wanted to be with him forever. But he had become my tormentor. What was once lust and then love was turning now to contempt and hatred. Over time, I grew defiant, and, on more than one occasion, I shouted out loud to Stefan how much I loathed him. There was not a trace of love for him left in me.

I could tell he, too, was growing increasingly miserable: he would curse me and say, "You ungrateful bastard! I gave you a new existence, resurrected you, gave you powers beyond your wildest imagination, gave you immortality—and now you're unhappy! I wish I had never transformed you—I wish I had never given you my dark gift!"

There were two things that kept me by Stefan's side: the power he held over me—the power of the vampire maker over the fledgling— and the fear of never finding another male lover. Was I destined to spend my life alone if I left Stefan? I didn't know. But in the end, I had to chance it. I simply could not bear to be tied forever to this animal. There were countless times when I begged Stefan to release me, but each time he would laugh and say, "You are mine for all eternity!" But then one day—abruptly, without any apparent reason—Stefan did allow me my freedom. All I could guess was that there was a small trace of human feeling left inside him—perhaps a trace of pity. Or maybe there was a part of him that did love me. Whatever it was, he did free me. But my freedom came with a price—with a command he made to me.

He warned me never to make a fledgling vampire of my own. If I did, he would infallibly learn of it, and then he would destroy both me and my creation.

I believed him. I said I would obey this command, but I knew deep down it would be impossible. I would not be able to spend eternity on my own. How could anyone ever agree to such a thing? In my hundred years with Stefan, I realized he was one of those beings who are capable of existing on their own, not needing to be close to anyone, not needing companionship, not needing connection. He did not need an equal, a friend or companion, to share his eternal existence with. I had been but merely an apprentice of sorts. I wanted to be more than an apprentice. Although I loathed the creature I had become, I had not given up on finding someone who loved me and whom I could love in return. I was not going to inflict on another man the cruelty that my maker had inflicted on me: that was a rule I had firmly established for myself. I felt in my heart that by following this rule, I had a chance of finding and keeping my soul mate.

CHAPTER 4

Laurent And Fabien (Laurent Narrates)

I'll always remember the first time I saw Fabien. It was a warm spring evening in May; the year was seventeen hundred and eighty-two. We met at the Parc Monceau. I was there for an evening of festivities celebrating the king's visit. There would be a fireworks display. Fortunately for all the attendees, the sky was lit up with a full moon, making it appear as if daylight had combined with the dark of night. Looking around the park, I noticed an interesting mixture of people from various social classes. There were families present, and the children were running around; there were jugglers and acrobats to delight and entertain us. It seemed that the park created a casual atmosphere, because everyone spoke to one another, regardless of social status.

There was one who stood out from the rest of the crowd: a man wearing a most elegant blood-red brocade suit that emphasized his extraordinary pallor. I found him extremely handsome. He appeared to be having a passionate discussion with an equally distinctively dressed man, who was accompanied by a young woman around the age of seventeen. This elegant man at once turned to meet my gaze— I froze. His gaze was prolonged. It felt as if he were looking right through me. Finally, I managed a smile.

He smiled back at me.

I hesitated at first, but then I walked over in his direction: something drew me towards him. His smile was warm and inviting. As I got close, I observed he had a peculiar skin color. He was the color of milk. I tried not to stare at his skin and instead concentrated on listening to the discussion.

"My apologies, I hope I'm not interrupting?" I said, however awkwardly. As the man with the oddly colored skin turned towards me to smile at me once again. I was assured by the handsome gentleman who had smiled at me twice that I wasn't bothersome; however, I sensed that neither gentleman wanted to lose focus on the discussion.

I stood there smiling at the young woman who accompanied them, waiting for them to finish. But eventually the other well-dressed man became so incensed that he took a hold of the young woman's arm, abruptly said goodbye, and left to go to another area of the park. The handsome man with the pallid complexion laughed and shook his head slightly at the other gentleman's abrupt departure and refocused his attention on me. He asked, "What are your thoughts on the latest Lully?" Taken by surprise, I said, "I'm afraid I didn't hear enough to contribute to the discussion. What is it you seek my opinion on?" "The latest opera by Lully," he answered. "Whether it was as good as his last. Our late friend is, I am afraid, one of those enthusiastic souls who cannot admit his idol ever falls short in the smallest way. Whereas I was saying I thought the arias in general somewhat inferior to those in the earlier works. Not an earth-shaking discussion, I admit. I quite forgive you if you have no opinion on the matter."

"I am afraid I have not been to the opera lately," I said. "My attention has been much engaged by tennis matches."

"Oh, dear, yes, tennis. All the rage among Those Who Count. The king is trying to ban it, saying it detracts from the practice of religion. Which is odd, because it was invented by monks."

I named various well-known people—courtiers, some of

them— whom I had seen playing; and I admitted I wanted to play myself. I was looking for someone to instruct me.

"I may be able to help you out there," said the pale gentleman. "I am no champion, but on the other hand, I don't think you'd call me a slouch at tennis, either. Do you have a racquet? Excuse me, my name is Fabien Levesque."

I introduced myself as Laurent Richelieu.

"Well, Monsieur Richelieu, I know where you can get an excellent racquet if you don't have one already. I do have to warn you of one eccentricity of mine. I only play tennis at night. There's a sort of romance to it. If you have enough fellows with torches, it's no more difficult than playing tennis by day."

I thought to myself, this must be the most handsome man in all of Paris, despite his dead-white skin. His eyes were so blue they looked like jewels as they gleamed and danced with the light of the nearby candles.

"I take it you have been to this park before?" he asked.

"No, in fact, this is my first time. I came here to attend the festivities in honor of the king," I replied. I noticed Monsieur Levesque merely nodded and didn't seem too excited about the events about to take place. "I take it you are not an admirer of the king?" I asked.

"Without getting into a lengthy discussion, no, I am not," he replied. "I came here this evening mostly for entertainment. Look around you, jugglers and dancers and children running around wildly it is quite entertaining, wouldn't you agree?"

I nodded in response.

We talked more about tennis, and then it was back to Lully, and somehow, we ended up talking about the American war on everybody's lips in those days. Could the Americans succeed in establishing a real democracy or were they too hidebound in their English ways?

As Fabien asked this, his hand touched my shoulder. An accident? No doubt it was. I had never met another man who was as excited by the male touch as I was. But there, his hand once again took a hold of my shoulder, and this time he looked me in the eye. My heart pounded. Was I at last meeting a man of my own kind?

It is one of the peculiarities of humanity that often when we meet with what we have been looking for all our lives, our nerves overcome us, and we turn and run. This was what happened to me. I could not say goodbye quickly enough, but before I left, Monsieur Levesque and I agreed to meet once again.

"Must you leave so quickly?" he said, sounding a bit disappointed. "Yes, I must," I said.

"I would like to see you again, if that is possible," he asked.

I hesitated at first but answered him with the words "I frequent a café, maybe we could meet there."

"Which one? Hopefully not the Café Alexandre? I used to frequent it quite a bit in the past— I am trying to avoid running into someone from my past," he said mysteriously.

"No, the Procope," I replied.

"Are you free tomorrow evening, shall we say seven?" he said. "Yes, I will look forward to it, Monsieur Levesque."

Did I see the shadow of a smile on his face as he bade goodbye to me? Did he know what was going on with me? I could not stop myself from blushing as I turned to leave. Involuntarily I looked back. Monsieur Levesque was still looking at me, and yes, he was smiling.

I wondered who else he would talk to and how late he would stay. Somehow I had a feeling he would not leave the park any time soon.

All the way home, I kicked myself. I had found out very little about Monsieur Fabien Levesque beyond his name, and that he did not want to run into someone from his past at the Alexandre. However, I would find out more about him when we met at the Procope. I was grateful I had a follow-up meeting with him.

I went to the café the next morning, and, thinking that I might see him before our evening rendezvous, I ordered coffee and breakfast and stayed all day. I ate lunch. Disappointed that he had not shown up, I drank more and more coffee. I ate pastries that were fresh from the bakery down the street. The hours ticked by, beyond the agreed-upon time of seven, and doubt began to fill my mind. I kept telling myself I was making a fool of myself, and I should leave but I could not make myself do it. Who was ever in love that did not make a fool of himself? I consoled myself by saying this in my mind over and over and over. And still Monsieur Levesque did not appear. Surely I was the most ludicrous fool who had ever lived.

I gave up. I had been sitting at that café for eight or nine hours. I have to say that no one remarked on my continued presence; there were some men who had been there almost as long as I had, playing chess, and talking politics. Nonetheless, I felt like a jackass. I was getting up to leave when Monsieur Levesque appeared right in front of me. I had not seen him approach, though I was sitting in the front of the café and keeping an eye on all comers. I did not understand how he could have shown up out of nowhere like that, but I was in no mood to raise questions: I was just glad to see him. I did not even try to disguise my pleasure.

"I thought you would never come!" were the first words out of my mouth.

"Poor Monsieur Richelieu!" he said teasingly. "Have you been waiting long?"

"All day. I had to see you. Please call me Laurent."

"Certainly, if you will call me Fabien. Why all day? We agreed to meet at seven."

I reached into my pocket for my watch and said, "It is eight o'clock, Fabien."

"I am so sorry, I was completely famished and realized I hadn't dined for quite a while; I thought it best to take care of my hunger, as I am not very pleasant company to be around without any nourishment," he said.

I looked at him with bewilderment, thinking to myself, *they serve food here at the café. Could he not have had something to eat here, with me?* Nevertheless, I feigned laughter and said, "Apology accepted," as I observed a bit of a rosiness to his usually white complexion.

"I was thinking we might take in one of the sights tonight," Fabien said. "What do you say to a trip to the Palais Royal? There are all kinds of new shops there."

I agreed most readily, of course.

We hailed a closed carriage for hire, and as soon as we set off, Fabien took my hand and held it in his. My excitement was tempered by apprehension, as I had never held hands with a man before; nonetheless, it felt good, and his touch felt warm and comforting. I tried to appear confident and would not allow my thoughts to ruin the mood. He was, after all, holding my hand.

At the Palais Royal, we found a covered place, an arcade, filled with small shops that all had glass windows, something I had never seen before. There was pavement underfoot—also a new thing for Paris— and you could walk up and down the blessedly dry ground and look in all the windows without ever going inside to buy a thing. The goods on sale were costly; cloth and furniture and paintings and books and statuary all had their place. Around the arcade there were gardens, and theaters, too. All of Paris, both middle and upper class, seemed to be abroad in this safe and convenient arcade. No one was in a hurry; everybody stopped to chat with their friends or to sit down at a café and have coffee with them. It was elegant and gay.

We spent the entire evening walking from shop-to-shop marveling at the exquisite things for sale. Against my protests, Fabien insisted on purchasing a beautiful silk scarf for me. It was blood red-like the suit he had been wearing the evening before. "For you," he said as he stood behind me, tying the scarf around my neck, his face only inches away from mine, his warm breath on my neck.

After that, we stopped at a shop that sold chocolate, and I drank some. Fabien, once again, consumed nothing. It had become evident he never ate or drank anything, or if he did, it was in private.

I did not mention this, of course, because it had also become obvious that I was never supposed to remark on it. I noticed and wondered silently.

Gradually, the crowds began to disperse, and another crowd, much less elegant, began to come out of the woodwork: soldiers and thieves and prostitutes. Fabien and I hired another carriage and took ourselves away.

"Do you enjoy the theater, Laurent?" Fabien asked. "Yes, I adore it," I replied.

"Wonderful! Then would you give me the pleasure of your company tomorrow night? There is a wonderful show at the Grands-Danseurs du Roi. I would like to take you." As I agreed, I tried not to sound too excited.

We were silent as the carriage drove us back to my rooms; there was no sound but the dull thud of the horses' hooves on the dried mud of the streets.

When the carriage stopped, I looked out the window and saw we were at my building. I looked at Fabien, uncertain of how to say goodbye. Fabien took my head in both of his hands and kissed me directly on the mouth. I had never felt anything like this before. Passion consumed every bone in my body; I felt as if I would burst.

Just as abruptly, Fabien pulled away from me. Formally, we said our good nights. As I knocked on the door for the servant to open it, I was so overcome with ecstasy at having been kissed by this handsome man, I could barely keep my hands from shaking. I was relieved when the front door opened and the carriage left, because I was afraid I would turn around again, and seeing Fabien, would rush back to him for another kiss.

Alone in my bedroom, I had wild thoughts about Fabien as I undressed, leaving on only the blood-red silk scarf he had purchased for me earlier that evening. As I stroked the soft silk scarf, I closed my eyes and pictured us in bed together, our naked bodies writhing around each other.

The next morning came faster than I expected. I awakened at the first cockcrow, still reeling from Fabien's kiss; I could not put the sensation out of my head. Collecting my thoughts, I got dressed and went to the café. I wasn't hungry: all I could think about was coffee, which I was beginning to feel the need for several times a day. What a strange substance it was—bitter, yet so delicious, and so enlivening to the mind!

More than coffee, though, I was there for Fabien. I did not yet know where he lived, so going to the café was the only way to see him. As I sat there emptying my pot of coffee, the sun rose. Fabien was not there. What was I going to do, spend another entire day waiting for him? I had an arrangement to meet him that evening to see the danseurs. I would find a more profitable way to spend the day.

After a breakfast of soup and bread, I paid and left.

I meant to do something very sensible and productive, but to tell you the truth, I have no idea how I spent that day. All I remember was that after supper, I got dressed in the most fashionable clothes I had: a new black velvet suit trimmed with lace, a gold watch, silk stockings, and black shoes with buckles of gold and diamonds. I stood in front of the mirror and powdered my hair, admiring myself, wanting to look perfect for Fabien.

My servant announced the arrival of the carriage. I descended the stairs at a dignified pace, preventing myself from running.

Fabien was there in the carriage. His skin color was less pale than usual; there was even a bit of rosiness to his complexion, I was glad to see. I realized I had been worrying about his health without even knowing I was worrying.

The coachman held the door open for me and I sat down opposite Fabien. After all the uncensored thoughts I had been having about him, I felt embarrassed to be in his actual presence. However, his smile put me at ease. Maybe he had been thinking about me, too. He reached out and grasped my hand. As if by instinct, I recoiled, expecting his hand to be icy—but I was pleasantly surprised to discover that it was warm. He must have been sick on those previous occasions; I was sure of it— because now he looked as healthy as my own reflection in the mirror upstairs. I was relieved.

How had I come to care about him so much in so short a time? "Yes, Laurent?" Fabien said.

"I'm glad to see you looking so much better. I was afraid you were ill."

"My health is unsteady," Fabien replied. "There are days when I am as well as anybody, and there are other days when my blood does not circulate properly, and I am as cold as a fish. It is a strange condition, but I do have a doctor to look after me. It must be frightening, but I assure you, the situation is not fatal.

"I look much worse than I actually am." He smiled again. "It is kind of you to take an interest in my health. There are people who fear and avoid me. I am glad you are not one of those."

We arrived at the Boulevard du Temple. The theater was up ahead, and a parade was going toward it. We were astonished to see that the parade was being led by a monkey. It turned out he was the famous Turco, whom we had heard of. We joined the parade, and once Turco got inside the theater, he ran up and jumped on the stage and began to perform. After I had watched for a little while, I realized that he was enacting the news of the day. He took the part of a well-known merchant who was known to be trying to get his daughter to marry a man she did not like, and he also played the part of the daughter, who was infatuated with an officer who did not pay his debts at cards. Turco next imitated a popular street juggler—and juggled as well as he did. Except for those that concerned the royal family, there were no current events that escaped Turco's mockery.

Filled with people, the theater was hot, and I found myself wishing I had worn something a little less warm than velvet. I noticed Fabien was observing me almost as if I were some kind of specimen— and that he had been observing me for some time. I asked him why. I was afraid he found some fault in me.

He gave me a strange smile and said, "Forgive me, my dear Laurent, but I was just noticing how handsome you are." I felt a flash of heat come over me, and I realized I was blushing.

Turco hopped off the stage and went up to the boxes to beg the ladies for candies, which they gave him, with delight. While everybody was watching this, Fabien leaned over to me and whispered in my ear, "If you think this is amazing, wait till you see what I have I store for you later."

I felt the blood in my cheeks increase once again, which caused Fabien to say "Why, you're blushing!"

I laughed and admitted it. I was no longer embarrassed. There was an air of innocence about our flirtation, as if this were a first love—and for me, it was. There was nothing to make me nervous, no suggestion that this was a pickup. Fabien was not looking at me as if I were a piece of meat hanging in a butcher's shop. It was quite the opposite: I felt cherished; I felt that there was no other man on earth he had these feelings for.

When the performance was over, we got into Fabien's carriage. We rode the entire way to my building consumed with laughter about the monkey's hilarious performance and happy to be in each other's presence. Once, Fabien placed a hand on my thigh, caressing it ever so gently. Despite his gentleness I could sense his strength. When we weren't engaged in conversation, I once again saw his intense gaze out of the corners of my eyes; it was as if he were transfixed by my presence.

As we approached my building, I lost my head. I had to get him to come upstairs with me; I had to—but I had no idea what to say to make it happen. I broke the silence by saying I was feeling a bit tired. As soon as I said it, I knew it was all wrong.

But Fabien answered smoothly, "That really is a pity, because I was hoping I might see where you live."

"Oh, it's nothing extraordinary," I said, blundering ever deeper. "On the contrary, I am sure there is much to interest me," Fabien said. "You have taste, and I'm sure you have been exercising it since you came to Paris. Have you bought no paintings? No Sèvres? No *objets d'art?*"

This time I successfully picked up his clue and admitted that there was an object or two he might be interested in seeing if he would be so good as to come upstairs to my rooms with me. The way he looked at me made it hard for me to utter the words.

As soon as we stopped, I jumped out of the carriage. I saw Fabien order the coachman to return home, which meant—*he was planning to stay the night.*

I became nervous all over again — nervous and yet profoundly pleased.

It was still quite early in the evening, so the servant who belonged to the building was on hand to let us in. He led us up the stairs with a lit candelabrum to my set of apartments on the first floor, and then Gaston, my manservant, met us with more lit candles. I went in, but oddly, Fabien hesitated on the threshold.

"Are you sure you want me to come in?" he asked.

Why on earth was he asking this? I had made my wishes clear— all too clear, I thought. "Of course," I said. "Come in and see this tapestry I bought yesterday. Gaston, some wine."

I wondered if Fabien would refuse, but he said nothing. He was examining the tapestry with interest. Gaston served us the wine in two silver goblets that were another recent acquisition of mine, and now I could not help but notice that Fabien looked at the goblet and ignored the wine. "Who made these for you, Germain?" he asked.

"Yes," I said with some surprise, but luckily I kept myself from saying more. I should have guessed Fabien would know his silver.

"Marvelous, the movement he conveys in a static form." Fabien set down his goblet. "Drink up; don't let me stop you. I am never thirsty or hungry at the times other people are. You mustn't embarrass me by taking note of it."

I was rather hungry, so, taking Fabien at his word, I told Gaston to bring us some biscuits and pâté and cheese and jam, and then to leave us for the night. *Please let Fabien stay, please let him stay*, I begged some unknown god.

While I ate, Fabien examined the paintings and tapestries on the wall and the curios I had in a cabinet. When I was done, he came and sat quite close to me. I looked into his eyes, and his gaze drew me closer and closer. He leaned towards me and kissed me on the lips. I decided to not allow the coldness of his lips and hands to ruin this romantic moment. The kiss drifted from my lips to my neck, which he began smelling and licking, moaning with pleasure as he did so. It was very odd, but if this what he wanted to do. I was not going to stop him.

Suddenly he pulled back from my neck and stood up as he looked me in the face. His blue eyes clouded over. "Forgive me, Laurent, I was about to do something I do not have the right to do, not unless you will it," he said. "I was overcome with desire. I will proceed only if I have your permission."

"Please, don't stop," I said.

He stepped back to run his eyes over my whole body, and I knew he was noticing my arousal. He walked over to where I was seated and took my hand, and I led him to my bedroom. Our lips locked in a passionate kiss as we undressed each other.

Hours passed. I marveled at every part of his body, as he did mine. Afterwards, we lay on the bed with our arms around each other. "I never thought I would meet anyone like you, Laurent," Fabien said as he kissed the top of my head.

"I feel the same about you, Fabien. I have always longed to be with another man in this way."

After a time — feeling safe and secure in Fabien's strong arms—I began to fall asleep. Outside, the sky was becoming lighter and lighter; it was nearly dawn. As soon as Fabien noticed this, he underwent a complete change. He leapt out of bed and put on his clothes in a flash. My jaw dropped.

"I'm sorry, but I must leave, Laurent. I didn't realize it had gotten so late!" Fabien said frantically.

"But why?" was all I could say, though I knew he would not answer.

"There will be plenty more of these moments to come, I promise," he said. And with that he leaned over and kissed me. In an instant he was gone.

"But when can we see each other again?" I asked the empty bedroom as I heard the door to my apartments open and close.

Who was this man, anyway, and what motivated his often strange behavior? All my questions began to add up. Why had he left so suddenly? Why had I never seen him eat or drink? Why had he never allowed me to know where he lived? Why did he agree to meet me only after dark? Above all, when would I see him again? I had no control over that last, since I did not know where to reach him; I could only continue to waste my days at the Café Alexandre, hoping he would show up. Happy as I was, I began to be a tiny bit miffed.

What was this big secret he felt he had to keep from me—me, his lover?

I lay in bed thinking I would be able to fall asleep once more, but it was no use: my eyes were wide open, and the sun hitting my face nearly blinded me; No, I decided it was time for me to rise, wash, and start my day.

I went to Café Alexandre simply because I always went there. There was no chance I would meet Fabien—a man does not rush out of one's rooms only to go around the corner and sit down and drink coffee. I finished the usual breakfast of soup and bread and then decided to take a walk. I hired a carriage to take me to the Tuileries, and I spent the entire morning there, listening to the chirping of the birds and marveling at all the trees. There was a statue that caught my attention. Titled *Renommée*, it represented Louis IV riding the winged horse Pegasus. I stood staring at every detail. The statue was made of the purest white marble, as white as Fabien's skin; and as this connection formed in my mind, I shivered, despite the warmth of the sun.

There was no point in thinking about Fabien now, no point in marshaling my questions about him. They would have to wait until I saw him again.

I wandered around and saw the most magnificent yellow rose. I bent over to smell the lush aroma and cut my finger on one of the thorns. Suddenly, a droplet of blood appeared on my finger. I was not able to locate my handkerchief accurately—I stuck my finger in my mouth, hoping that would stop it from bleeding any further. I remember thinking how odd the taste of blood was. I marveled at the beautiful assortment of roses a while longer, till dinnertime, and then I had an inspiration.

I had heard people talking about a new institution, called a restaurant, where people could pay to be served a meal. The restaurant I had heard of was the Grande Taverne de Londres. It was like the kitchen of some nobleman, only the chef worked for the restaurant owner, not a member of the nobility. Restaurants were open to the public. You could go there and order any one of a great number of dishes, and the kitchen would make it just for you. There was also a fine wine cellar; and the proprietor, one Antoine Beauvilliers, would take the cellar key out of his pocket and go get the wine he felt would go best with your dish.

I decided to try out La Grande Taverne de Londres. Some small, spiteful part of me was glad that I was going without Fabien. If he was going to abandon me at sunrise, I would show him I wasn't dependent on him for entertainment.

I did myself proud at that meal. I will not bore the reader with a list of everything I ate, but I did order every delicacy on the menu that appealed to me and I had room for. I also drank several different wines, at Monsieur Beauvilliers' suggestion. I took my time, so that I did not get sated early and so I did not get drunk. By the time I finished the meal with a slice of tart of *fraises de bois*, I was so satisfied with the world that I was telling myself that Fabien was sure to turn up in a day or two, and that there was no reason for concern.

As it happened, he did show up, and we resumed our love affair. Our bond grew more durable and more reliable with each passing day. He consumed my every thought. We spent time together nearly every evening. We went back to the Palais Royal several times. We went to the opera, something I had never done on my own. We were invited to elaborate dinner parties, where Fabien introduced me to the most exciting friends of his. But I never saw him eat anything.

One evening that stood out was a masquerade ball Fabien asked me to attend with him. He had purchased intricately decorated masks for us. Naturally, when we participated in the dance—we each chose a female dance partner. However, our gaze was always returning to one another across the ballroom.

We spent many months together. There were so many unanswered questions, so many mysteries that remained. I found it more and more curious that we never were able to meet during the daylight, much less dine together in a restaurant. However, it seemed Fabien always had business to do. From time to time, I would question him, and at times he was short with me. He told me he felt as if he were being interrogated.

We decided to take a pause in our relationship.

I cannot begin to describe how miserable I felt. I was thrown back into the life I had had before I met Fabien, and I now saw what a poverty-stricken life that was.

One evening, weeks after I had seen Fabien last, I got home and found him waiting in the lobby for me, seeming agitated. I was much more agitated than reassured. "Fabien, what is it? What's wrong?" I asked, forgetting all about showing him I could survive very well on my own.

"I must speak to you," said Fabien.

"Of course. Come upstairs," I said, and when we reached my front door, I insisted that Fabien go in first and make himself comfortable in one of the upholstered chairs. I was going to get him a brandy before I remembered he would not drink it. I sat down near him and waited for him to talk.

"I have missed you, Laurent. I need you back," Fabien said, but he seemed to find it challenging to go on.

"I have missed you as well, Fabien; I hope you realize that"

He didn't respond, but said instead, "There is something I need to tell you. It is essential. All-important, you might say."

"Are you going to tell me why you felt we needed to have such a long separation from one another?" I asked with more than a touch of waspishness.

"Yes, I will explain that. Everything will be explained." "Go on, Fabien," I said, more gently. "I'm listening."

Fabien took a long moment to answer. "Laurent, this is very hard. I have not been truthful with you."

At once a sense of betrayal had come over me, was this handsome gentleman someone other than he seemed to be? This man I had spent so much time with and grown to love. Someone who consumed my every thought. My head was swimming with doubt, but I was determined to hear his confession, perhaps it would shed light on the many mysteries surrounding this handsome, yet mysterious man with the pale skin.

"I'm sure you've found it rather odd that we have never been together during the daylight—that we always meet at night," he said. "And that I have never eaten or drunk anything in your presence."

"Yes, I have found it most odd," I said, relieved that the matter was now coming out into the open. "I'm sure you are ill, but it is not any illness I have ever heard of."

Fabien turned and looked at me. "No, I am not ill. It is something much worse. I hardly know how to tell you, so bizarre will you find it. I am not sure you will believe my story at all."

"And yet you are going to tell me the truth."

"Yes, of course, Laurent. That is why I have such misgivings. Let me say, before I begin, that from the first time I met you in the park, I have begun to feel alive again—for the first time in a long time. In your company I have enjoyed myself as I have not for…well, many longer years than you would find possible. And then there was our first night of intimacy," he said, almost dreamily. "I have never had those feelings with anyone else, Laurent. It was a new thing to me." By this time, I was all tenderness to Fabien.

"To me, too," I said. "I thought maybe I was the only man in the world to crave another man so intensely. I wondered why I was made so different from other men. Do you feel that, too? Is that what made you want to separate yourself from me?"

"No, I had another reason for fleeing. A much more serious reason." He pulled his chair close to mine and took my hand. Once again, his was like ice. "I am not the man you take me for. In fact, I am not a man at all—that is, I am not mortal."

I could think of no reply to this, since I could make no sense of it. Not mortal? Since Adam sinned, all men have been mortal. Surely Fabien was not going to ask me to believe he was a demon— or an angel? If so, I was going to have to try hard—and probably unsuccessfully—not to laugh in his face.

I left my hand in his and stared into his blue, blue eyes, waiting for him to resume talking, to explain what could not be explained. My heart began to beat faster and faster; it felt as if it would burst out of my chest. I stared at him in anticipation. He looked at me and began to explain. "Laurent, I am one of the living dead, more commonly known as a vampire. I was made into one over a hundred years ago by someone I have grown to loathe," he said.

"I don't understand. Living dead? —Vampire? I have never heard that word before. What does it mean?"

"I will tell you everything, and I ask that you allow me to talk uninterrupted. "What is a vampire, you ask? A vampire is the body of a dead person that is reanimated by regular infusions of blood. A vampire is neither alive nor dead, but undead. A vampire is a creature of the night, who must sleep by day—and is free to roam only when the sun has set, because the sun will kill him. A vampire never grows old himself—so he is cursed to have to witness the deaths of all his family and friends. The only nourishment a vampire can take is blood. He cannot eat the foods humans eat.

"The vampire has many supernatural abilities. He can transform himself into certain kinds of animals—bats, rats, and wolves. A vampire can see in the dark, and his senses of smell and hearing are so keen that he can detect things humans cannot. A vampire can turn into mist or fog and can move much faster than any mortal eye can detect or follow. A vampire can hypnotize humans and can summon them using telepathy. A vampire can levitate and can fly through the air. If a vampire decides to move far away—he must be transported in a sealed container or box filled with the soil of his birthplace." Fabien turned to me. "You must think vampires are quite invincible."

I did not know what to say, so I waited for him to continue. "There are several ways that human beings can guard against vampires. Crucifixes and holy water are proper tools. A cross is usually held up towards the face of the vampire, driving it away, while holy water—if unleashed on the vampire, will burn, and disintegrate its skin. Garlic also works as a deterrent against vampires. There are ways that a vampire can be killed—as I mentioned, sunlight will. Fire also will kill a vampire. You can behead a vampire or drive a stake through his heart."

"As for how I became a vampire, I was bitten by one— who then forced me to drink his blood. That's how a new vampire is made: one who is already a vampire brings a human being to the point of death by drinking all of his blood and then reanimates him by forcing him to drink the vampire's blood. I tell you all of this because you must know the facts to make a free choice to accept my offer or to refuse it."

"What is your offer?" I asked, though I had a glimmer of a guess. "I want to make you a vampire, Laurent, so you will never die—so that we can be together always." Fabien paused. "I know this sounded horrible, and indeed it is horrible in many ways to be a vampire. Not for nothing does everybody fear us. But since I was made a vampire—against my will—it is the only way we can be together. And I need you, Laurent; I love you as I have loved no one else. I know I am being selfish, but perhaps you need me, too. Or perhaps you will have pity on my love for you."

I reflected on every word he said and contemplated my life before I met him. There hadn't been a life, or one that meant anything, I had never met another man who longed for the physical touch of another man, even if he wasn't indeed a man, yet a creature of the night. I felt anxious and became confused, asking myself, what kind of existence would I experience? I felt apprehensive as I remembered tasting my blood after being pricked by the thorn of the rose in the park. I thought about how this would become my nourishment, blood. A substance that would sustain my existence if I were to join Fabien and become as he, one of the undead.

As he gazed at me tenderly and longingly, I could not have loved him more than I did at that exact moment, I felt as if Fabien had bared his soul to me, had finally been truthful, yet his dark secret frightened and intrigued me.

I looked at him without concealing the love and compassion I felt as I stood up, reflecting deeply on his words. For a while, we said nothing to each other. There was nothing but silence between us. I walked over to the window and looked at the darkened Paris night, thinking, *This is what my reality would become if I were transformed into a vampire: it would be all night.* Finally, I gave him my answer.

"Yes, Fabien, I am willing to become a vampire," I said. "You'll never know exactly how happy you have made me with your decision. You shall come to live with me—I don't want there to be any physical distance between us," he said.

"Nor do I," I replied as he came closer to me.

"Are you ready to begin your journey with me now, Laurent?" "I am ready, Fabien. Give me the gift of immortality."

"It is a gift, but a dark one," Fabien said. "You must be sure this is what you really want."

"I am sure, Fabien."

His face turned from a somber expression to one of complete happiness—and then, in a moment his eyes went from deep blue to a crimson red as he opened his mouth to reveal two abnormally large incisors. As he told me to tilt my head over to one side. Then I felt excruciating pain as his incisors bit into my neck, as my blood ran down my throat. The room spun around as he sucked the life force out of me.

I grew weaker and weaker. I was barely able to whisper the words, "Am I going to die?"

"Yes, Laurent, you will die a mortal death. Then you will be reborn," he said.

With that, I lost consciousness.

When I awoke, I knew I had a few drops of my mortal life left. Fabien was saying, "Now that I have drained you to the point of death, you must drink my blood. It will resurrect you to eternal life." He bit into his wrist, and the blood trickled out. He put his bleeding wrist to my mouth. I was so weak it was difficult for me to open my mouth, but I managed to drink a drop or two—three— four. I felt a new power enter me, a new strength, but along with this power came convulsions—I screamed in pain, but I heard Fabien say, "Fear not, Laurent—you are being reborn!"

The convulsions stopped, my eyes closed, and I saw nothing but blackness. Then suddenly a sea of scarlet red washed over my brain, and I began to gasp for air, as if I were drowning.

"Breathe," Fabien said.

One large gasp for air was enough.

When I opened my eyes again, my eyesight had a clarity that it never had before. I gazed at Fabien's face, able to make out every pore in his skin—even down to the intricate detail of his hair follicles, as he knelt over me softly cradling and stroking my head with his strong hands. Fabien helped me to stand as if I were a small child about to take its first steps. I felt like a newborn, at first, a bit unsteady but quickly regained my strength and walked over to the window and opened it.

The coolness of the night no longer chilled me. Fabien walked over to where I was standing and tenderly put his hand on my shoulder, in an unspoken way of displaying his love for me. The crystal clarity of my vision was profound. My hearing, too, was greatly enhanced: I was witness to sounds I had never heard before, creatures stirring in the nearby park, leaves that brushed up against each other.

I looked down at my hands, which were now as bloodless as Fabien's. I walked to the mirror on the wall and saw that I cast no reflection. The mirror was as empty as if no one at all were standing in front of it.

Then an overwhelming hunger made me double over in pain. It felt as if it would tear me in half; I felt as if I hadn't eaten in a lifetime— there was an overwhelming thirst, as well.

"My God! What is this hunger?" I yelled at Fabien. "It is the vampire's lust for blood," he said calmly.

"Well, then, feed me! You made me into a vampire—so feed me!" "Yes, I shall, but you must first listen to what I have to say. I have one rule, which for me justifies our very existence. There are some human beings who prey on others, who rape, pillage, and murder— it is those criminals, and only those, whom I feed on: the criminals human society fears—and do not search for once they go missing. If there is such a thing as evil, surely it is those who prey on innocent, law abiding and unsuspecting citizens. I have chosen these evil humans to be my lifeline, and now they will be your lifeline as well. We will kill no others. Are we in agreement, Laurent?" he asked.

"Yes! Yes! Please, for the love of God, feed me! I cannot take this torture!"

Fabien opened the window. "Remember, I told you that vampires can fly. That is what we are going to do now. Observe." He climbed onto the windowsill and glided down to the darkened sidewalk. He motioned me to follow. I hesitated.

"Laurent come to me!" he called.

I jumped. I flew, thinking to myself, My God! I am airborne! I felt a slight tickle of excitement in my stomach all the while laughing in amazement and disbelief as I landed next to where Fabien was standing.

We decided to take a stroll in the park. Under the trees there was total darkness—but now that I was a vampire, I could see all there was to see, trees and shrubs along with various creatures, such as birds, nesting in their branches in the dark. Walking in the park was something I had always wanted to do with Fabien, but I had never imagined that it would be at night. I thought briefly about never again being able to feel the warmth of the sun. I had taken it for granted, but now sunlight was something that would kill me.

"How was your first experience flying?" "It was beyond my wildest imagination!" I said excitedly. "Good, and about your hunger; has it subsided a little, Laurent?" Fabien asked, sounding concerned.

"Yes, a bit for the moment," I replied.

"We shall find someone deserving of death soon. Paris by night has many criminals roaming the streets" he said, reassuring me.

"Fabien, there is one thing you mentioned just before you turned me I would like you to explain," I said.

He gave me a curious look and said, "Oh, what is that?"

"You mentioned earlier that there is another vampire loose in the world—in fact, the one who turned you over one hundred years ago," I said, but his attention had been caught elsewhere.

"Listen!" he said.

I heard a scream nearby.

"Let us investigate," Fabien said, as a glimmer of excitement appeared in his eyes.

We ran faster than any mortals could have done, and we arrived at the scene of a crime. A man wielding a sword was threatening another man. When he saw us, the victim screamed, "Help me!"

The would-be assailant raised his sword and said, "There is nothing these two can do to help you—tonight, you're going to die, so prepare yourself! Once I finish with you, it shall be their turn!"

"Wrong, it is you who will die tonight!" Fabien cried, his eyes turning red.

"Run! Save yourself now while you still can!" I said to the victim. The assailant was distracted by Fabien's threat, and his victim ran away into the night. Fabien grabbed him by the neck, lifted him in the air, and proceeded to choke him as he struggled against Fabien's vise-like grip, despite that, the man was still alive.

"Laurent, here is your nourishment," Fabien triumphantly proclaimed.

Instantly, we began to tear at the murderer's body, Fabien at his throat and I at his wrist.

Conflicting thoughts flooded my mind. On the one hand, Fabien had taken a life, and that was a sin, then again—this was not a life worth preserving. The assailant had attempted to murder someone. We had saved the life of a man who would otherwise have been his victim. If we were to limit ourselves to feeding on criminals, then we would be helping to rid society of them—and that was all to the good.

Fabien dropped the body to the ground and retrieved a handkerchief from his waistcoat to wipe his mouth. He handed it to me so I could do the same.

"Quickly, we must dispose of the body," Fabien said as we picked up the corpse and started digging with our hands until we had dug a deep enough hole to bury the body. If this man had a history of criminal activity, the authorities would undoubtedly search for a while and then give up and label it as an unsolved mysterious disappearance.

Once the hole was dug, we carried the body over to it and placed it in the freshly unearthed dirt. We covered it within seconds using vampire speed and strength. As soon as the plot was covered with dirt, we wiped the dirt from our hands with Fabien's handkerchief.

"Shall we return to your apartments, Laurent?" Fabien asked.

The color was coming back into his face. I looked down at my hands and saw that the color was coming back into them, too. It was because of the blood we had drunk.

We returned to my apartments, entering by the same window that we had left through only a short time ago.

"How was your first experience as a vampire, Laurent?" Fabien asked with genuine concern.

"All I was thinking about was feeding myself," I confessed. "This is my new reality—I accept it."

Fabien nodded and said, "I struggled with my first experience as well. Stefan forced me to kill anyone and everyone in our sight, even families with little children." He turned away from me as if in shame.

After a moment, as if he needed some time to compose himself, he turned around to face me and said, "Now allow me to tell you about another vampire I know. He is the only other to my knowledge; however, there may be others—such as the vampire that made Stefan. It was Stefan who made me a vampire. He, too, was my lover—to my everlasting regret." I intently listened as he told me how he and Stefan had met at a café, the Alexandre, which is why Fabien preferred meeting at the Procope, careful to avoid the other café altogether for fear of the two of us running into Stefan.

Fabien shared with me that he felt he was tricked into becoming a vampire without his consent, that he had met Stefan and was drawn to him by how handsome he was, with his wit, and charm, which soon turned to unending cruelty. The two of them had attended cultural events together; and finally became physically intimate together. As I heard, I became enraged in jealousy, making me hate this creature even more. Fabien described how Stefan delighted in torturing Fabien, primarily through wild and endless killing sprees. From the many attacks—Fabien explained there were two that stood out in his mind, which brought him to tears.

The first was the killing of Fabien's trusted servant Jacque, forced to witness Stefan brutally and savagely kill him, and that there was nothing Fabien could do to stop him. He paused for a bit before continuing to share the other killing, which had so upset him. An attack on an entire family, including the family's coachman and small children—of hearing the parent's cries for mercy to spare the children, and finally, the children who discovered that monsters genuinely exist, which lead to their deaths. Fabien had reduced himself to performing horrific acts all under Stefan's command; deciding never to do this to anyone else. When he found his soul mate—Fabien intended to give that man a free choice whether to become a vampire or remain mortal. And he had seen me and given me the option.

Upon hearing this, my love for Fabien grew, I couldn't contain my sadness upon hearing what torture Fabien had endured at the hands of Stefan, as blood tears ran from my eyes, as I reached out to wipe the ones running down Fabien's cheeks as well. Once I had finished wiping away Fabien's and my blood tears, I thought a change of scenery was in order. I had recalled how fond Fabien was in frequenting the café. I suggested we take a stroll over to the Procope to lose our thoughts of Stefan in a game or two of chess once we composed ourselves, As he smiled at me and said, "What a wonderful suggestion, yes—let's stop all of this talk about Stefan. Instead, let's enjoy the solace of our café and each other's company."

I could tell Fabien had become emotionally drained in describing to me their tortured history together.

I walked over to the window, hearing thunder as I gazed out into the blackened night as lightning lit up the sky, looking out, thinking I saw someone looking up towards our window—in an instant the figure had disappeared, as Fabien came over to join me. Fabien was by my side looking out of the window and saying,

"What are you pondering, Laurent?," Fabien asked softly as he gently placed his hand on my shoulder.

"Strange, I just thought I saw an image of a man staring up at our window," I answered.

"A man?—I think your imagination may be playing tricks on you; there is no one out there. All this discussion of Stefan has the two of us on edge," he tried to assure me. As hard as he tried to calm my nerves, I couldn't help but have this dark and foreboding feeling come over me. "Come, let us go, I feel as if I shall beat you this evening at chess" Fabien proclaimed. I replied with a faint laugh as we left the apartments arriving at the café in a matter of moments.

As soon as we entered the café a feeling of calm and normalcy came over me; I could tell Fabien felt equally at ease; little did I know these feelings would return to doubt and fear. We spotted a table towards the back of the café; it was a busy night; there were many patrons; we felt fortunate to be able to locate a place to sit. Fabien proceeded to set up the chessboard and all its pieces. Hearing the laughter of the patrons and sometimes, arguments, were not so much a distraction, but instead comforting as we began our chess game.

"It's your move Laurent," Fabien said as he sat there feeling content.

So soon after locating our table, I noticed someone sitting across the room from us, appearing to have the same deathly pallor Fabien and I had. The man seemed to be transfixed by the two of us, watching our every move.

"Laurent, what has you so distracted?" Fabien asked, sounding slightly annoyed.

I turned away from the man's gaze, which appeared as if he were looking right through me. I wondered whether that man was a man at all, or if it were another of our kind, possibly Stefan?

"My apologies. Yes, for a moment, I became distracted; I thought I saw a man who appeared to have our skin coloring," I admitted.

Had I detected an expression of panic on Fabien's face? — I pointed in the direction that the man had been seated.

"It appeared he has left Fabien; he seemed to be quite interested in our chess-playing," I said anxiously.

Thinking about this strange man I had seen observing the two of us so closely, caused that dark and ominous feeling to return—as I tried desperately to hide those feelings from Fabien, which proved to be pointless. It was as if he could read my thoughts, and despite my efforts in remaining calm, I could sense that Fabien was beginning to feel fearful, knocking over some of the chess pieces to show how unnerved he had become.

"Let us return home Laurent, I suddenly have lost any interest in pursuing any further chess matches," he said, sounding almost defeated.

It pained me to see Fabien this way; he appeared to me to display feelings of torment and that Stefan once again was not only observing us but most likely stalking us, if not plotting something against us.

We left the crowded and bustling café—with the mysterious gentleman nowhere to be seen. As soon as we were outside, the weather had changed dramatically. The skies were lit up with lightning as thunder echoed in the background as it began to rain. We decided to use our vampire speed, rather than stroll home, especially given the uncertainty of the yet unknown man who appeared to be following us. Once in the comfort of our apartments, we were greeted with the fireplace ablaze with warmth and color— my servant Luc must have made it shortly before retiring for the evening. We sat next to the fireplace, merely observing how the flames danced and flickered while hearing the crackle of the wood as it burned.

I became mesmerized by the flames, knowing that something so beautiful could also be so tremendously destructive, and end our existence. I don't remember how long the silence lasted; it seemed to be an eternity until Fabien finally spoke.

"This man you claim you saw at the café, do you remember what he looked like?" Fabien asked.

"He was quite handsome and had the same skin coloring as you and me— as white as milk," I replied.

"No mortal has the color of our skin, it must have been another of our kind, perhaps even Stefan!" Fabien said.

I cringed at Fabien's suggestion, not wanting to accept it, but deep down inside—both of us know who the stalker was; it was Stefan. The tension felt as if either of us could use a knife to cut through it. Suddenly, our wonderful time spent together seemed consumed with the looming threat that Stefan posed.

"I have been so careful to avoid him. We must—or he will destroy both you and I should we be spotted together," Fabien said.

"What are you suggesting, Fabien? I refuse to become a prisoner here in our apartments; we must still be able to roam about freely," I said almost in defiance.

"At what price Laurent?" Fabien asked.

I didn't reply to Fabien's question but instead responded to his question with a question of my own—"Isn't there anything we can do to stop him? Surely with your strength and mine combined, we could overpower him and" I angrily replied as Fabien interjected.

"There is nothing you or I can do; Stefan is one of the ancient ones, his strength is the equivalent of fifty mortals, your strength and mine amount to half of that," Fabien said, sounding once again defeated.

I walked over to where Fabien was seated and put my arms around him—holding him as if I were protecting him from anything that would choose to harm us.

Just then, a thought occurred, *For Stefan to have become a vampire, he had to have had a maker as well, another vampire. If there were some way we could locate this creature and perhaps meet with him, maybe we could enlist this creature's help to control Stefan, and surely this vampire would be older and even more powerful than Stefan.* However, a few obstacles remained: whether this vampire maker of Stefan's still existed, and where would we locate him?

My thoughts consumed me until Fabien spoke. "What are you thinking of, Laurent?" Fabien asked.

I shared my thoughts of attempting to locate and meet with Stefan's maker; I pleaded with him to go along with my plan— I felt it was our only chance in dealing with Stefan.

"It is our only hope," I said.

"Say I agree to this, then how do we locate this other vampire, do we know if this creature still exists?" Fabien asked.

"Fabien, you shared with me that vampires can summon mortals, did you not?" I asked.

"Yes, that is correct," Fabien replied hesitantly with a questioning look on his face.

"Well, for example, if a vampire can summon a mortal— why wouldn't a vampire be able to summon another vampire?" I asked— feeling a newfound excitement and hope stir inside me once more.

"There is only one way to determine this; we shall begin this experiment tomorrow evening, as the time is drawing near for us to rest—observe," Fabien said as he pointed towards the window. The storm had passed hours ago, and the sky was starting to grow more and more illuminated with the approaching dawn, hours and hours had gone by; we had lost all track of time with many lengthy pauses of silence during our discussions of how to contact Stefan's maker. Time goes by so quickly to those of our kind, which are not bound by it.

We entered our bedroom and quickly got undressed and lay on the bed, side by side, holding each other's hands as we drifted into an undead slumber.

Once sleep set in, I started to have a dream about a man with a white beard; he appeared to be quite ancient. I had no idea who this man was, only in this dream there was another that appeared by his side, the same mysterious man that had observed us in the café. This man, who turned out, wasn't a man at all, turned to meet my gaze and hissed, exposing his two large vampire fangs.

I wondered who the man with the white beard was. It was as if he were warning me that, despite this only being a dream, it felt as if it were truly happening. I woke up shaken by the vision, careful not to awaken Fabien, and determined more than ever to see my plan through.

The next evening, after I had given my servant the evening free, no sooner had he left, we began our experiment. Before we began we left our window open—thinking that whoever would show up by means of being summoned, would naturally enter through the window. Fabien and I sat on the floor with three black candles, arranged in a circular pattern. We held hands as Fabien called out to the maker of Stefan.

"We gather here this evening to ask the vampire maker of Stefan, Baron of Vitré, to appear before us; if you can hear us—I ask you to come to us."

Outside the wind had intensified and began to moan. Fabien called out three more times. My heart began to sink—I was beginning to doubt this experiment; perhaps only vampires could summon mortals, and not others of our kind?

A mighty wind rushed through the window as thunder and lightning lit up and echoed through the black of night, startling us both a bit. A man with a long white beard appeared before us; but this was no ordinary man, or a mere mortal at all. I recognized him from the dream I had had the previous day, and then he spoke.

"Why have you summoned me here?"

The white-bearded man asked as he bared his two large incisors. We each greeted the vampire by baring our fangs in return.

"Are you the vampire maker of Stefan, Baron of Vitré?" Fabien asked forcefully.

"Who wants to know?" the white-bearded vampire replied.

"It is I, Fabien Levesque— Stefan was my maker," Fabien replied, as I continued to hold onto Fabien's hand. To suggest my unease by this experiment with the actual appearance of Stefan's maker would not be inaccurate.

"Why have you summoned me here?" the white-bearded vampire demanded.

"Ancient one, we need your help in dealing with Stefan," Fabien said forcefully.

"Why should I want to help you? And who is this other vampire, if you are the fledgling of Stefan?" the white-haired ancient one asked.

"My name is Laurent Richelieu, I am Fabien's fledgling— but much more than that—he is also my lover," I said, answering the ancient vampire's question.

"What is your name, ancient one?" Fabien asked commandingly. The white-haired vampire grimaced upon hearing those words and said "My name is Thaddeus— I am indeed the maker of Stefan; he was my fledgling— until I cast him out."

"I don't understand?" Fabien replied.

"For many mortal years, I had been a very close friend of Stefan's family— before I became this creature of darkness. I had sworn to Stefan's parents that in the event of their untimely demise I would look after their child—they knew nothing about my becoming a vampire; Stefan lost both of his parents because of the black plague, Stefan became infected as well— it is I who saved him from mortal death—he became as I."

"So now we understand how Stefan became a vampire; what we do not understand is, why did you cast him out?" Fabien asked the white-haired vampire.

"If you must know, it was after I had turned Stefan—he began making physical advances towards me. Misinterpreting my feelings of love for him—similar to a mentor, or father figure, than the love he had sought from me—I was disgusted by his physical advances and banished him from my presence, never to return!"

It was becoming clearer and clearer to Fabien and me how Stefan's feelings of rage and jealousy had developed. It was the feeling of rejection and being cast out by Thaddeus, along with Stefan finding another man to turn into his everlasting, immortal fledgling— ending in Fabien's rejection of Stefan as well— which helped ignite an almost inextinguishable fire of rage in his heart.

"So now that I have shared this with both of you, what more is there left to say?" Thaddeus said as he was preparing to leave.

I heard Fabien as he pleaded with the ancient vampire.

"Wait! We need your help, Thaddeus— if you have one trace of compassion left inside of you, please, help us. We love each other; yes, I forbade Stefan's command of never making another vampire, but I was miserable with him—you have no idea what he made me do—the torture he put me through. Then meeting Laurent, who changed my very existence and has shown me how love truly can be please—I beg of you!" Fabien pleaded.

The ancient white-haired vampire shook his head and said "You will have to contend with Stefan yourselves; I don't agree with your kind of love, I must be off!." He departed as quickly as he had arrived.

Summoning Thaddeus hadn't accomplished anything. It merely provided a bit of insight into Stefan's thoughts and what motivated him to act out with such unrestrained cruelty and hatred for everyone it seemed. I looked at Fabien and said with a heavy heart, "All hope is lost."

"All we need to do is to avoid Stefan" Fabien replied sounding defiant.

"And how do we do that? —Did he not spot us at the Procope? How did he know we would be there? —And was it not the reason you chose to avoid going to the other café, the Alexandre for fear of running into him there?" I asked with a bit of agitation in my voice.

"Yes, I had no idea he would come to the Procope; however, we must continue doing the things we have enjoyed together," Fabien replied, sounding equally frustrated.

I paused a bit before I replied to Fabien— waiting for my mood to soften. "I guess you are right, Fabien, as long as we remain vigilant and on the lookout for Stefan, then and only then, may we continue to enjoy what we once had; otherwise, we are prisoners of our own making," I said.

We agreed we would attend a play entitled "Agis" by Laignelot, at the Comédie-Française the following evening. Perhaps there we could lose ourselves in the performance, and quite possibly, forget about Stefan at least until we should happen upon him again.

The next evening, we decided our transportation to the theater would be using a hired coach rather than take flight and arrive at our destination with the help of our vampire abilities. We arrived at the theater and quickly made our way inside. Fabien and I looked around the theater's spacious waiting area expecting any minute to see Stefan leering at us; however, Stefan was nowhere, or if he was, he had not yet made himself visible.

As desperately as we tried to pretend as if this were merely an evening out, as so many others, each one of us, felt a certain amount of anxiety. We looked nervously in one direction and then in the other direction, each time meeting each other's gaze with the same anxious expression and ending with a faint smile. Both of us felt distracted. I was beginning to wonder whether coming to the theater was such a good idea.

The performance ended, and we got up to leave once again, feeling the ominous threat of Stefan, as if he were watching us, plotting his next move, until he would eventually strike. We made our way out of the theater and entered the waiting area, still Stefan was nowhere to be seen.

"You see Laurent; there is nothing to worry about— it's not as if Stefan can read our minds, how would he know we were here?" Fabien said, sounding as if he were trying not only to convince me of this but also himself— as we walked out of the theater towards one of the hired coaches, that same feeling of foreboding came over me, feeling as if we were being watched.

We entered the coach and gave the driver our address, and we were off. We sat in the carriage in silence, both of us preoccupied with thoughts about Stefan—each of us feeling as if at any moment, he would appear and end our existence.

Nearing the location of our apartments, suddenly, there was a jolt and a loud thud, as if something had landed on the roof of our carriage.

I reached for Fabien's hand, as a look of terror overcame both our faces.

Then the long-anticipated and dreaded appearance of Stefan's face, as he bent over from on top of the carriage and displayed his grotesquely twisted face of anger in the window of the carriage, bearing his long incisor's as he hissed at us with rage.

We exited the carriage as we turned to witness Stefan attacking the coachman as he cried out for help. We made our escape by air, arriving at our apartments in mere seconds, with no trace of Stefan; luckily for us—he had become distracted by taking the life of the coachman, which provided our opportunity to escape.

Entering inside, I could tell that Fabien was as visibly shaken by this incident, as was I.

"He is coming for me— I feel it in the depths of my soul!" Fabien said, his eyes wide with terror.

"Fabien, if he wanted to attack us, — why would he have stayed behind feasting on the coachman?" I asked.

"Stefan is ruthless, to him— it's all a game, he enjoys instilling terror—he will stop at nothing until he has destroyed me, avenging himself for my disobeying his command to never make another vampire."

"I will protect you Fabien," I said, trying desperately to comfort him with no success— as Fabien walked over to the window. The weather had once again turned violent— as the sound of thunder echoed in the distance, becoming louder and louder as the lightning lit up the sky.

"This cannot be!" Fabien shouted after another flash of lightning. "My God "It's him! — It's Stefan, he has followed us here! Quick, you must hide! —he must not find you here!"

Instantly, Stefan was seen hovering outside our window. There was a menacing animalistic look on his face that twisted and distorted his features— the blood that he had consumed recently from the coachman, still trickling down either side of his lips. Before either of us could move, Stefan crashed through the window.

"So, you thought you would rid yourself of me, didn't you, Fabien?" Stefan said as he brushed the glass off his jacket. "You know that I have been observing you for quite some time, and who might this be? — He doesn't appear to be one of your victims," Stefan said. Apparently he could tell by my appearance, that I was a vampire. "Could it be? Is it possible that you have disobeyed my command? —have you made a vampire fledgling of your own?"

"Why have you come back, Stefan? I thought we were to remain apart!" Fabien said ignoring his inquiry.

"Well, neither one of us held to our bargain— I knew you would not stay true to your word," Stefan said, sounding sarcastic.

"Laurent and I are happy, Stefan," Fabien said.

"Silence!" Stefan said. "Who made this young vampire? Who is his master?"

There was a moment of silence; then Fabien answered defiantly, "He is mine. I created him, and I'm in love with him."

Stefan reacted by picking up a vase and smashing it against the wall. "Because of that, I will destroy him."

"You lay one hand on him and it is I who shall destroy you Stefan!" Fabien shouted.

No sooner had Fabien warned Stefan— I jumped on top of Stefan and tried to wrestle him to the floor. Stefan merely laughed and threw me off as if I were as weightless as an article of clothing. "I will destroy you, fledgling!" he repeated— as he knelt over me, preparing to end my very existence.

But Fabien was there between us. "If you must destroy someone, destroy me," he said, "but spare Laurent."

Stefan had become so enraged upon hearing Fabien's confession of love for me that he took his hand and tore through Fabien's shirt, ripping the fabric apart, seeking to rip Fabien's heart out, as he screamed out in agony. Finally, clawing his hand deep into Fabien's chest, who then slumped to the floor with a thud.

Fabien was dead, finally at rest— however that was not a comforting thought. I couldn't believe what I had witnessed. Call it what you wish— survival mode— or animal instinct; however, I knew I had to get away from Stefan, or I would suffer the same fate. I vanished instantly, using my vampire speed to exit out of the window Stefan had entered from only moments earlier. Even so, I sensed I was only seconds away from suffering the same fate at Stefan's mighty hands.

CHAPTER 5

A Narrow Escape (Laurent Narrates)

I narrowly escaped the horror, destruction, and wrath of Stefan by materializing into mist. I made my way to Pere Lachaise cemetery seeking shelter in a family crypt— thinking I would be safe from Stefan locating me. My blood-soaked tears running down my pallid face was quite a sight to behold. I was in shock; I found it hard to believe that my Fabien was gone, destroyed in front of my eyes. The vile creature known as Stefan had fulfilled his threat— that he would ruin Fabien if he dared make a vampire fledgling of his own. And now I was alone. The unbearable feeling of that overtook my emotions. I looked around the crypt, barely seeing through the red film of blood streaming out of my eyes like a fountain.

What now?— I asked myself. *What am I to do? Where am I to go?* I knew I would never be safe anywhere in Paris, much less anywhere else in Europe, Stefan would hunt me down and destroy me as he had Fabien, ending my wretched existence—and even though my grief was unbearable, the animal instinct of survival soon overcame my pain, I tried to suppress my blood lust as a thought entered my mind, *Some of my relatives had left France for the new world as it was known. To a city named New Orleans named after the town of Orleans in France. I had heard that many other French nationals, as well as Quebecois, had settled there. Perhaps I could start over— try to forge a new beginning for myself and leave Paris and the heartache of losing Fabien to start anew— remaining anonymous and escaping Stefan.* I couldn't stop thinking about Fabien; I felt heartbroken and defeated.

Unbeknownst to me, a mist started to develop near one of the stone coffins, as the ghost of Fabien appeared. Transparent but with his distinct features visible to my vampire eyes.

"Fabien?" I asked, not believing what I was seeing. The entity looked at me with a loving glance and nodded.

I was confused as to whether this was an illusion, or what I was witnessing was the actual spirit of my departed soul mate Fabien. Then I heard the apparition speak, I was convinced he had returned.

"Fear not Laurent; our love is eternal— it is our destiny to be with one another. I shall always be with you— and you shall always be with me, I shall never leave you".

I stared mouth open as he stepped towards me, extending his hand; I longingly reached out my hand to meet his— but felt nothing but extreme cold and watched as my hand went right through his transparent hand.

"You cannot touch, nor embrace me, Laurent, however soon— very soon we shall meet again, and I assure you, this time we shall be together for all eternity. I must go now," the apparition spoke reassuringly, he looked at me with tenderness and love.

I cried out, "Don't leave me Fabien; you must not leave me again!"

But it was no use, the spirit of Fabien had vanished as suddenly as it had appeared. I felt a second sense of loss— the first— naturally being— the body of the deceased individual and its destruction. Now, this final blow, appearing then disappearing, not knowing if I shall ever see Fabien again? I wanted so desperately to believe what he had shared with me— that we would be together, but how was that to be? *Would his spirit haunt me for all of eternity, or was he alluding to something else?* I felt confused, saddened, and somehow through it all, the blood hunger reared its ugly head once more. I had to put an end to this thirst for blood.

I stepped out of the crypt feeling I was safe from Stefan, he couldn't have followed me I told myself— and if he had, I most certainly would have encountered him by now. In the distance, I heard a dog panting, a mangy-looking dog that someone had abandoned. It stopped, saw me, and growled, bearing its fangs at me as if to warn me.

Had I been a mere mortal, I would have feared for my safety— but a vampire does not worry about animal attacks. I glared back at the dog and beared my fangs for the dog to see, it made a whimpering sound, within seconds— I was at the dog's neck, as it yelped and struggled to get away to no avail, I tore into the dog's neck, the taste of dog's blood spraying the back of my throat. I didn't care much for animal blood, but I would not seek a human as my food source.

I drained every drop of blood from its body—the dog fell silently into my arms.

Glancing up at the sky, I saw that the sun was about to rise— I had lost all track of time. I released the dog's corpse to the ground and quickly made my way back into the family crypt and hoisted a sizeable concrete slab from a nearby coffin— which displayed skeletal remains.

I removed the bones, tossing them in the corner of the mausoleum, and made my way into the coffin. Instantly, I was at rest, dreaming of a lovely place. I was picturing buildings with their wrought ironworks, plantation homes with pillars with magnificent magnolia trees, and weeping willow trees. I felt at peace in this special place and thought it was calling to me as a lover might by some unforeseen force.

Was it destiny? I thought.

After a week of hiding out in the crypt, I decided to return to our apartment cautiously.

I knew it was time to leave France and begin a new chapter that did not always remind me of my previous existence with Fabien.

New Orleans in French Louisiana, or New France, would become my new home— but just how long it would take to find a new home I did not know.

I left the cemetery no longer feeling the threat of Stefan looming over me. Surely after a few days spent at the crypt, Stefan would have moved on, ending his search for me, at least for the moment. I transported and materialized myself in front of our apartment, quickly entering the front door. There on the threshold, I noticed a letter. I opened it immediately, seeing the return address of New Orleans. It was a letter written to me by my grandfather Pierre, who had immigrated to New Orleans five years prior— after the passing of my Grandmother. In the letter, my Grandfather disclosed that he was gravely ill and would not survive much longer; he most certainly will have passed on before I was to receive the letter in the mail.

It was his dying wish; I was to inherit his plantation and furnishings and the servants' sworn loyalty. His second wife, Josephine Jacobson, an American, would stay on at the estate until my arrival and afterward relocate to Virginia's newfound American colony.

The plantation known as "Le Petit Fleur," named by my late grandfather, was located just north of New Orleans in a small community called Vacherie; in the St James parish district, it was everything I could have imagined. My eyes turned to the blood-spattered remains— seeing where just a short time ago, my lover Fabien had been destroyed in front of my eyes, as I dropped the letter out of excitement.

Stefan had undoubtedly taken the body and disposed of it in some cruel and horrific manner— of that I was sure. I began the unpleasant task of cleaning up Fabien's blood and cleaned the mess.

I broke down on more than one occasion, cursing Stefan over and over, all the while shedding blood tears over my destroyed soul mate. I left absolutely no trace of blood or anything that would raise questions for anyone responsible for packing my belongings. I began the task of focusing my attention on my new home. The next evening, I made my way into town to arrange a crate transport, which would serve to house me across the high seas to the new world.

Naturally, all my belongings would come later— after I had made my acquaintance with my late grandfather's wife, Josephine and secured her departure from my inherited estate. I instructed the shipping company that the crate needed soil. They did not question why— thinking perhaps I was a bit eccentric for this unusual request—nor did they want to do anything to anger me or jeopardize the arrangement as I had paid them handsomely.

CHAPTER 6

The New World (Laurent Narrates)

The day arrived when I was to be transported to the New World, and my new existence in New Orleans— or rather a small village in the north called St James parish and the small town of Vacherie where I was to reside in my estate. I would make my way on board the vessel without being detected, find the crate containing the soil of my homeland, and lie in this container until the ship reached the shores of the Mississippi River.

I knew I would survive the lengthy and treacherous journey across the sea— fed enough blood from dogs— cats— and vermin before the sea journey. This blood would sustain my appetite for the long adventure.

Nightfall came, and I made my way to the long vessel, the workmen had just about completed loading the crate.

I chose to transform myself into a mist, which would cause me to go undetected by the workmen. Spotting it at the other end of the vessel— and making sure none of the workmen were around, I materialized and lifted the heavy lid of the wooden crate as if it were light as a feather and secured myself inside. A few hours later, the vessel was in motion, and I knew my journey was beginning.

I had many strange visions while I was self-contained in my wooden refuge. Was I perhaps starting to grow mad being trapped in this wooden box—or were these visions a part of my vampire abilities? Seeing the apparition of my beloved Fabien in the crypt of the cemetery gave me pause. It isn't typical for the living—or the undead to see ghosts of the dearly departed. Was Fabien sent to warn me or comfort me through my grieving process? I didn't know, which troubled me significantly.

One more than one occasion— I had recurring nightmares seeing Stefan destroy Fabien repeatedly, each time screaming as I awakened to find myself in this temporary home, alone. My guilt and anger consumed me, thinking, *I should have tried to do more to protect my eternal soul mate! But how? I was no match for Stefan—his being over two hundred years older than myself made him much more powerful than I— much like a full-grown person's strength compared to that of a child's.*

I swore to myself—I would exact some revenge against Stefan— perhaps as I grew in age, my strength and vampire abilities would increase? For now, what mattered was to seek out a new existence in the New World and plans for revenge against Stefan would need to wait.

The ship made its way across the rough and treacherous sea, bobbing and weaving along the Atlantic Ocean, lasting an entire month, finally settling into the harbor, in the city—known as New Orleans. The workmen hoisted the wooden crate and carried it off the ship and onto the pier—it was left as ordered, no questions asked. As soon as I sensed, the sun had set— which seemed to be an uncanny ability of mine—something I assumed other vampires had —as I broke open the wood crate as if it were made from kindling wood.

I was ravenous after the long sea voyage, and having spotted a stray dog near the harbor, I seized the opportunity to feed, making certain there was no one else around to witness this. I descended upon the animal, much like a rabid animal myself, snarling and baring my fangs. The dog recoiled, growled— and then a whimper, then nothing. The dog's blood was spraying the inside of my neck as I tore upon its jugular vein, feasting and draining its red life-force. Even though I detest animal blood, it served its purpose until I could find a human involved in a criminal act, as I had learned from Fabien.

I had been given the location of my new estate in the letter sent by my late grandfather. I took flight— landing close to the center of town. My flight ability meant I was able to transport myself to other locations but not over water; otherwise, I would have spared myself the unpleasant and long journey over the Atlantic.

I made my way into town, looking for a room to stay in that didn't have a window to shield myself from the sunlight. I would travel by horse so as not to mysteriously appear out of nowhere—and call on my late grandfather's widow the following evening to work out the details of her departure and to acquaint myself with my newly acquired servants. I located a room in the center of town known as the French quarter. It was being rented out by the proprietor of a bar, and while it was noisy due to the patrons of the bar who seemed to congregate there regularly, the room provided me the privacy I required.

The bar was owned by a French-Canadian man in his mid-twenties, Claude Boucher, who had emigrated from Quebec a few years prior. Monsieur Boucher and I had struck up a conversation as the last of the bar patrons were preparing to leave. Once the last of the bar patrons left, he showed me the room, indicating that the place would be private and, as I had requested, would not have a window.

"Here is the room, as you can see, there is a washbasin as well for you to freshen up," he said. I looked at him and gave a slight smile while looking around the dingy room, thinking it would serve its purpose as I feigned a yawn indicating I required rest and privacy.

"I can see that you are tired Monsieur, it must have been a long journey, I will excuse myself, if there is anything you require, please do not hesitate to ask," he said graciously, as he turned to leave.

"There is one last thing I will require Monsieur Boucher, a horse, for purchase. I have business to attend to outside of town tomorrow evening, and I will not be returning. Will you arrange this for me? I will pay you handsomely for your troubles," I said.

"Yes, of course, Monsieur Richelieu."

The next evening, as promised, Monsieur Boucher arranged for the horse to be delivered. It was a beautiful, muscular black Arabian horse; I was introduced to my horse and told its name was Mercury. I made my way over to the horse, stroking it a few times to acquaint myself with the horse and develop its trust. It responded with a neighing sound. And as if by instinct, the two of us bonded as I climbed on top of the magnificent creature. I thanked my host and paid him handsomely for his troubles as promised, we said our goodbyes, and in an instant, I was off.

With my vampire night vision, I was able to steer Mercury in the right direction. We made our way through the trees and wetlands for hours. I knew Mercury would not make the journey from New Orleans to Vacherie in one evening, after riding for what seemed several hours, I found a house along the way. I decided Mercury would need water and rest, and I would need shelter during the scorching daylight hours. I made my way over to the house and knocked on the front door.

A man who appeared to be in his mid-thirties answered the door. "Yes, can I help you?" he asked as he looked me over suspiciously. Instantly meeting his gaze, I drew him in and began to hypnotize him.

"I require lodging for the night, a darkened room or cellar will suffice, as well as water for my horse, you will provide me all of this," I said as I held his gaze.

He naturally agreed as he was under my hypnotic spell. I knew that I would be able to rest here until sunset and complete the remainder of my journey arriving at the estate the following evening.

I found refuge in the man's cellar. It was dark enough to shield me from the punishing rays of the sun. Luckily for me, it was also rodent infested. I quickly seized upon one of the scurvy creatures tearing it apart with my sharp teeth, draining the blood of the rat, which ran down my throat, instantly satisfying my blood lust. As soon as I had nourished myself, I gave Mercury his water, I had found some hay to feed him as well and settled him in for the evening. I walked the owner's property and gazed up at the stars, feeling anxious to begin my new existence in the new world.

I rested during the day in the man's cellar, it was dark enough to protect me from the sun.

Nightfall came, I boarded my horse, and Mercury and I were off. I knew it would not be long before I arrived at my newly acquired estate.

Arriving at the estate late that evening, after tying Mercury to one of the trees, I made my way around to the front, taking in the splendor of my new home, it's majestic, massive columns, and the many oak trees lining each side of the very long walkway leading to the front door.

To describe my newly inherited estate as grand would be an understatement.

Despite my late arrival, I noticed a flickering candlelight coming from inside the great house; I suspected my late grandfather's widow, Josephine, had not yet gone to bed, and perhaps was up reading.

I made my way over to the massive front door and announced my arrival using the door knocker. After what seemed to be several minutes, an attractive woman in her mid to late forties answered the door. Soon I would meet the woman my late Grandfather had married after my Grandmother's untimely demise.

"Yes, may I help you?" she asked with a concerned look on her face.

"I am Laurent Richelieu, your late husband's grandson; I believe you were expecting me?" I replied.

She looked me over and broke into a flirtatious grin. "My! Pierre never mentioned what a handsome man you are," she said, almost gushing. I found this spectacle to be embarrassing and rude, and so soon after my grandfather's death.

"May I come in?" I asked— as I ignored the woman's flirtatious advances.

"Why, of course, where are my manners," she said as she stepped aside to make room for my entrance.

"This is exquisite" I said as I looked around at every detail in the great house, noting the many crystal chandeliers, as well as the magnificent, polished mahogany of the grand staircase leading upstairs.

"Please follow me into the drawing-room," she said, continuing to flirt with me as she batted her eyelashes.

We entered the drawing-room, complete with a magnificent fireplace, as she sat on a settee and motioned me towards a wingback chair, as she picked up a fan and began to use it on herself. *Soon, all of this will be mine,* I thought to myself.

"May I be candid with you, Monsieur Richelieu?" she asked as I noticed she had dropped her flirtatious manner, perhaps sensing my disinterest, and was apparently getting down to business.

I was impressed by her knowledge of French, despite being an American. I was sure my late grandfather had taught her everything he knew.

"Yes, by all means, Miss?" I asked, not remembering her surname.

"Miss Jacobson," she said, sounding somewhat irritated as she continued, "I find it odd that during our entire marriage, your late grandfather very rarely, if ever, mentioned you," she said, perhaps alluding to questioning the legitimacy of my inherited estate.

I looked at her as if the two of us were engaged in a strategic game of chess.

"I can assure you, Miss Jacobson, my Grandfather and I were very close back when he lived in Paris married to my Grandmother," I stated, almost defiantly.

"I'm sure you were," she replied rather coldly.

"What are you implying, Miss Jacobson? —If there is something you would like to share with me, then by all means!" I said as I looked at her rather sternly.

"With all due respect Monsieur Richelieu, I believe it is I, as your grandfather's widow, who am entitled to this estate, or at the very least, half of it," she said in a challenging manner. I looked her over carefully and responded in a calm, collected manner. "Miss Jacobson, I appreciate your candor, however let me remind you that I am a blood relative and the rightful heir to this property and all of its belongings according to my late grandfather's last will. I understood from my late grandfather's letter that you were to be in the process of relocating to the commonwealth of Virginia?" I said sternly. I sensed her mood switch to once again being flirtatious.

"Perhaps you and I can work out some arrangement?" she said, batting her eyelashes and fanning herself at the same time.

I got up and walked over to the window, looking out at the darkness, and making out everything with crystal clarity.

I turned to her and said, "You are not a relative of mine; I have no affinity for you—you are merely the second wife of my late grandfather. You will pack up your belongings and leave first thing in the morning; naturally, I will leave you a small payment to help facilitate your relocation efforts," I said in a commanding way. "However, before you leave, you will introduce me to all of the servants that reside on the property so there is an orderly transition, do I make myself clear, Miss Jacobson?" I said with a stern expression on my face as I leaned over in her direction so close I could make out the features of each of her long eyelashes she used up until a short time ago to flirt with.

"Yes, I understand perfectly, Monsieur Richelieu," she replied as she backed down from her challenge, sensing her efforts had failed and she was defeated.

"Now shall we go out back so you can introduce me to all the servants?," I suggested.

"With pleasure, Monsieur Richelieu," she replied, sounding almost sarcastic.

I knew that my offering to add to her fortune my late grandfather had left her with, would help facilitate her timely departure. I knew she had been an opportunist and merely cared for my grandfather because of his wealth; there hadn't been any real love, as my late grandfather never wrote about his second wife ever. Quite frankly, the one thing we had in common was that neither of us knew much about the other—the thought of her flirting with me so soon after his passing! I theorized she didn't care too much to play the role of a grieving widow.

She walked over to pick up one of the candelabras to light the outside pathway, as we made our way over to a gigantic bell used to gather up all the servants, she proceeded to ring the bell repeatedly.

The servants streamed in, a large group totaling roughly twenty of them—both men and women. Miss Josephine shared with them that the plantation was in transition and that I was their new owner. I introduced myself to them, as they, in turn, presented themselves to me. There was no need to speak to them in English, a language I had not yet studied— many understood French and had come from the French West Indies in the Caribbean as well as from the French colonies in Africa.

I instructed them to begin preparing my room and that my bedroom required dark velvet curtains, which would ensure complete privacy, as well as sufficient shielding from the sun's rays during daylight, a thought which I did not share with them.

I surveyed the twenty-room estate; there would be enough room for my belongings once they were brought over by ship to add to the furnishings I inherited from my grandfather.

We bid our goodnights to the servants as well as to each other. I shared with Miss Josephine my exhaustion of having made the long journey from France to Louisiana a couple of days ago, as well as the days-long journey from New Orleans to the estate, and that I would not be able to see her off come morning. She told me she understood and noted my pale complexion and suggested that perhaps I was becoming ill.

My, how her mood had changed after I gave her a small fortune of my gold coins as promised, she had become downright agreeable, almost pleasant.

I had seen the last of Miss Josephine. As per our arrangement, she had left the next day making the days-long journey by carriage to her newfound home in Virginia. She had left me a letter leaving me her forwarding address, which confused me a bit, what was she expecting of me? I thought, *Why would I need to be in contact with my deceased grandfather's much younger widow?* I started to question her sanity and morals at this point, as I shook my head in disgust, I picked up the paper and began to tear it up and toss it into the fireplace where I felt it belonged.

I waited one month for all the treasured antiques and paintings to arrive. There was one possession that was the most prized, the portrait of Fabien. It took three days until the entire estate and my furnishings sent from France, were moved in and set up. I instructed my servants to hang the picture of Fabien on the wall inside my master bedroom. That way, I would be able to gaze upon it just before I lay down to rest, and it would be the first thing I would see as I rose.

As I walked around the enormous mansion, examining each artifact, every painting, and inspecting each room, I voiced my approval much to my servant's relief. It is essential to gain the appreciation of their master. They all carefully scanned my face to see if I approved or not, finally with a calming and tender voice, I said, "You have all done well," to which they all replied in unison, "Thank you, Master Richelieu" I felt at home, in my new country and excited to explore this city already vibrant with African, Island, and French influences.

I must have appeared as different to them, as they seemed to me, as I had never seen anyone as dark-skinned as my servants, nor had they ever witnessed anyone as pale as myself. It's highly unlikely any of my servants would suspect that they were laying their eyes upon one of the living dead.

I won't call them "slaves" as I loathe the word—I do not feel superior to them in any way; they are my servants, to serve me, but not slaves. I felt grateful they were there taking care of my needs, and at some point—I would have to confide in at least one of my servants and reveal my true self. That day would come sooner than I had ever dreamed.

It was a hot, humid summer night, the kind of weather that you could almost cut the air with a knife.

Thinking I was alone in the back of the estate, when suddenly I spotted a Jackrabbit meandering in the bushes, I immediately seized it in my hands, tearing into its neck—blood running down my throat, not realizing that my trusty servant Barthelme was standing outside smoking observing everything.

He was a big man who stood taller than me. A French creole servant with bulging biceps, which would make any woman swoon.

Barthelme cried out, "Master!"

I quickly dropped the now deceased Jackrabbit, instantly appearing in front of him, before the blink of an eye. He scanned my face with his mouth wide open in horror at my appearance and what he had witnessed.

"You are to tell no one about what you have seen tonight, your very life may depend on it! —is that clear?" I said sternly.

His speech began to stammer. "Ye Ye Yes, Master! Why is your mouth covered in blood?! Are you injured? What has happened to this animal?" He inquired.

"Never mind, Barthelme!" "You best not ask questions that you will later regret asking!" I warned. "I repeat you are not to disclose any of what you have seen to anyone, do you understand?" I commanded menacingly.

"Yes-Um Master", he replied.

I was curious as to exactly what Barthelme had witnessed, so I decided to ask him directly, "What did you see Barthelme?"

After a brief pause, he answered with his head bowed down, saying finally, "I saw you bite an animal with blood smeared on your mouth."

I could have ended his life in that exact moment, but given my moral dilemma of indiscriminately killing, as taught by Fabien, and knowing I would need Barthelme as a trusted servant—I chose to employ a more controlled response.

I demanded Barthelme look deep into my eyes. I repeated over and over and over again. "You saw nothing; you saw nothing, you saw nothing!"

Then asking once again, if he had witnessed anything strange the past evening.

"No, nothing I can remember, Master!" Barthelme said, shrugging. After a brief silence he spoke, "Master Laurent, May I be excused? I still have some chores to attend to", he said.

"Yes, you can leave," I said coldly.

It was too late, the seeds of doubt and mistrust had been planted in my mind. *How could I trust Barthelme?* I thought. I decided he needed to be made into a servant I could trust my very existence with—he would become my immortal mortal servant.

The next evening, I summoned Barthelme telepathically; he would come to me only hearing my voice call out to him, beckoning him to the vast mansion where I would anxiously await his arrival.

He arrived holding his hat, the sun had just set, and I could see Barthelme's clothes had been stained due to the fierce summer heat of the day.

"You wanted to see me, Master Laurent?," he asked sheepishly. "Yes, Barthelme, let us go into the drawing-room, which offers more privacy," I said.

We entered the drawing-room, and I was lost in thought, thinking of the few short nights of chess playing and roaring fires with my beloved Fabien—as Barthelme's words led me back to the present and away from my thoughts of the past.

"Master, what was it you wanted to speak to me about?"

I paced around the room a bit before giving him my answer. Finally, saying, "Barthelme, I feel the only way I can trust you utterly and completely is to have you as my immortal servant. Rather than have to destroy you for what you witnessed—it is the only way, I need you Barthelme."

"I don't understand Master; immortal servant?" he asked.

I knew by biting him, he would live much longer than a mere mortal, and never grow old or prone to sickness—I would need a servant sworn to secrecy that knows my dark secret, a gatekeeper. I told him to remove his shirt. I would bite Barthelme on the shoulder so the two puncture wounds would not be visible to the rest of the servants.

"Take off your shirt, Barthelme," I commanded.

He did as I instructed him to do, revealing a muscular, chiseled chest with strong pectoral muscles and a hard rock abdomen. I leaned over, and bit him—he seemed stunned and tried to escape my powerful embrace, but I was too strong even for someone of Barthelme's build. He tried to speak, but I held my hand over his mouth—he struggled but quickly ceased. I drank only a little bit of his blood, combined with hypnotizing him, would make Barthelme my eternal servant—shortly after I finished drinking his blood, I began the hypnotism.

"Barthelme, you are growing tired, so tired you can barely stand up," I said, as he slumped slightly in my arms. "Barthelme, I command you to secrecy; you will be my immortal servant, to guard me against anyone who may wish to harm me, for I am your eternal Master. Do you understand?" I asked "Yes, Master," he uttered in a hypnotic slow reply, his face expressionless.

"I am one of the living dead, a vampire; I require your services at all times. During the day I must sleep, you are to guard me and protect me, have I made myself clear, Barthelme?"

"Yes, Master, I swear to you my undying loyalty, your secret I will defend and guard with my life," he stated as he kept his promise throughout the years, which brought us into the civil war between the states.

The war ended in 1865; a proclamation order ended slavery; nevertheless, Barthelme stayed on as my trusted manservant, as he had no choice. Quite suddenly, we approached the early 19th century.

CHAPTER 7

Just The Two Of Us (Laurent Narrates)

Nearly seventy years had passed, and Barthelme and I witnessed many inventions of the 19th century, such as the steam engine— Trains that could take a human from New Orleans to New York. The light bulb, although I chose to stay with candlelight— call me old fashioned. I allowed for only one modern invention, the telephone, which is a requirement for Barthelme's dealings with the outside world.

There were other inventions as well, the telegraph and many more wondrous devices—one more spectacular than the other! Photography was popular during this time, and whenever someone asked to take my picture, I graciously declined as being not very photogenic, no one asked any further. A vampire's image does not appear on film; anyone who would have taken a picture of me would not have believed their eyes in seeing nothing in the image except for whatever background I chose.

There was one thing that shook me to the core, approximately thirty years later, when in 1897, a book by the name of "Dracula," written by an Irishman named Bram Stoker, was written.

The book told the fictional story about a Romanian Count who was a supposed vampire—king of all vampires, existing amongst ordinary mortals. I read it; it alarmed me as there were a growing number of individuals who started believing in the paranormal. If people started believing in the existence of ghosts, then why not vampires?

I knew quite well after seeing Fabien's spirit that ghosts do exist. I wondered how many would believe in vampires after reading "Dracula," and if any of same individuals crossed paths with me, how many would think me to be as odd as the Count in the book? —I decided to stay extra cautious and not to expose myself to the public. Ironic as it may seem—many of the things that Bram Stoker wrote about in his book were correct. I thought; *Was this man psychic? A shaman, perhaps? How could he know such intimate details about our kind?*

Every description in the book, everything from the two puncture wounds on someone's neck after a vampire bites the victim—as well as a vampire's ability to change into a wolf, bat or mist, and many other things.

I suspect the author perhaps knew of or possibly came into contact with someone of our kind. The rest of the book was, fiction, all except— the infamous Count, who impaled invading Turkish troops from the Ottoman Empire, legend has it, and he bathed himself in blood!

The years kept melting away, my loneliness for companionship grew to be almost intolerable. I knew I needed to get out of my relative seclusion. Barthelme was a poor excuse for a companion. After I put him under my control nearly a hundred years prior—he hadn't aged physically.

He was an excellent gatekeeper, he dealt with and hastened the departure of anyone showing up unexpectedly looking for me. Barthelme was instructed to tell everyone I was away on business. It did take nearly four or five days to reach New York or Boston, so most did not question my absence whenever someone would come to call.

As suddenly as the nineteenth century arrived, it departed, I found myself, along with my trusty servant, in the late twentieth century. The year was nineteen hundred and eighty-three. I had resided in New Orleans, or rather Vacherie, for nearly one hundred and eighty-seven years. Despite the numerous television shows and movies about vampires, I needed to get out and meet some of the inhabitants of the city called "The Big Easy." Barthelme became my driver. From time to time, I had thought about Stefan's possibility of tracking me down; I knew I would need more than my vampire skills to defend myself against him, as that alone would not suffice.

I became intrigued with the ancient Martial Arts of the east. I decided to locate a Martial Arts Academy to learn the art of hand-to-hand self-defense—I enrolled in a nightly class in the ancient East Asian art of Karate. My speed and agility impressed my instructor, as did my hand and eye coordination. I quickly adapted to an accelerated training, always fearing Stefan would show up at any moment looking to fulfill his promise of my destruction. If he were to—I would be ready for him!

A few months later, I earned a second-degree black belt. I not only enjoyed getting out of the confines of my secluded estate, but training in hand-to-hand combat, along with my vampire abilities, gave me the confidence in knowing I could withstand an attack by Stefan. When I was not training at the academy, my other passion involved attending the many jazz clubs in town, where I would be seated at a dark table near the back.

Each Friday night, Barthelme dropped me off in the center of the city near any one of the many jazz clubs. I cannot operate a motorized vehicle—I am getting used to an automobiles' concept, or better known presently as "cars" instead of the horse and carriage of my day.

I quickly became fond of jazz. It seemed to be so captivating and alluring, a brilliant mix of instruments, horns, strings, and typically a sultry vocalist to accompany the band. Listening to this music made it seem as if it had transcended into my soul. I made it a point to visit all the long-time jazz bars, including "Snug Harbor," "the Bombay Club," and "Preservation Hall."

I did not ask Barthelme to join me as I wanted to be alone, to listen and contemplate my existence, and lose myself in the music entirely.

Besides—would he not think it strange to accompany me, as if we were on a date together?

Barthelme accepted my preference for male company, but I couldn't picture him and me attending something together.

The thought of that made me laugh. Not that Barthelme wasn't engaging—I hired some of the most exceptional tutors in Louisiana to be able to master the English language, so he and I could converse in English. As for my teachings, I decided to study English through "*Berlitz,*" which were audiotapes and booklets designed to help those— like myself, learn a particular language. Barthelme had secured a modern device called a tape recorder; I used it to listen to the instruction material, quickly mastering control of the English language.

Once a week, usually on a Friday, I was driven into town by Barthelme. I marveled at the world around me and wondered what Fabien would have thought of all these modern-day human-made inventions? I could only imagine. Oh, how I missed him! It had been so long since I had any male companionship to embrace another male, smell a man's essence, and feel the taut muscles, much less the deep bond that can exist between two men.

As for finding any male companionship; I frown upon casual sexual encounters or "hooking up" as it's referred to in its modern-day expression, which meant meeting a gentlemen caller purely for sex.

Of course, I appreciate physical interaction, and even longed for it. However—there was something brutishly animalistic in today's world about meeting a man. Most of the emphasis was purely on the sexual, rather than genuinely trying to connect with another individual. I had frequented some of all gentlemen saloons—also known as "gay bars," listening to whatever recording artist was famous at the moment. *How truly awful!* I thought. *Is this music?*

And how awkward was the approach of many gentlemen in these

establishments? I was propositioned many times, each time declining their advances.

Rather than face endless encounters such as these, I decided to avoid these establishments altogether in place of the jazz clubs where mostly males and females frequented, at least at these establishments, there appeared to be decorum.

I was hopeful that at some point in my existence, I would find a companion who once found out my dark secret would invite me to turn him so he and I would be together for all eternity. I had no idea what to expect and how soon the situation would present itself.

CHAPTER 8

Jack's Story (Jack Narrates)

When I was growing up in Baton Rouge, Louisiana, in the 1960s, a man couldn't live openly as a homosexual. I knew I was different, but I strived desperately not just to hide but also to overcome who I indeed was. I tried to dominate my two other brothers, besting them in wrestling and other forms of hand-to-hand combat. My father taught me how to box and told me, "I don't want my son to become a 'sissy'!"

But I always knew the story of my life would be different from his. My earliest recollection of being different was in junior high. I would furiously try not to look too long at my classmates as they undressed after gym class, especially when we all took showers together. I was hell-bent on fighting that desire to watch and diving headfirst into passing as a straight guy.

I joined the football team at my high school, hoping that would change things and toughen me up, make me more of a man. So, I decided to try out—and I became a linebacker.

I was athletically blessed, with good hand-eye coordination, speed, and a muscular body. I became a football player—but the physical attraction to other boys remained.

You may ask, did I have any experiences with girls? Of course, I had girlfriends—I even had what you might describe as enjoyable sex with them, but what was lacking was the emotional connection. I remember making out with girls in the backseat of my dad's car, imagining that they were the hot guys on the football team.

As a good Roman Catholic, I prayed to God every night that the attraction to my sex was only a phase and that I would soon blossom into a full man with carnal desires for women.

I was not too fond of stereotypes and wanted to distance myself from all myths of what a gay man looked and sounded like. Whenever I saw a gay male character on television or in the movies, it was a negative portrayal. Swishy and effeminate. Seeing those characters made me hate myself that much more. I guess you can thank my good old-fashioned southern upbringing for that. Some would say I was a self-loathing gay, and I wouldn't dispute it. I would ask myself over and over, *Why has God done this to me? Am I being tested in my faith?* I convinced myself that no one, including family and close friends, suspected anything, as my voice was deep and masculine, and I didn't display any effeminate behavior. And while I cared about fashion and looking good, I wasn't obsessed with fancy clothes and didn't groom in front of a mirror for hours. Despite having done well financially, our family didn't provide me with much money for clothes anyway. When I graduated from high school, I went out with my straight friends to straight bars, where I received attention from women. I treated heterosexual encounters like a game—but they were, equally playing with me, as if I were a toy. I thought foolishly that if I slept with a lot of women, my feelings of loneliness and not belonging would go away, and that I could bury in them the pain of hurt and isolation.

I knew I couldn't stay in the confines of Baton Rouge with my large family all around. I wanted my freedom; I wanted to move to a place where I knew no one, and no one knew me, and I would be free to live my own life and follow my desires. I decided to move to the Big Easy, the big and bawdy city of New Orleans, where I could act upon my urges and satisfy my hunger for encounters with men.

I found out quickly just how the city lived up to its name. I slept with whoever I wanted without having to be afraid my family would find out. My sexual encounters were with both men and women. For a while, I decided I was bisexual—which was more comfortable for my mind (polluted with narrow-minded thinking and religious strictures) to accept than being gay.

Whenever I found myself in bed with a man, the guilt was so intense that I hated myself. To ease my mind, I held off on any further gay encounters; I decided I needed to "stabilize" my life, which meant sleeping only with women, at least for a while.

I certainly wasn't looking for a relationship, but the relationship found me. I met Lisa at Maison Bourbon, a jazz club, and a local and tourist hangout on Bourbon Street, where lots of liquored up women and men listened to great jazz.

Lisa was sitting at the bar with a couple of girlfriends. Her laugh was what drew me to her; it was intoxicating. I heard it across the bar. I looked over in her direction, and our eyes met and locked, I nodded, and she winked at me. I got up and walked over to the table where she and another woman were seated. I attempted some bad humor and introduced myself as Jack and said I wasn't looking for three's company. She gave me her name. She was attractive enough, big smile, strawberry-blonde hair, and pale-blue eyes. She asked me to join them at their table, which I did.

The evening progressed. The girlfriend sensed Lisa and I were beginning to make a connection, and she politely excused herself and left. Lisa loved to hear me tell jokes, and yeah, I'll admit they were terrible, but somehow Lisa found me interesting. I must admit; I felt comfortable around her. For once, I didn't feel as if I was being lusted after just for my looks. I thought of Lisa as a friend, even as if she might have been my sister— but Lisa was starting to develop serious feelings for me. If truth be told, I did lead her on. I was only thinking of myself, so I thought, what the hell? I tried to bury the gay part deep within myself, however tricky, as I was tempted daily by the men around me.

I pushed away the gay part of me every day and night, mostly through prayer. I can't tell you exactly how many times I had prayed to God to save me from becoming a queer—more times than you can imagine. My faith was essential to me; I believed, as I learned, that homosexuality was an abomination in the eyes of the Lord. No one ever told me, in that context, that Jesus Christ had come not to condemn the world but to save it.

When I was with Lisa, it indeed was like being with my best friend. The only problem was the sex, or lack thereof. Poor Lisa, she thought I was impotent! When we were out, my eyes always searched the room, connecting with other men and some women. I was able to read their thoughts with merely the prolonged glance or the wink of an eye.

On more than one occasion, I followed up with whoever provided me with their number. There were, in fact, a couple of times Lisa caught me in bed with a woman—with that, the same scenario played out every time: she would get upset, leave crying hysterically, scream and yell and tell me to "go to hell!" and that "I was no good!"

She always came back, begging for forgiveness, I guess Lisa and I were relatively evenly matched as far as self-loathing went. I figured at the very least, Lisa would be a companion, and at least then I wouldn't feel so lonely all the time.

I asked her to go steady and told her I would mend my ways and be a good boyfriend. I could finally announce to everyone that I had a regular girlfriend and that she very well might become my wife someday, hoping that would convince everyone that I was heterosexual. To that, I usually received hysterical laughter from friends. "What, you? The confirmed bachelor?" they would scoff.

Feeling that I had no choice, after three months of dating, I asked Lisa to marry me. She was overjoyed and cried with happiness, but I felt as if my heart were breaking. I wanted to cry with her; only my tears would have been out of misery and self-loathing. I felt all the oxygen in the room go out and thought to myself, *What the hell have I done?*

We set a date for a year later. During that time, I miraculously remained faithful, as I had promised Lisa.

The date came, and we had the prominent Roman Catholic wedding at St. Louis Cathedral. It was a large wedding, at my father's insistence, with over two hundred and fifty people in attendance. I'll never forget that day. It was an unusually hot, humid Louisiana summer day with dark storm clouds gathering in the sky, perhaps a hint of how rocky our marriage was to become. I felt I would have made a great actor because no one suspected how miserable I was.

Lisa looked radiant in a white dress with a cathedral train. For one of the few times in my life, I had on a tuxedo. It must have been the heat and humidity, combined with my nervousness that produced two armpit stains the size of ponds under my arms. I put on my jacket to hide those unsightly stains. My father came over to me and said, "Son, I'm proud of you—congratulations, I thought you'd never marry!" To that I feigned a smile and caught a glimpse of myself in the mirror, which made my heart sink. I told myself, *You'll probably be dead by the time you reach sixty, because that's thirty-seven long, miserable years of living a lie with Lisa.*

Once we were married, our life together dragged on, each day and night being the same as every other day, miserable. I was as strong as an ox, so I applied for a job in construction. The pay wasn't great, more importantly, it helped me to feel like a real man. I landed mostly day jobs. My not having gone to college prevented me from getting a high-paying office job. I left the house early each morning at five to be on the construction site at six, grateful not to have any interaction with Lisa so early in the morning. She was usually still asleep when I left.

Lisa got a job at a local department store called Maison Blanche as a salesclerk. We had little money which made our marriage even more miserable. At night we would watch mindless television together, mostly family sitcoms and game shows, anything to avoid having to speak to one another. Whenever we did interact, we ended up arguing—mostly about money or lack thereof, and about sex and lack thereof. The only time I could escape from her was when I was asleep and dreaming—that was an escape into another world, away from Lisa. On occasion, I would have a nightmare, which sometimes involved flailing my arms around and almost hitting Lisa.

"Wake up!" she would yell. "You're having a nightmare!" Most often she was annoyed that she had been so fiercely awakened.

"Perhaps you should lay off the Jack Daniels you drink every night before you come to bed, before it destroys you and your liver, and maybe you wouldn't have bad dreams. Now turn the light off and go back to sleep. I have to get up early tomorrow," she said as she settled back into a fetal position with her comforter wrapped snugly around her. The next morning at work, guys on the construction site looked at me and said,

"Man, you look like shit! Ain't you been gett'in' any?" "That's the least of it," I said.

"I guess I would be having bad dreams too if I was married to your wife," one of the workmen said.

"Knock it off, Rafael!" I said.

"Yeah? What are you gonna do about it, Jack? Sic your wife on me?" Rafael said, laughing.

I thought about what he was saying, and even though I was miserable being married to Lisa, he had no right to talk to me about her like that, especially around a group of the other guys on the site.

"Naw!" I said, "I don't need my wife to deal with you, asshole!" I feigned turning around and then suddenly twisting towards him—my fist clenched, and I knocked him one. Rafael landed on his ass with a bewildered look on his face. I have always been a good fighter—I had my Dad to thank for that. *At least he had tried to do everything not to raise a sissy,* I thought. The guys kept us separated for a bit and eventually we got back to work, forgetting our emotional outburst.

My marriage to Lisa dragged on into days, weeks, months, and finally into years. Except for one or two indiscretions, I had been mostly faithful for nearly an entire decade. Here I was thirty-five and nothing to show for it, except a lousy construction job, a beat-up old wreck of a truck, and a wife I didn't love, living a lifestyle I had become more and more of a stranger to. I couldn't take it any longer. I encouraged Lisa to visit her folks in Shreveport, and she jumped at the suggestion. Which meant I could finally take care of some much needed and delayed business for myself. The only way I was going to hook up with another man was to go to one of the dreaded gay bars, filled with men who were there with their friends; men who felt as if they had a connection to one another. I felt connected to no one.

Looking around the first bar I went to; I made eye contact with this guy by the pinball machine. I walked over and asked him if I could join him. We traded smiles, and I offered to buy him a beer. He told me his name was Sam, and he admitted to me, as if he were confessing to a priest, that Sam was closeted as well; he had been married for five years. Him being closeted, was to be our bond, beyond the physical attraction, of course. Sam stood about five foot eleven, had a slight, yet muscular build and a boyishly handsome face, and blond hair and brown eyes. He must have been in his early thirties.

We made small talk as we played pinball. Once we finished, we went over to the back section of the bar, where it was a little quieter to talk. He told me he liked sports but that he was also into culture. Sam liked art and music and was also into fashion. He described himself as "a ladies' man," which made me suppress a chuckle, because it was clear to me that he was completely gay. Then again, who was I to judge him? My smirk disappeared from my face as quickly as it had come. With that, I put my hand on his thigh and rubbed it as he looked at me and leaned over to kiss me.

We agreed to go back to his place because his wife was out of town. He had a beautiful apartment in the French quarter. No sooner had we entered his apartment, he suggested that I slip off my shoes and make myself comfortable. He gave me a full and beautiful smile. I knew the suggestion of slipping off the shoes meant we were going to be getting down to business—so I kicked off my shoes and sure enough, we began to make out.

We made our way to the bedroom, which was a Laura Ashley flowering nightmare. I knew the household linens belonged to the wife— but even so! Sam had left the television on, and President Reagan was challenging another leader to "tear down this wall." I asked Sam if he could switch it off, as I felt the broadcast would interfere with our mood.

I don't know why those flowered sheets raised such hostility in me; I guess it was the idea that Sam's wife claimed that bed for her own, whereas I wanted it to belong entirely to Sam and me, with no female interference. I made it a point to get those flowering sheets as sweaty as possible! Call it a mission of mercy for Sam.

We got undressed, Sam's body was slender and muscular, and a swimmer's build, although I don't think any swimming pools were involved — it was more probably regular trips to the gym. When I undressed, I told him to get ready to see fireworks. He laughed and begged me to show him. And I did.

I made my escape as soon as I started to hear Sam snore. I didn't like the awkwardness of small talk after a sexual conquest, and I didn't see myself as the cuddling type. If I wasn't going to do that with my wife, why would I cuddle with a stranger? I figured he had his wife to do that with.

When I was back in my own home, I turned on the radio, and AC/DC's "Highway to Hell" blared out—I thought there couldn't be a more appropriate song to describe my current situation.

Lisa returned home the following week, exhausted from having spent the entire weekend with her parents and two siblings. She was speaking to me, but all I could do was look at her, or rather, look past her. I didn't hear a word she had said.

"Are you paying attention to me, Jack Deveraux?" she asked, sounding irritated, like a parent addressing a child who wasn't listening. I must admit; I probably suffered from some arrested development or at the very least a prolonged frat boy mentality while Lisa took on the role of the adult—almost of a parent, in our relationship.

About a week later, the shit hit the fan. Lisa was making dinner for us, or instead heating dinner in the microwave. It occurred to me, Lisa, and I had been married for ten long years. I was so miserable! I couldn't take this charade any longer, despite my self-loathing and Catholic guilt. In addition to homosexuality being a sin in my faith, so was divorce. I couldn't help it. I had had enough of the lies, the denial, and the unhappiness. It felt as if I were leading two separate lives, which I was. I looked Lisa squarely in the eyes and said, "We need to talk."

"Jack, I'm a little busy at the moment, as you can see," she said in an irritated manner. I reached for her hand, holding it, and looking intensely at her with eyes wide with concern. She finally returned my gaze and asked, "About what?"

"Lisa, I'm unhappy, and I know you are too—let's end this marriage before it kills either one of us!" I said, trying desperately to sound compassionate.

"I don't know what you're talking about, Jack, except that you're distracting me from making dinner for us," she said as she pointed to the yet unprepared frozen food she was holding.

"Lisa, put the damn food down and listen to me!" She looked at me with a puzzled expression and said, "I know one thing, Jack: I know you're no longer attracted to me!" Her hands began to tremble as she continued fumbling with dinner. "We haven't had sex in over a month," she continued.

I cut her off before she could finish. Brutally, I said, "That's right, Lisa, I haven't been attracted to you since our wedding night, and even then, I was thinking of someone else while we made love!"

"Who, Jack? The waitress at the diner? Or some other slut you've been screwing around? I know you've had affairs, don't tell me you haven't!" she retorted.

"Lisa, I know you're going to find this hard to accept, but it isn't another woman. It isn't any woman at all. I'm not sure I can accept this myself, yet this is the truth: Lisa, I'm gay." Lisa stared at me, unable to speak—so I went on. "For a long time, I've been lying to myself, trying to make myself think I was bisexual—but I've had to face the truth at last. I'm not bisexual; I'm gay."

Lisa dropped a frozen TV dinner on the floor. "What?! You've got to be kidding me! You, the big athlete on the football team? The big bad macho construction worker? The same guy I caught several times screwing some slut in our bed? Don't make me laugh, Jack Deveraux! You're not gay!"

"Lisa, I know this is hard to hear when we've been married for ten years—even if they haven't been the greatest ten years. I was in denial; I was lying to myself, so I ended up lying to you. I hated myself so much that I couldn't admit the truth to either one of us."

Lisa sat down at the table across from me. I could tell she was beginning to believe what I was saying. "But I don't understand this, Jack. We had times in bed that were good. Okay, maybe not for a long time, but I never got the sense that you rejected the female body. And now you're telling me you do. You're interested only in men. I'm finding this hard to grasp, Jack."

But I'm done with that; I'm only going to say this one more time, listen, and listen good! I am a homosexual; I like guys! I denied it for too long, I've fought it all my life! I always have been and always will be until the day I die. No woman on this earth can change that. Even if I wanted to, I can't change who I am! And I won't change!" "Dammit! Lisa, I'm thirty-five years old! It's time for me to live my life for myself. I can't take the lying, the deception, and the self-loathing any longer! It's isn't fair to me, and it certainly isn't fair to you either!" I yelled.

"Stop it!" She said, "what about me?! You son of a bitch! You mean to tell me I wasted ten years of my life with you?! Cooking and cleaning and loving a man sleeping next to a man, who's not even a real man!

With that I saw red, all my pent-up rage and anger became directed at her as I knocked the still frozen container of food on the floor and yelled back, "shut up Lisa!"

She looked at me with disgust and spat out her words saying, "I hope you rot in hell Jack Devereaux!" She screamed. "Get out! Get out! Get out of my sight."

I looked at her with rage and said, "I'll be out in the morning; just give me some time to pack up my stuff!" I suddenly thought to myself how devastating this must be for her, "Lisa, I'm sorry! I'm sorry for hurting you!" I broke down and cried, "I didn't mean to, you remember the first time we met? Your laugh was what attracted me to you, your gentleness. I delighted in making you laugh; I tried Lisa. I tried!" I said, desperately reaching for any emotion beyond just anger.

"Yeah, well, you should have thought of that before admitting you're gay! Instead, you've done anything but that, Jack! Jack Devereaux, I want you to leave tonight! I can't bear to look at you; you disgust me!" She said with a cold reply.

Wow! I hadn't thought about being thrown out of my own house; with that, I went into the bedroom, packed a few items into a suitcase and left. I was leaving most of my possessions and Memories of my former straight life with Lisa behind.

I exited our front yard, trying to think of where I would go and check my wallet for cash. Fortunately, I had enough to stay in a cheap motel, way across town, in the seedy part of the city, I had driven past it one day on the way to a construction site. I got in my old wreck of a truck and started the ignition several times with no luck. *Wouldn't it figure?* I thought to myself, so I got out and started walking. The humid night air was miserable; it took me nearly a half an hour to reach the motel. I knew I didn't need a reservation.

The Stardust Motel never looked as good as it welcomed me that night. I checked in and headed to my room. It was dated and tired looking in the late nineteen sixties early nineteen seventies design, but I didn't care as I barely had the strength to remove my clothes, leaving only my underwear on as I climbed into bed. I had a good night's rest and a dreamless sleep.

The next morning, I went to work, keeping hidden the fact that my marriage had just ended; after all, it wasn't their business to know.

I put in a full day's work and headed back to the motel that night. I was sitting on the bed with just my underwear and socks on. Another head, other than the one on my shoulders, was thinking for me. I was horny and needed some company, desperate to have someone, anyone, by my side. The loneliness was becoming unbearable. I decided it was time to get lucky. I hadn't had sex since my encounter with Sam and decided to make up for it.

So, I headed over to another dreaded gay bar known as the "Golden Lantern" in the French quarter. If Sam were there, I would ignore him, as the awkwardness of having a conversation with a past sexual encounter just wasn't in the cards for me, as emotional intimacy with another man

100

was alien to me. Call it too close for comfort; my conservative, Catholic upbringing to be more specific.

From the moment I walked in, I felt as if all eyes were on me, it didn't help that Madonna's "Like A Virgin" was blaring in the bar. While I wasn't exactly a virgin to same-sex encounters, I was practically a virgin to going out and being seen in gay bars.

I felt as if I were doing the wrong thing, thinking to myself, *What the hell have I done?* Just as I turned to leave, I stood there and asked myself, *Then what Jack?* I froze in my tracks, lost in thought.

To some who know me, or think they know me, they might think I'm arrogant and self-centered, and while I certainly possess some of those traits, there is another side that I don't show too often, if ever—a shy and scared and insecure man at times, especially around other gay guys. Rather than saunter in my usual way, I felt as if I was an altar boy about to be molested by a priest or like sheep to slaughter. This bar had older men who were more secure in their own sexual identity with the usual good looking younger man hanging on their arm.

Making my way through the crowded bar, I finally reached an empty chair at the bar. I asked the bartender for a shot of Jack Daniels; call it my comfort drink. I saw the other guys checking me out and undressing me with their eyes until one of them walked over to me and said, "Hey there, Cowboy! You look like you're new around here?" *Cowboy?* I thought to myself, *who the fuck is this clown?* "Um, yeah, I don't get out much," I said in a disinterested way, hoping he would get the message and leave while I turned away from his gaze.

"Well now, Drew Phillips here, please to meet ya!" he extended his hand... which he kept extended while I continued to ignore him.

"You can consider me, one of the welcoming committee; we've been eyeing you ever since you entered the bar!"

"Hey, Drew, I'm Jack,"

"Jack, what?" Drew said sarcastically. "Ain't you got a last name,

Cowboy? Never mind, I guess you're playing hard to get!" He continued, "Well, pleased to meet you, Jack! Can I buy you a drink?" "Nope, I got one coming," I said as I continued my gaze towards the bar and away from his eyes, I could see him checking my body out as if he were buying a brand-new car, I was disgusted by this. Still, then quickly thought about the many times I had done the same checking someone else out.

"Say, I hope you don't mind me saying this, Jack, but ah, those jeans fit you nicely!" he said as he whistled.

He wasn't exactly a troll—he was modestly handsome enough, mid to late forties, balding, with a slight beer gut—guess it does catch up with men of a certain age.

"Hey, Jack! I've got a great idea, why don't we blow this pop stand, and go somewhere where you and I can get better acquainted?" He suggested excitedly. I think I held back a trace of vomit in my throat at what he had proposed and cleared my voice before saying, "Hey, Drew, what's your rush, man? I just walked in the door; I haven't even gotten my damn drink yet?" I said, sounding annoyed. "Well, you see Jack, I have this cute little place in the Bywater, and I've got plenty of booze and I just scored some pot from one of my buddies here—I promise you we'll have a real good time, Jack."

This guy was starting to annoy me, all I needed was a little time to think—besides, if there were someone in the bar that I wanted to hook up with, and it certainly wouldn't be with this character.

"Look! Drew, was it? What are you not understanding?"

As I turned to face him while raising my voice, "Why don't you knock it off? I told you, I'm waiting for my drink; besides, you're not my type!" I said as I turned around to face the bar.

"Hey, Jack, relax!" he said "No, man, you relax!" I replied as I shoved him hard, he staggered back and looked somewhat bewildered

"Fuck you!" he said as he left me to join his bar friends circle, as I felt all eyes on me—knowing he and his buddies were talking about me.

"Fuck you," he yelled from across the bar once again, feeling like a big man amongst all his other bar buddies.

I stood up and walked over to him and his group in a menacing way and said, "You know what? You're a pathetic human being! Completely and utterly pathetic!" I turned to walk out of the bar.

There I was, alone and out on the street, still feeling horny as hell!— But nothing but my growling stomach to remind me I hadn't eaten anything all day! My being horny far outweighed the urge for food. So, I decided to try my luck at another gay bar, which was known to be a lot less pretentious. I proceeded to the Rawhide 2010 a couple of blocks from the other bar.

"The Rawhide," as locals know it—is a casual leather bar. Even though I wasn't into the leather scene, I felt as if it would be more welcoming and not as prissy as some of the other gay bars in town with the patrons of the bar stinking up the place with their Polo shirts and cologne.

No, these were real men—just soap mixed with sweat and the smell of beer, call it man's- man bar.

As I entered, not one guy looked my way—I immediately felt relieved and at home. *Now, this is more like it,* I thought, where guys aren›t undressing you with their eyes the minute you walk through the door—Oh, there were guys there and plenty of hot guys, but they were all involved in conversations telling jokes, laughing—a game of pool had started in the back of the bar, it struck me as being a gay version of "Cheers," it felt real, a bit dirty and I felt completely at home, probably for the first time in a gay bar.

"What can I get ya?" said the ruggedly handsome bartender dressed in leather from head to toe.

"A shot of Jack Daniels, I didn't get to finish my other drink at the other bar."

"Coming up," he said as he poured my drink… in less than a minute, he returned—"Here you go, man."

I shot him a shit-eating grin. "Cheers!" I said and drank it down in one gulp. "Hit me again!" I said.

He gave me a look, grinned, and said, "You got it, boss!" The bar was a casual place filled with ordinary looking guys in every shape and size.

Suddenly, from across the bar, I spotted the perfect male specimen; he looked to be about twenty-three, blonde hair, tanned, real honest to goodness California surfer boy, or so it seemed. He had one leg propped up on one of the cigarette vending machines, enjoying a smoke. I took my drink and walked over to the cigarette machine and said, "You mind?" Which meant share the space and move the fuck over. He looked at me somewhat dismissively as he walked away from the cigarette machine.

"Thanks!" I said sarcastically and took a large gulp of courage, also known as my Jack Daniels—as I shot him a glance, finally getting up the nerve to ask him.

"I know this might sound like a cliché, but do you come here often?" I said sheepishly, with a grin.

He let out a huge laugh and said, "Man! That line is as old and as tired as some of the queens in this bar!"

We both laughed as it helped cut the tension.

"Yeah, ain't that the truth!" I replied. "So, what's a nice guy like you, doing in a dump like this?"

He just shook his head as his perfectly styled blonde wavy hair flowed from side to side.

"Man, oh, man! Will your clichés never end? He said teasingly. "Well, if truth be told, it isn't to drink!" he inferred.

"Naw?" As my eyes narrowed to a squint, as I said, "Isn't that a coincidence, me neither!" My reply and my self-assuredness seemed to arouse this hot surfer boy. He had the bluest eyes I had ever seen, pale blue, which seemed to dance with the light hitting his eyes with wisps of pale blonde hair, bleached out from the sun.

"Look, I'm just gonna come out and say it—I find you incredibly hot, you're probably the hottest guy in this dump, and I want to take you back to my motel room to do wicked things to you!" I said.

He looked somewhat surprised and said, "Whoa! Hold on! I don't even know your name? Besides, we just met!"

"Does it matter?" I asked, after a bit of silence, finally giving in— "Okay, I'll play along, name's Jack Devereaux. Your turn!" I insisted.

"I'm Trey Jones."

"Guess you're not from around here," I said.

He replied instantly. "No, I'm not, I'm a California boy, San Diego born and raised—I'm just out here visiting my aunt who moved out here with her husband a few years ago from out West."

As I sized him up before saying, "Well, nice to meet you, Trey!" "Yeah, nice to meet you too, Jack Devereaux!" he replied.

"So, what's next, my friend?" I said as I shot him a wide grin, hoping he would catch my hint and noticing his lips parted to reveal the whitest teeth I had ever seen!

He was licking his lips and suddenly said breathlessly, "You know what comes next! —let's get out of here!" he said, barely being able to speak.

We left the bar with the heavy humid Louisiana night air hitting us like a wave crashing unto a beach. We walked together without uttering a word the sexual tension so high you could cut it with a knife.

Coming upon a darkened alley just around the corner from Bourbon street, and so we were out of the public's plain sight—I threw him up against the wall, as if he were a rag doll.

All the muscles straining against my tight short-sleeved shirt, the veins of my arms protruding as I kissed him passionately, finally ending the pent-up lust since the last rendezvous with Sam. After what seemed an eternity, we both came up for air.

"Lead the way, Jack Devereaux!" he said breathlessly. "Right this way Trey!" I replied.

We both laughed, seizing on the moment's silliness, as we realized what we had just said, rhymed.

The walk back to my motel was hurried and full of anticipation, we walked on without a sound, only glancing at each other from time to time. Finally, arriving, we entered my room at the motel.

"Nice place you got yourself here, Jack!" He said sarcastically as we both broke out in laughter.

I picked him up as if he were light as a feather and threw him on the bed. We wrestled and squirmed with our clothes on what seemed like an eternity as I quickly overpowered him and pinned him down on the bed.

He looked up at me innocently and said in a hushed manner, almost purring the words, "So what are you going to do to me?" He asked. I answered back, sensing the size difference between us and my being so much larger: "Everything and anything I can!" as I felt the adrenaline rush of an intense sexual attraction. I ripped his clothes off in a matter of seconds, to reveal a small speedo tan line. He had smooth legs and a light dusting of blonde hair on each of his legs, except for two small patches of dirty blonde hair under each armpit. I devoured him; every inch of him, he smelled of cologne, sweat, and a hint of soap.

He responded by moaning, which enticed me even more. I always got off on hearing my sex partner moan with pleasure.

"Yeah, that's it! That's it!" He let out, barely being able to speak. After three hours of doing everything imaginable, and exploring and enjoying each other's bodies, we collapsed into each other's arms. "Damn!" He said, "Jack, you're incredibly hot!"

He heaped on the praise. It felt good to feel needed, if only in a physical way.

I laughed and said, "Thanks," sounding almost embarrassed—in an empty hollow-sounding voice, at which point I could no longer connect with his admiring eyes.

He sensed my being distant," Hey, what's on your mind, Jack?" I shook my head and said, "I'd rather not talk about it, Trey, it's a bit complicated you wouldn't understand!"

But he kept pressing on as he propped himself up on a pillow on the bed "Yeah?! Try me! Come on, Jack! You might feel better!" he said sounding as if he were genuinely interested to hear.

I became increasingly agitated and felt as if he were prying, finally saying.

"Okay here it is Trey, I just separated from my wife of ten years, ten long wasted years of my life. I'm a practicing Roman Catholic and self-loathing homosexual, and even though I find you incredibly hot, and we had an amazing time—now all I want is to be left alone! Aren't you sorry you asked?" I said as I continued to avoid meeting his intense stare. After a brief pause finally saying, "So, I think it would be best if you left,"

He started to frown; I could sense it without looking at him. "Why?" He asked, "Man! Talk about making a guy feel cheap!" He said resentfully with a forced laugh.

"Look, I'm sorry, you're a real nice guy and all—I just need some space right now, here's twenty dollars for a cab" as I reached for my wallet and handed him the twenty dollars in his direction.

"I don't want your damn money, Jack! I just want to stay here a little while longer," he said.

"I don't think that's a good idea, Trey; I think you better leave," I insisted.

"Give me a reason why?" He pleaded

"Do it! Don't ask me why, I don't owe you a damn reason! You hear me?! Leave! Before I throw you out!" suddenly becoming so angry, I nearly broke into tears as I shouted the words.

"But I don't understand, what did I do?! Aww, screw it! Whatever! Okay, Jack, have it your way!—yeah, I'll leave Jack!"

He yelled, Go to hell!" "You're pathetic, you know that?! No wonder your wife divorced you!" Trey got up, dressed himself in lightning time and left storming out the door without closing it.

I reflected on his words as I spoke these words aloud in an empty room, *"Yeah, too late, kid, I'm already living in hell!"*

Once more, I found myself alone and feeling abandoned, a flash of lightning and a loud crackle of thunder came from outside the motel window.

Here I was sitting on the bed, feeling as if I was the last person on the earth's face—it all seemed too much to bear, I broke down and began to cry. I hated to cry, it made me feel weak and vulnerable—the last thing my Dad would have wanted to see was his son cry. I couldn't remember the last time I shed a tear, I felt as if I couldn't fight it, and quickly became a blubbering mess!

Images came flooding into my mind. My high school days on the football team—meeting Lisa for the first time, all the trysts with other married self-loathing Bi and Gay men. All my pent-up emotions, all my repressed desires—were coming out at once. As soon as the tears subsided, my sadness was replaced by anger. In the form of my fist going through the cheaply made wall of my motel room!

It madea sound so loud, that it woke up one of the other occupants of the motel, they yelled, "Knock it off next door, or we'll call the manager!"

I asked myself, *Is this what my life as a gay man was to be like? — To live alone and seek out other men only to hate myself every time I did?*

I couldn't stomach the thought —this almost animal-like urge that

I hadn't felt with a woman before. I enjoyed the physical contact with men—all except for the afterglow, there wasn't any— it was more guilt than anything.

I felt as if I had let my dad down and my desire to become a real man. Guilt in knowing that God must see me as an abomination— merely for having my guilty pleasures. All that was left was self-hatred, loathing, and the emptiness and feeling as if I was a sexual deviant— an unclean animal performing carnal acts, and living a lifestyle most people despised!

I felt a tremendous amount of emptiness and thought about Lisa. How empty she must have felt when I came out to her—it certainly didn't help me feel any better about myself or how I had left things with her. I asked myself, *what the hell am I going to do?*

I walked into the bathroom, and stepped into the shower; the hot water felt good on my skin. I slathered myself up at least two or three times—never really feeling thoroughly clean.

I stepped out of the shower and toweled myself off, glancing at my reflection, my chiseled chest, six-pack abs and bulging muscles and thought, *How can someone as good looking as myself be so completely and utterly messed up in the head?*

I was too tired to dwell on those feelings any longer and crashed into bed. As I lay there staring at the ceiling and listening to the rain hit the roof of the motel and the window of my room, I heard the sound of thunder one last time before I fell asleep.

I was startled awake by someone honking their horn outside in the parking lot, and realized how pathetic my life had become. Staying in this dump of a motel. I felt guilt, cheap and disgusting—my life meant nothing to me.

And to make matters worse, I was without a life partner and my truck was out of commission— I was in a sorry state. And couldn't stay in my room any longer.

I glanced over at my alarm clock sitting on the nightstand next to my bed; it read midnight—I thought, *The witching hour has begun.* I knew it was late, but I didn't care. I had to go back out, find somewhere, or someone to get my mind off my sad existence. At the very least, the bars stay open until two in the morning, but decided to skip the gay bars— my Catholic guilt had messed with my head for too long. I went back to my comfort zone—the straight jazz clubs that I had frequented in the not too distant past.

I thought, *Who knows?! Maybe I could hook up with the right woman? Perhaps I could try and bury the gay deep within me one last time?* I told myself, *Perhaps they were right after all? Maybe I just hadn't "met the right woman" to be able to "change me" into the man I dreamed of being—which was a straight guy.* Just before dawn, I paid a visit to a club called "Snug Harbor". Little did I know, a chance encounter with a mysterious stranger there would alter my life and destiny forever!

CHAPTER 9

Haiti's Queen (Raphaella Narrates)

For the record, let me state, I am not royalty, or at least I don't think I'm related to anyone of importance—so I'm not technically a Queen. It's just a nickname my parents gave me growing up in Port de Paix on Haiti's island.

My parents would kid me and say, "I think we gave birth to a Queen, you sure she belongs to us?"

I always thought I came from the wrong family, the feeling as if you didn't belong in your surroundings—or perhaps born into the wrong body?

Life in Port de Paix was dificult; in English, it means port of peace, although my childhood was anything but peaceful. My family came to the island of Haiti from Africa (specifically Senegal) in the nineteen sixties, to escape extreme poverty for somewhat less— I describe it as substituting one living hell for another.

My father Ayomide (his name in African means happiness is coming) was an alcoholic— my father never fully lived up to his name's meaning. We were dirt poor as most of our village was, and poverty was a way of life for my family. My father worked the sugar cane fields along with my Mother, (Asha,) toiling away ten to twelve hours a day in the hot Caribbean sun, when he was sober enough to stand.

I was often left alone in our palm-thatched mud hut when I wasn't in school. Even though my parents had left me alone, I wasn't truly. Some visitors entertained me and sometimes frightened me. Of course, I was too young to understand the gift I possessed; I would learn as I got older it was the ability to connect with the "other world." How shall I say this? I'm what you might describe as a medium; everyone assumed I was conversing with myself. When in fact, I was speaking with "the other side," the dearly departed, ghosts, spirits—or whatever you want to call these often-conflicted souls.

They would appear before me and tell me to warn someone or avenge their passing, or just to come and talk with someone. Even as a child, I wasn't frightened most of the time, but there were those tortured souls so overcome with their grief and anger that it was difficult, if not, impossible to look. Their contorted faces showed their anger, and some had a dark energy, which was too much to bear at times.

At times I would scream at them, "Go away! Go back to where you came from!"

Some of the entities would taunt me; others would leave out of mutual respect. Some possessed powerful and frightening energy— such as opening doors or windows and cabinets. When they were upset, they would throw objects across the hut. Any number of cups and dishes would smash against the walls. I quickly cleaned up each mess they had made before my parents came home, many remained calm simply not wanting to be forgotten.

Once my parents came home after a long day of tending the fields, they would simply shake their heads and look at me, saying "What has the Queen been up to while we were gone?" I simply replied, "Just talking," My parents wouldn't understand if I had told them. They were Catholic—converted by missionaries back in Senegal. I never considered myself to be very religious, more spiritual than anything. It was easier for me to imagine somehow a spirit world or "other side" than it was to envision Heaven or Hell. I thought, *If Hell truly exists, then we are living it!*

You might ask, had I ever envisioned angels? I never did unfortunately, despite my Catholic upbringing—my fascination with the supernatural intensified as I grew to be a teenager. I felt I needed to explore all the realms of the occult.

My interest expanded into voodoo; what island teenagers hadn't dreamt about raising a dead person's body? I would attend these groups— usually calling on a recently deceased villager or loved one. We were trying to make the spirit appear.

We would cast spells cast using an object called a "pentagram," drawn on a piece of paper, and candles were placed carefully at the corners, with a purple one at the top, then a blue, green, red, and white one. An object placed in the middle, and ash sprinkled around it; once the candles were lit, we would think about a deceased person. We meditated for five to ten minutes as we all chanted in unison "I call to the spirits; I call to the dead let me see my dear again. I call to thee, come to me to reunite once more. I wish to see whom I seek, whom I miss so much."

Eventually, we progressed to using a recently deceased body and trying desperately to resurrect it; in essence, we became grave robbers, not looking for valuables other than the corpse itself. Mostly we failed, until one incredibly humid summer evening, I managed to reanimate a dead body!

Call it a zombie, a non-thinking, non-feeling, reanimated corpse, missing their soul. Once it rose, and after a couple of minutes, it fell to the ground, but the fact that I had brought a corpse back to life was a miracle! I could barely contain my joy, not to mention my smugness with my ever-increasing abilities.

"Well, look at that! The Queen has resurrected a dead body!"

one of the group members said. That was the nickname I was given, "the Queen."

Most of the group were considered friends of mine, all except one; she was a sworn enemy; her name was Fabiola "Quiet!" I commanded as she and the others shuddered; I knew Fabiola's abilities, and the rest, could not equal my skills; I knew I frightened and intimidated her and took great delight in this. I hated her! Fabiola was prettier than me, had many more male callers than I— and her parents were esteemed and well respected if that weren't bad enough. They were in local government, not field workers like mine, and having an alcoholic father made it even more unbearable. To make matters worse, her French was perfect! Her French instructor was someone from Paris! What afluence and power can get you! But I knew I had this talent, which was making me feel invincible. I felt I would make something of myself and strengthen my gifts— while poor Fabiola, her looks would fade, she would undoubtedly be stuck on this miserable island for the rest of her life and hopefully end up married to an alcoholic field worker like my father was—she deserved no better!

Until the day that catastrophe hit our island as if life hadn't been miserable enough—a health epidemic called "AIDS," which stood for acquired autoimmune deficiency syndrome.

We had heard news reports from America describing a disease called "the gay cancer," which hit metropolitan cities such as New York, Los Angeles, and San Francisco. It restricted itself to mostly homosexuals and intravenous drug users.

Our people, or at least the vast majority, were neither. How wrong we were to assume the disease would limit itself to only those two groups of people, as the infection started spreading in the heterosexual community. Our island became infected relatively fast and soon became a pariah. Tourism died off, as did a lot of our native islanders. Shortly after the official announcement in our official newspaper, "Le

Nouvelliste" (Haiti's largest newspaper publication) the headline across the front page read "La est arrive en Haiti!" (AIDS has arrived in Haiti!)

I'll never forget the day my father came down with a mysterious fever and purple lesions forming on his back, shoulders, and legs. At first, my Mother and I thought Father was working too hard and that the purplish blotches covering his legs were due to extreme sun exposure. My Mother demanded to know what was going on, and told my father to go to a local doctor, which for us, was in Port Au Prince, the capital. My father begrudgingly agreed.

Our local doctor seemed perplexed and strongly urged my father to seek treatment in a hospital. We visited him a few days after his admission. The attending doctor, originally from France, came to help our besieged island, and diagnosed my father with "AIDS." in other parts was labeled the "gay cancer" even though my father wasn't gay. It had worked its way down from the US mainland and invaded our island, not caring who was gay or who was not.

Asha was naturally troubled and concerned for her husband and daughter's father; my mother ignored her symptoms, slowly beginning to appear, which included swollen lymph glands and fever.

My Mother continued to provide my father with sexual pleasures, which I understood to mean sexual intercourse. Our doctor suggested my Mother receive a test for HIV—she reluctantly agreed and tested positive. My world came crashing down all around me.

I felt powerless despite my occult abilities. I thought *If I am so "gifted," why didn't I see this coming?*

I was angry and bitter; I shut myself off from everyone. I couldn't think and could barely breathe. I thought, *What am I going to do? How will I care for my parents? With both sick and what on earth will I do if I lose them both?* Both eventually ended up in L'hopital General in Port Au Prince, laying in beds side by side in the same room; they lay next to each other, hands extended, holding each other's hands as if to form a never-ending bond, "till death do us part" as the saying goes.

Then the unthinkable happened, my father passed away at two o'clock in the morning, clutching my Mother's hand. Her hands showed his nail marks and how they had dug into her flesh. It was as if to hold on to her and one last breath of life. My father professed to be a practicing Catholic; he truly believed he would go to "a better place" I hoped he would, as his life here on earth had been hell on earth. And as with some spouses who die within a short time of losing the other, so did my Mother. She had lost her battle with the AIDS virus a week after my father passed. I nearly lost my mind and felt lost and abandoned and thought, *What am I to do? How will I reinvent myself?* At that moment I decided I needed to leave this wretched island, reimagine a new life for myself, and chart a new course for America. But where exactly? I had heard stories about the city of New Orleans, and heard its inhabitants were of French, Caribbean, and Creole backgrounds living in a historic place that dated back to seventeen hundred and ten! I also learned about the voodoo shops and the many paranormal experiences people had there. It intrigued me and seemed to draw me in as if by some unforeseen force. The fact that I had zero money to make this relocation possible made this impossible for the time being. I knew I had to make money and make it fast. I did what most women would do on our island, when faced with a desperate situation, I resorted to prostitution.

I'm not proud of the fact I had to sell my body for money. My body was still young, supple—and firm enough to entice a few privileged white men who dared to "walk on the wild side." Those rich men being the east coast men from New York, Boston and Miami who wanted to go to bed with a local girl, despite the risk of the dreaded AIDS virus.

Remembering my late parents and how they died, I insisted on condom usage while engaging in sexual activity. I did not want to end up as they had by becoming a vague memory to some. It felt as if I had my whole life ahead of me; my world was my oyster. I was still in my late twenties and reasonably attractive.

I had encountered many wealthy, out-of-shape east coast executives, willing to pay big money to have sex with an island girl and saving every dollar from every sexual get-together. It wasn't cheap; I demanded a high price, which they agreed to pay.

Whenever I encountered even the slightest protest from any number of men, trying to pay more for unprotected sex, I reminded them that AIDS was severe and that our island was rampant with the disease. There was nowhere that was safe from the scourge of this dreaded disease. They reluctantly agreed, as they tugged and pulled, licked, and penetrated me as I kept dreaming of my new life; looking past their lustful gazes, I kept thinking about my escape, my new life. It was sheer torture! I hated feeling like a sex slave. Forced to do unspeakable acts, it made me hate myself. They didn't consider me a human being, merely a sex toy.

Finally, a year had passed—and I had enough! A particularly obese businessman with foul-smelling breath and ill-fitting trousers came into my hotel room in Port Au Prince, forcing himself upon me, wanting a sexual encounter. I knew I had saved a good deal of money to transition to my new life, as I had been entertaining primarily rich white men. This bloated pig wanted to have sex with me and insisted on not using condoms, despite my warning him of AIDS running rampant in our once tropical paradise—and that my parents had died of the disease, still he insisted and wouldn't take no for an answer! I snapped; I couldn't help myself! I told him "Fuck off!" and pulled out a six-inch knife I had been carrying around for protection. I threatened to kill him if he didn't leave immediately, telling him I didn't need his stinking money.

Haitian women are known to be tough, and I was no exception. I had never used my trusty knife before, which I had nicknamed "Pierre", but I felt I had hit a new low and was quite prepared to use it, and so ended my short-lived profession as a high-paid prostitute. I decided I needed to visit the "Bank de la Republique" (Haiti's central bank), where I had opened a savings account only a year prior, and collect my hard-earned savings and purchase my one-way air ticket to New Orleans. The city beckoned me like a lover might. I knew I would make my dreams come true and leave to start a new life in this exotic city, which seemed different from any other American city.

As I arrived at the bank, I could hardly contain my excitement. I was in total disbelief that I was finally leaving this wretched island, with all its poverty and this disease running rampant, taking my parents with it.

I thought, *Why didn't their spirits come to me? Why have I been cursed with this "gift" of seeing other entities and not my parents, so they could comfort me and let me know they had passed to the other side?* I felt alone and abandoned—but still determined to start a new life in America. The land of opportunity, fame, and fortune. I held my head high as I walked into the bank.

A well-dressed woman by the name of Monique assisted me in closing out my bank account. I had amassed nearly $30,000 US dollars, giving me enough cash to purchase a one-way plane ticket, pay for rent and food. I had her issue my withdrawn savings in a cashier's check, which I would cash once I arrived in my new city of New Orleans.

I had made a reservation that day for a one-way plane ride to New Orleans, as luck would have it there was one seat left on board the DC-10 aircraft.

I went back to my hotel room, packed all my worldly possessions—and made my way to the airport via a taxi and boarded the plane. I was seated, shortly after that, the big silver bird took off in flight. As I glanced out the window, muttering under my breath a final goodbye to my island, as I shed a single tear thinking of the family and friends I would be leaving behind.

I closed my eyes and tried to rest on the relatively short flight, which lasted a little over two hours.

I opened my eyes as the airline captain announced some expected turbulence we were about to experience and looked over to the empty seat next to me. I couldn't believe my eyes! There she sat, my deceased Mother! I stared at her struggling to find the words, any words; she merely smiled and spoke these words to me,

"Go forth into the world knowing your father and I and all of your relatives have passed over to the other side, be a help to those that are anguished, both the living and the dead, as you have a special gift, my child and you must share that gift."

Those were her last words; as she faded away, I didn't even have the chance to tell her how much I loved and missed her and my father. I drifted back off into a deep sleep with the aircraft's rocking motion due to the turbulence. I was abruptly awakened by the Captain's announcement that we were preparing to land and that everyone must take their seats.

My flight connected through Miami. That's where I had to clear customs and enter the US. I gathered all the identification papers and my passport and the necessary paperwork documenting my recent HIV testing status—which was negative. This procedure was required as the US authorities carefully screened Haitians as a potential risk of spreading AIDS. I passed through US customs without any delay. The US customs authorities were welcoming and not too rude as they searched my bags, possibly for drugs and not finding anything, not even an aspirin! My connecting flight to New Orleans got delayed due to a storm approaching New Orleans. I wondered if this was a foreboding of what my life was to be in my new city; I shuddered at the thought as I made my way through the terminal and found a bar—as I had two hours to kill before my flight would take off.

I sat down at the bar and ordered a Mai Tai; I had never had one before and felt like a tourist on a tropical vacation. I asked the bartender for an extra shot of rum—he winked at me and assured me the drink would be to my liking. He was right; it hit the back of my throat, and suddenly I felt relaxed. Finally it was time to board the connecting flight to New Orleans; I stood in line, or instead attempted to stand because of the three Mai Thai's I had at the bar just a short time ago—I figured they were starting to take effect.

I presented my ticket with my boarding pass attached to it and stepped onto the aircraft feeling slightly woozy from the Mai Tai's effect, and settled into my seat for the two-hour flight, drifting off to sleep. This time the trip was as smooth as silk, having waited for stable weather patterns to return. We landed at Louis Armstrong International airport in New Orleans. I saw the most radiant sun that was about to set; the sky was ablaze with red and purple colors announcing the arrival of twilight. I could hardly believe it. The euphoria swept over me. We disembarked the plane, and as soon as my feet hit the pavement, I knelt on my hands and knees to kiss the ground: to celebrate my arrival to my new home and a new beginning. A new journey was starting.

I quickly retrieved my bags, heading outside to where the taxi cabs waited for passengers to go into the city and beyond. The cab driver pulled up—asked me where to? I had no idea; I didn't have a reservation for a hotel, not even at a motel. I asked the driver if he were a native of the city and could recommend a place. He asked me what my budget was—I told him low, extremely low. He suggested the Stardust Motel; I figured that would do until I found my apartment. As we made our way into the city center—a group had gathered and was protesting, shouting, "Fight AIDS, not people!" "What do we want?!" "AIDS funding!" "When do we want it?!" "Now!" "Act up, fight back!" "Fight AIDS!" Another foretelling, I thought. Being greeted by a bunch of protestors after having just immigrated from AIDS-infested Haiti? It seemed all so surreal to me.

The car pulled into the Stardust motel's parking lot—I saw a good-looking man checking in at the reception desk. A tall man who appeared to have a muscular build. I paid the cab driver and thanked him for his recommendation, as he made a pass at me! He asked if he could call me. I was shocked! Was this man expecting a sexual favor for merely suggesting somewhere to stay in New Orleans?, And somehow I got the impression this guy might be married.

I yelled, "No!" as I gave him a dirty look. He sped off—but not before he shot me the middle finger. I had seen tourists in my own native Haiti do this with some of our locals and quickly learned what this one finger obscene gesture meant. I shook my head and went inside to inquire about a room. The tall, good-looking man had already left as I approached the reception area's front desk, somehow I had the feeling that I would be seeing him again!

A sixty-something man at the reception desk looked up without uttering a word to me. I politely asked if he had a room available.

"Yup!" was his response in a cold manner.

"Well then, how much is the room per night, and do you have a weekly rate—just in case I need to stay for a bit?" I asked.

"Twenty-two dollars a night or one hundred and fifty dollars a week," he answered. I told him I would take the weekly rate.

"You have a funny accent' where ya from?" He said as he squinted his eyes, looking me over suspiciously.

"I'm from Haiti. I just arrived into this country today," I replied, looking towards the ground. Why was I allowing this overweight man with perhaps the education of a nine-year-old, intimidate me?

Finally I looked up at him and said, "Look, I can assure you; I am not infected with AIDS if that's what you're thinking?" He ignored my reply and instead said, "Cash or charge?"

"Cash!" I said, as I paid him the full amount.

I thought, *Some welcoming committee! AIDS protestors, an*

oversexed cab driver, and a rude motel clerk all in one day Welcome to New Orleans, Raphaella!

"Room thirteen, it's upstairs," he said as he threw the key down on the desk. I shot him a dirty look, and as sarcastic as possible said, "Thanks!" I made my way up to the room and opened the door to lucky number thirteen. The first thing to fill my nostrils was a stale, moldy smell of many years and past sexual encounters over the decades that had passed. Perhaps the Stardust Motel lived up to its name in the nineteen sixties—but that was twenty some odd years ago, and the place had grown stale and tired. Ugly shag carpeting, a floral bedspread, and a pink tiled bathroom greeted me.

I bought a city map and studied it—choosing to walk to my interviews rather than take taxis to acquaint myself with the city better and save money. I took in the sights of my new city, with people rushing about, a marching band was playing the theme to "Happy Birthday," and I wondered if it was a birthday celebration or a memorial service on the birthday of the deceased?

I arrived at the "Ruby Slipper" on Burgundy, and Stephen, the restaurant's assistant manager, greeted me.

We sat at a booth in the back; he started the interview by asking me several questions: Did I have any experience? Would I consider myself a decent cook? How well do I handle stress? He told me the pay was four dollars and eighty cents per hour—plus the staff usually pooled tips with the kitchen staff. Feeling distracted, I looked around and noticed the interior, which resembled a bank.

Suddenly, a cold air enveloped my physical space—much to my surprise, there stood a gentleman with a handlebar mustache, wearing a bowler hat and a suit with a watch on a chain that hung outside his jacket. He was transparent and merely stood there, observing me.

Stephen offered me the position I had ignored due to the distracting presence intrigued by our conversation.

"Do you want the job or not?" he said, looking slightly irritated. I quickly accepted and apologized for having become distracted. I told Stephen I could start tomorrow; he told me to be here bright and early at six in the morning as the kitchen staff needed to prep the food and the restaurant needed to be open by eight in the morning for business. We shook hands; he welcomed me "into the family." I told him I was very excited to start working in such a fine establishment. I left the restaurant on cloud nine, finally something was going my way! Perhaps things would turn towards my favor?

With a job secured, I could start the next phase of my move, locating an apartment, which would finally get me out of that dumpy motel!

I rushed off to the apartment viewing, which was in the French quarter on Ursuline near the renowned "Ursuline convent." I heard a rumor the convent had taken in four or five women suspected of being vampires back in the eighteenth century due to their ghostly pallid complexion and blood smeared across each one's mouth. I had experienced many strange sightings in my life, ghosts and zombies— but I had never encountered a vampire! I wondered if these creatures were a myth. If these creatures have been written about for so long in numerous television shows and movies, even existed?

The studio apartment was on the second floor. It had charming shutters outside the two large windows facing the street; it was a furnished studio apartment with a small kitchenette and rented for six hundred a month. I took it without seeing the rest of the flats; call me spontaneous, but I had a good feeling about this apartment, and the best part was I couldn't detect any spirits there.

Don't get me wrong; I appreciate my gift to see and communicate with the "other side." Still—it is also physically exhausting to communicate with spirits; it takes a lot of energy.

"When can I move in?" I asked the nice lady named Florence, who was showing me the studio.

"Tomorrow, if you wish?" She replied with a smile.

"That's wonderful!" I said and could barely wait to get back to the Stardust motel to tell the welcoming committee there to go to hell and demand my money back for the rest of the week.

Walking back to the motel, I kept practicing what I would say to the man at the front desk who had been so rude to me upon my arrival.

I marched into the front reception area and said, "I'm in number thirteen; I'll be moving out tomorrow—I want my money back!" I demanded.

He looked at me with a smug expression.

"I don't give no refunds, you done paid up, and that money is mine," he said with a chuckle, feeling as if he had the upper hand.

I looked at him at once, turning aggressive, and said, "I won't ask you again, you fat pig!" as I reached inside of my pocket to pull out my trusty companion "Pierre," which was my six-inch knife, and I held it firmly against his throat.

His two eyes, which looked more like two pig eyes, had a sense of terror in them as he knew I wasn't joking, and if provoked, I would use this knife to slit his throat. I had a determined look in my eyes as if I meant business and would not back down. I knew in my heart that I was right and that money belonged to me.

"Sure, take it. But I want you out tonight," the man resembling a pig replied, handing me the money as I spit in his face.

"I wouldn't waste one more hour in this dump; I'll be out within the hour, as soon as I pack up my stuff; that soon enough for you?" I snapped.

He nodded, giving himself two more chins to the two he already had.

I made my way up to number thirteen and quickly emptied all the drawers of clothes and belongings into a suitcase and made my way down the stairs, I could hear the police cars' sirens approaching, and I decided to exit through the back of the motel.

I thought, *That pig called the police on me,* as I laughed to myself. Where was I going to go? I wouldn't be able to move into my new apartment until tomorrow afternoon. I figured one night on a park bench wasn't all that bad—as I made my way to Louis Armstrong Park and found a park bench under a half-burned-out streetlamp. By this time, it was sunset—it would be dark in a matter of hours.

I took out some clothing articles and bunched them up to form a pillow to rest my head. I didn't need a blanket as it was a mild seventy-four degree out at six in the evening. It would be dark in less than three hours—and I could rest, hoping for enough sleep to be able to endure my big day tomorrow—starting a new job as a cook and moving into my new flat on Ursuline.

I could hardly wait! I sat on the park bench, mesmerized by the beauty of the park and nature on display. I heard the birds chirp and watched them chase each other in flight as squirrels hopped about and families out trying to enjoy the last remains of the daylight hours.

Sunset came, similar to the one I saw upon my arrival into New Orleans only a short time ago. It was as beautiful as before, appearing like some exquisite abstract painting. Shades of crimson-red, along with purple. My mouth was open in amazement, then suddenly the darkness arrived with a now empty park—as everyone had left, except for me. I suddenly felt a slight chill in the air; perhaps I needed that sweater after all?

I reached for it, having bought it upon my arrival in New Orleans as there was no need for a sweater in Haiti. It never got cold enough to need one. I sat up as a transparent figure of a man walked past my park bench and stopped looking right at me, then vanished in front of my eyes.

I typically see spirits milling about for the record, but few approach me unless they need something from me. I wondered whether the entity was having difficulty transitioning over to the other side and asking me for my guidance to help with that... I was sure I would encounter plenty of other spirits here in New Orleans because of its sordid and often violent past—with slavery and many other tragic events that had occurred.

I awakened the following day from a dreamless sleep. I checked my watch, a fancy "Swatch" that I had purchased at the Miami airport. It showed the time five, I had to be at work at six. I discovered an outdoor restroom where I began to wash from head to toe. One thing I knew about this newly adopted country of mine, bathing was a necessity; I didn't want to appear or smell like some hired hand from the islands.

I was ready in no time and reached the corner of Burgundy and Conti, where my new job as a cook was to start at "The Ruby Slipper" No sooner had I arrived; I was introduced to the rest of my co-workers by the manager Stephen. Right away, I was made to feel at home and welcomed warmly and genuinely.

Stephen was a fine-looking man; he stood at roughly 1.75 meters tall with African style braids and a big smile with teeth as white as snow. He shared with me—the restaurant staff felt more like a family than just a group of people working together; I couldn't have agreed more. I longed for some bond or sense of family, especially given the fact that I had no other family.

Stephen gave me a sheet of paper for me to look over containing the daily menu. It didn't seem very interesting, just the usual food served at a diner. I came up with an idea and called in the manager, "Hey Stephen! —you got a minute for me?"

Stephen appeared right away as he was a very attentive manager. "You mind if I add to some of the lunch items?" I asked sheepishly. "Nah! That's great! I like that! Stephen said.

"Was there something you wanted to whip up?" He asked My puzzled expression was giving away my confusion about his using American slang.

"Whip up", it means to create, cook up," he said.

"Yes, I want to add a lunch item to the menu. I cook a mean Jambalaya," I told him. "What would we call it on the menu?" he asked, clearly open to the idea.

"I know! We'll call it the Queen's Jambalaya!" I said.

"Better yet, how about Queen Raphaella's Jambalaya?" he inquired excitedly.

"Perfect!" We both said at the same time as we broke down laughing.

"I'll tell you what, you make the staff and me some for lunch— and we'll be your guinea pigs," he snickered as he walked out of the kitchen.

"You got it, Stephen!" I yelled back. I got busy making all the other items on the menu, "prepping the food," as it's known in the restaurant business.

As soon as I had finished, I began to make my jambalaya, which my parents used to love eating. After the breakfast crowd left —it was time for the staff and manager, and I to eat. I served up the Jambalaya to each server, six in total, to Stephen and lastly to myself, as we sat down to eat, Stephen had put the closed sign on the front door at eleven, and we all had an early lunch as the restaurant would reopen at noon.

I was a bit nervous as the others pitched their forks into their meal, as did Stephen when suddenly yelled, "Here's to the Queen's Jambalaya!" Stephen leaned over to me and told me it would be a big hit on the menu. I looked at him with a smile and teardrop in my eye; I had found my new home and my new family.

Eventually, everything turned sour. I started to have more visions of spirits coming towards me at work—did I mention the restaurant was an old, converted bank? Stephen would always be present when I would "talk to myself," as he described it. He isn't gifted—or "receptive" to the other world, which meant he neither sensed nor witnessed the restless spirits I did.

I had worked nearly a year at this place, but then mistrust and anger on Stephen's part bubbled to the surface. He began to doubt my sanity, he told me. It scared the other workers whenever I would talk or yell out to no one, or at least, that anyone could see, but I saw them—the many restless entities begging for my attention. What was I to do?

I managed to save up quite a bit of money in my savings account, nearly thirty-five thousand dollars; perhaps the time had come to part with this now dysfunctional family.

What I wanted was to open my shop—where I would focus primarily on doing readings for people to help them connect with their dearly departed loved ones on "the other side." I gave up voodoo but I figured calling it a voodoo shop would attract more customers; I hadn't practiced actual voodoo since I was a teenager back in Haiti.

So, I searched the newspaper for shops for sale—at the very least, I would have enough for a down payment. Perhaps I could secure a loan, as the thirty thousand dollars, along with my saved earnings from the diner, which was pretty much spent paying rent and daily expenses.

The following day, I made up my mind—I was going to quit my job and give Stephen a piece of my mind.

I decided to do this before the others started arriving so they wouldn't witness this spectacle. I found Stephen going over the menus in the back of the café—I approached him and held my head up high. "Stephen, you're a fool! It would be best if you respect those who have an eye to the other world as I do—everything I have encountered here is true. Your very own Mother has visited me here to tell me how much she misses you and how proud of you she is,"— I said.

Of course, he didn't believe me and asked me for my Mother's name to prove my sighting. "Your Mother's name is Shaniqua. She was born in nineteen thirty-two in Mobile, Alabama to two African slaves brought over here before the civil war. She had a scar on her left cheek—an injury from a bully at school when she was just a little girl of the age of seven. Her nickname for you is "Curious Stevie," as you were always such a curious child full of wonder and a zest for life— now, what else would you like to hear?" I said as I grinned from ear to ear.

His stunned facial expression said it all, both his eyes and mouth wide open—like he had seen a ghost, unfortunately for him, he hadn't, and never will. There are skeptics, and there are non-believers—and Stephen qualified as a non-believer. I felt sorry for him.

"I don't believe it! How can that be? You're crazy!" he said, growing increasingly angrier by the moment.

"So, you think I'm crazy, do you? After everything, I have shared with you? Fine! I quit! Find yourself another cook! —Good luck to you," I yelled out as I exited the door.

Fortunately for me, I had received my check from work just the other day, so I wasn't expecting anything else in terms of pay. I made my way back to my apartment; along the way, I stopped at a newsstand and picked up the local newspaper "The Times-Picayune", and looked at the real estate section. Instantly spotting the ad which read: "Storefront for sale, contact Tom Renaud," including his phone number.

The ad had a picture of the storefront; it looked perfect, but the price! A staggering one hundred thousand dollars! I thought, *Where am I going to get that kind of money?*

I slumped into my chair, dropping the newspaper to the floor; the heat of the day and the emotional roller coaster that had played out at the café just a short time ago had taken its toll. A feeling of complete exhaustion poured over my entire body. As quickly as I had dropped the newspaper, I fell into a deep sleep.

In my dream, my Mother appeared, offering me her pearls of wisdom, which comforted me.

"Raphaella, you have a special gift; your talents are needed by those less fortunate, do not despair! Do not give up your dream to own your own space. You will prevail; you must never lose faith; do not waste the gift you have!" she said.

In an instant she was gone, I awakened myself crying and saying, "Mama, don't go! Don't leave me alone!"

CHAPTER 10

A Dual Perspective At A Chance Encounter (Both Laurent And Jack Narrate)

I made my way to a jazz club called Snug Harbor. Happily listening to an evening of soulful music and losing myself in the music temporarily.

In the nearly two hundred years, I've existed in New Orleans, I have taken a particular liking to this sort of music.

Somehow, the music reached deep into someone's soul, tugging on a person's heartstrings. On occasion this music has inspired me to blood-soaked tears—each time having to shield my face from the other patrons of the club, so they didn't witness such a sight!

You might ask yourself, *Do vampires have souls?* I can assure you, I do. I cannot speak for the rest of my kind. I have tried desperately to retain some of my human emotions. Such as tenderness, compassion, and even love, despite the loss of my soulmate, Fabien. Perhaps some others of my kind may not care to retain any human emotions— it's considered a sign of weakness, and for many vampires, absolute power is everything. Still, I would rather perish than become nothing more than a bloodthirsty creature that merely lusts after blood with no feelings other than rage and the immense powers vampires yield.

Before my exposure to this sort of music, I restricted my music to listening to classical and opera. However, I made a conscious decision to expand my horizons—to embrace the sounds of my surroundings. To become more open to present-day life, even though living is a word I would not describe my kind.

Let me clarify some things for you—a vampire straddles the line between life and death; we merely exist, hence the expression the "living dead."

I was seated by the hostess in the back, as I requested, at a table for two. I observed the club's patrons escorted to their seats; one couple drew my attention. In her early thirties, a reasonably attractive woman with a gentleman her senior who must have had a disagreement before entering the club as both the woman and the man seemed angered and somewhat distant from one another.

Others were smiling and laughing and seemed quite excited to be at the club, awaiting whatever band was about to play.

I had come to hear the style of music, I hadn't sought out a particular group or singer, and I wouldn't describe myself as a fan or "groupie."

I continued to watch the flow of people enter the club, thinking to myself that my fellow patrons had no idea of the creature seated amongst them. If it were not for my teachings from Fabien—to not kill indiscriminately and retain some semblance of morals—I would have the power to end their existence. Lucky for these individuals, that was never my intention.

I'll admit, I struggled with that at times; the blood lust urge can frequently make a vampire lose control. The fact that I had not dined before going out only intensified those cravings.

Having missed nourishing myself before my outing—I couldn't help listening to their heartbeats, occasionally glancing at my fellow patrons— mostly, they ignored me, shifting my gaze instead towards the front door. There I spotted standing in the doorway—someone who made my world stand still. I became motionless, thinking, *My mind must be playing tricks on me! How can this be?*

Appearing in the doorway was a tall man with wavy golden brown hair, perfect skin, and the most piercing blue eyes—I recognized his face at once. I remembered the same face from the first time our eyes made contact at the Park Monceau in Paris over two hundred years ago. As he passed by my table, I looked at the man, thinking foolishly perhaps he would recognize me!—I couldn't help but say the name of one who had consumed my endless nights since his destruction so very long ago.

"Fabien!" I said as the man turned and looked at me.

"Excuse me?" he asked with a confused look on his face. "Forgive me; I thought you were someone else," I replied as my smile faded.

He cleared his throat, gave me a brief smile, and asked me if he could join me at my table—I thought this was so very much like Fabien, being the aggressor and taking charge of the situation.

"Yes, of course, where are my manners?," I said as I motioned towards the empty chair.

"Thanks, I know this must sound like a line, but do you come here often?" he said awkwardly. We both laughed, exchanging flirtatious glances, both our eyes dancing wildly. He had those same azure blue eyes I remembered so well. His smile was bright and cleverly disarming.

"No," I said after a long pause. "Neither do I," he quickly added.

"Allow me to introduce myself to you; my name is Laurent Richelieu," I said as I stuck out my hand. He took hold of it and had the oddest look on his face as he physically shuddered a bit. I knew it was his reaction to the coldness of my skin.

"Sorry—I must have caught a draft or something. Happy to meet you, Laurent; my name's Jack Devereux."

Shortly after our introductions, the room fell silent as the band began to play. The music seemed to put my new jazz companion in a sort of trance—I was captivated by this man and watched his every movement. I thought, *How Jack embodies the essence of my beloved Fabien!*.

I caught a glimpse of Jack closing his eyes and swaying to the music; then he sheepishly gazed at me with a smile that could melt even the coldest heart—I wondered if I still had a heart to melt? I felt at that moment we no longer were strangers; I was sure of this. I sensed a connection to Jack and felt as if it were destiny that he had walked into the same jazz club as I.

I decided to be the aggressor and reached under the table to put my hand on his thigh; he did not resist but merely looked at me and flashed a wide, pearly smile approvingly.

I felt that same excitement the night I met Fabien so long ago at Park Monceau in Paris. It felt as if I were given a second chance. In over two hundred years, I found that I very much retained feelings of love, excitement, and, naturally, a physical attraction.

***

(Jack narrates)

What was it about this gentleman that drew me to him? Was it his refined elegance? I have never felt so completely at ease around another man. He made me feel comfortable in my skin for the first time.

He wasn't the usual guy I wound up in bed with on so many occasions—yet there was something incredibly mysterious about him—I just couldn't put my finger on. The way he looked at me so tenderly and lovingly, as if we've known each other longer than just having met this evening. I knew this didn't make sense—my imagination must be getting to me. I thought, *Don't overthink it, Jack, you don't even know for sure this guy is gay. He did touch my leg, but what did that mean?* I was dying to find out—I wanted to know as much about this man as possible.

I thought, *Would he ask me back to his place?* It wasn't just lust; I felt like I wanted to get to know everything about him—and I wanted him to get to know me! I said to myself. *Well, Jack, you're making some progress. Here it was just a few short hours ago, and you were ready to dive back into the closet, possibly for good, not now!*

***

(Laurent narrates)

The band finished their performance as I looked at Jack; he seemed to be a bit preoccupied with his thoughts. He had consumed nearly three drinks presumably to lessen his nervousness and lose some of his inhibitions, *Oh how I detest alcohol! It makes fools out of most mortals; perhaps in the not-too-distant future, Jack will not need it,* I thought to myself.

"Wasn't that magnificent, Jack?" I asked. He didn't reply.

"Is everything alright, Jack?" I asked with a concerned look on my face.

"Yeah, I guess so." His speech sounded slurred as he was became intoxicated. "I just need to know one thing before we continue with all of this," Jack said with a stern look.

"Continue with all of this?" I asked, feeling confused.

"This small talk, your hand on my leg," he said with a grin from ear to ear. I remained silent and looked at him with a blank expression. "Ok! I'll just come out and say it—are you gay?" he yelled out. "Gay?" I said in return with questioning eyes.

"Sorry! Maybe they don't use that word where you come from— are you a homosexual?"

"If you mean, do I prefer another gentleman's company, then the answer would be yes," I stated.

Jack let out a sigh of relief. "Whew! That was tough!" he said and let out a loud laugh. I looked at him, somewhat puzzled. Most of the other bar patrons had left as we continued our private conversation.

A young woman, possibly in her twenties, came over and addressed us as "Gents."

"Hey, if you Gent's want to hang around here a while longer, you'll have to buy another round of drinks," she said.

I shook my head and promptly paid our tab, "No, thank you, Miss—keep the change," I said as I handed her a twenty-dollar bill.

"Hey! You didn't have to do that," Jack said, "Hey do you want to"…

And before Jack could finish his sentence, I invited him back to my estate.

"I guess you beat me to it," he said with a grin.

Barthelme was to pick me up at ten in the evening. We stood up; I looked at Jack—and asked him, "Are you feeling alright, Jack?"

"I'm fine; let's get back to your place," Jack replied.

As suspected, there was my trusty servant Barthelme waiting in front of the club.

"Wow! That's some set of wheels you got there, Laurent!" Jack said, I assumed he was impressed with my Rolls Royce.

"So, where are you taking me kind, Sir?" Jack said, trying to sound aristocratic—which amused me.

"My estate is an hour north of here, Jack, in the town known as Vacherie."

"An estate, eh?!" He said, seeming impressed.

"Good evening, Sir," Barthelme greeted me as he got out of the vehicle to open our doors. "Where to, Sir?" He asked.

"Home Barthelme," I replied. "Right away, Sir," he assured me.

"Jack, perhaps you should ride with the window open; the fresh air will improve your condition considerably," I suggested.

"What condition" he muttered under his breath.

We sped off into the darkened night. We exchanged few words between this handsome, unrefined drunken young man and me. After all, I thought, *what would the topic of our conversation be? Sports playoffs? What kind of beer he drank?, I already knew what his hard liquor of choice was.*

I thought about this, and the realization of Jack being who he was, compared to Fabien—which gave me a moment to wonder, *was I doing the right thing? Perhaps Jack was merely himself, only a striking resemblance to Fabien and nothing more? No, it wasn't mere coincidence that we so happened to be in the same place, at the same time—and Jack bearing the exact resemblance to my beloved. No, this was destiny, of that I was sure!* I was going to make certain that nothing would separate us again—I was to learn much more about Jack once we arrived at the estate.

We pulled into the long driveway past all the magnificent Oak trees, which lined the driveway up to my plantation's front entry.

By this time, Jack had regained some sobriety, the cold night air blowing in his face must have brought him back to some of his senses.

"Wow!" Jack said as he stepped out of the Rolls.

"Do you approve, Jack?" I asked playfully There again that gorgeous smile that washed away any doubts I may have had—perhaps I could groom this "diamond in the rough" so Jack could become my eternal mate, as we laughed and entered the mansion.

I witnessed Jack's mouth open in amazement at the sight of the many paintings and antique furnishings—most of which dated back to France in the late seventeenth and eighteenth centuries.

"Jack, let us adjourn to the drawing-room," I instructed.

"Yes, let's!" Jack replied, once again trying to sound aristocratic. For a moment, I had an image of myself as a mortal entering Fabien's drawing-room. His entrusted servant offered us an aperitif— never suspecting what that was to lead to, and as quickly as my thoughts returned to the past, I refocused my attention to the present—and Jack. This time it was Barthelme who was fetching our drinks.

"Man, oh, man! You must come from money, Laurent! I've never seen a place like this before; it's like the White House, or how I would imagine it to look!" he said.

How he endeared himself to me almost every time he spoke, sounding simple-minded at times but always straightforward, with a hint of intoxication.

"Jack, I'm going to come out and say this as delicately as I can; you've consumed way too much alcohol—I think it would be best if you spent the night sleeping it off. I have many guest bedrooms—I'm sure you'll be more than comfortable—you're welcome to stay in any one of them you see fit, and on second thought—perhaps we should skip the aperitif—Barthelme will take you home in the morning" I instructed.

"I was hoping you'd invite me to stay over," he said, grinning from ear to ear as he came towards me.

"Jack, I think you're getting the wrong idea—I'm not one to rush into physical contact right away if that is what you are implying? While I find you most handsome Jack, I wish to get to know you a bit before we proceed into the next phase if that's alright with you?" I said, rather gently.

I observed his facial expression, which seemed to convey confusion mixed with disappointment. A man such as Jack was not used to being turned down from his advances.

"Aww, you're just trying to play hard to get," he replied sheepishly and gave me that come hither look, as he studied the expression on my face, which was stone-faced. I didn't respond to him. After a few uncomfortable moments, he backed down.

"Yeah, maybe you're right; perhaps I did hit the sauce pretty hard." "Come now, let's put you to bed, Jack," I instructed.

Once again, Jack was becoming sexually playful, saying: "Are you joining me?" as he began to giggle like a child.

I looked at him and shook my head "I will put you into the room next to mine—that way, should you require anything in the middle of the night, I will be able to hear and assist you with any of your wants."

"Here is your room, Jack," I said as I opened the massive mahogany door.

Inside the room, a large marble fireplace with a giant mahogany canopy bed draped in the most beautiful silks—the window coverings were out of heavy velvet fabric, in a rich red wine color. Near the fireplace was a Louis the fourteenth chair with an embroidered scene, next to it was a small mahogany end table with a small porcelain figurine of a woman holding a basket.

On the fireplace mantle sat a silver candelabra—there was no electricity in the house. The light coming off the fireplace danced upon the crystals of the chandelier hanging from the ceiling.

I could quite literally see Jack's mouth open upon viewing what would be his room for the night.

I broke his thoughts with an offering of kindness. "Is there anything else you require, Jack?"

"No, you're so kind—all I need is a good night's sleep, and I'll be good as new!" he said as we hugged good night.

"Sleep well, and pleasant dreams!" I wished him.

***

(Jack narrates)

Man! I had only seen rooms like these in the movies! This guy must be beyond loaded! Sure as hell beats the Stardust Motor inn! But why wasn't this guy into me? Or if he is, maybe he's just trying to play hard to get? Nah! This guy is a gentleman. He's from Europe, for Christ's sake! No wonder! I've only met street trash or any guy willing to give it up upon the first meet-up. What would Lisa say about this? Fuck her! Why was I even thinking of my ex-wife? The same woman that denounced me as an "abomination of God" well, she would most likely include my new friend Laurent in that category and that he had most likely made a pact with the devil to live like this. What does it matter anyway? I thought. *Stop thinking about her, Jack; focus on getting a good night's sleep, and let's see what tomorrow brings.*

I thought about my new friend Laurent. *How dignified he was, what manners! A sense of grace, a true gentleman. I could tell he was into me, but he didn't want me to think he's promiscuous. Maybe he's only been with a handful of guys, if that!* I thought, and with that, I started to laugh.

I looked around the large guestroom and couldn't find one mirror! I thought, *That's strange? Not a single mirror?*

I began to undress; Laurent had been kind enough to leave me a pair of silk pajamas; I thought, usually, *I sleep naked, but tonight's different. You're in a beautiful place; to sleep on such luxurious soft sheets naked would be downright wrong!*

I shrugged and started to put on the silk pajamas. They felt so comfortable and soft on my skin.

Laurent's servant must have left the large window to my room open—as a slight breeze made its way through the window, making sleep much more pleasant. I climbed into bed—no sooner had my head touched the pillow than I was asleep.

I dreamt of walking around a dense fog; I appeared to be in some mausoleum—the only thing visible was a coffin. Walking over to it, sensing dread and hands shaking, I carefully lifted the coffin lid to reveal myself laying in it—suddenly awakening with a jolt, only to find my elegant silk pajamas wet with sweat.

I looked down at my watch; the time was six o'clock in the morning— the sun was about to rise in half an hour. I couldn't stay in bed, not after the nightmare I had. I decided to get up and wander around the gigantic estate, hoping to familiarize myself with my new friend's stately home. I wanted to learn more about this mysterious European man. As I opened the door to my guest bedroom—the door creaked a bit. Barthelme, Laurent's trusty servant, immediately greeted me.

"Is everything alright, Master Jack?"

"Yes, thanks for asking Barthelme; I just want to get some fresh air; I didn't sleep very well, now if you'll excuse me," I said.

"Of course, Master Jack. Please let me know if there is anything I can provide for you?" Barthelme said. Looking at Barthelme's face, I noticed he appeared a bit anxious.

"Good night Master Jack, or what's left of it," he said.

Barthelme walked back into his room, glancing back at me one last time before closing his door.

I decided I needed to see my new friend, Laurent. Perhaps he was an early riser and was up waiting for me. I carefully opened his door—a large ornate, heavy mahogany door which made no squeaking sound, as mine had made. There was nothing but silence—dead silence.

Naturally, Laurent's room was even more majestic than I had imagined. A sizable wooden canopy bed, heavy velour curtains in blood-red color, several antique chairs, and that familiar marble fireplace, the flames of which were starting to die off in the early morning hours. There appeared to be a massive painting of someone—a portrait.

I chose to make my way over to Laurent's bed before going over to the portrait to get a better look.

There he lay, motionless—I hadn't awakened him. It seemed all the coloring of his face had left him, appearing chalk-white! I looked at his chest and couldn't detect any breathing. I took his hand, thinking that might awaken him, but no, he continued to lay there as if he were dead. I lay my head down on his chest to hear his heartbeat. There was nothing! *Every living thing on this earth has a heartbeat. Why doesn't Laurent?* I screamed out as I began to panic.

Barthelme, Laurent's trusty servant, came to my call. He flung the door open.

"You shouldn't be in here!" he shouted.

I stood there, paralyzed for once in my life. And felt utterly helpless, throwing my arms up in despair.

"I think he's dead! There's no heartbeat, and he's whiter than a ghost!" I was barely able to speak those words.

"Get out! Leave! I will drive you back into town, Master Jack, but you must leave if you know what's good for you!" Barthelme warned me.

"How can I leave when he's in a state like that? Aren't you going to call a doctor or an ambulance? Are you going to let him die just like that? What kind of servant are you?" I yelled as I tried to reach for any level of sanity left in my brain.

"There are things that you do not understand, Master Jack; it is not my position to explain them to you, leave at once! —I have been instructed by Master Laurent to drive you back to your place. Once the Master has awakened—he will contact you".

"He's dead! —I tried to listen to his heartbeat, he doesn't have one! He's not waking up, and here we are yelling at each other and still nothing? What kind of madness is this?" I said as beads of sweat started to appear on my face, my voice trembling as I spoke.

"I will only ask you one more time—gather your belongings so we may leave! Master Laurent is fine; it is not what you think! I have been Master Laurent's trusty servant for a very, very long time—I know him best! I have experienced what you have many times before. Now go pack, and we shall leave immediately!" Barthelme instructed.

I did as he told me, probably for the first time in my life. All I wanted to do was leave—to get away from Laurent and Barthelme.

Something was going on here that didn't add up. Last night I had too much to drink—I wasn't thinking with a clear mind. Now being "stone-cold sober," my thoughts became more precise. There was a painting in Laurent's bedroom, a large picture in the room with a man in it whose features I couldn't make out because of the darkened room except for the candlelight beside Laurent's bed.

Before I could walk over to it—Barthelme entered the room.

I thought there were so many questions that needed answering. *Why wasn't there any electricity in the house? Why wasn't there a mirror anywhere to be seen? Only a telephone, and an old rotary phone at that!*

I was dressed in an instant and decided to shower once I got back to the motel.

I wondered if I was still recovering from my drunken state and the series of events that occurred once we arrived at Laurent's estate, thinking, *Had all this happened—or had I imagined it all?*

I gave Barthelme the address as he opened my passenger door and closed it, then entered the driver's seat as we drove off. There were no words exchanged during our drive back; I was relieved as my head was swimming.

Soon we were pulling up into the parking lot of the Stardust Motel. Barthelme wished me a pleasant day and told me the Master would be in touch soon. Laurent and I had exchanged telephone numbers—curious that he had a telephone but no electricity, it seemed this man wanted to preserve some things of the past and not all things? I made my way to the construction site—just barely, and started work. I was lifting heavy steel bars and carrying them to their *final resting place*. I contemplated the sentence; it sent a shiver up my spine. I thought about Laurent. I wondered if he was okay—and whether I would ever see him again.

I called Laurent a few days later from a payphone near the construction site; during my lunch break, I was expecting a call from him which never came. I was becoming concerned something terrible had happened to him.

The number rang and rang until Barthelme picked up.

"Hello Richelieu residence, Barthelme speaking, how may I help you?"

"Barthelme, it's Jack," I said frantically, "Is everything alright with Laurent?"

A brief silence—nothing more, it seemed to last an eternity.

"Yes, Master Jack, I had to rush Master Laurent to the hospital— it appeared the Master suffered from a seizure, which would explain the lack of a heartbeat—he had gone into cardiac arrest. You are to be commended, Master Jack. Without your help, Master Laurent might be dead! He's doing fine and is back safe and sound—I'm sure you'll be hearing from him as he will undoubtedly want to thank you personally for saving his life".

"Expect to be hearing from the Master very soon. Goodbye, Master Jack, and thank you for all of your efforts and concern!"

I heard a dial tone as Barthelme had hung up before I could utter any other words or a goodbye. I raced back to the motel as soon as I had finished my shift. I soaked in the bathtub to relieve my aching muscles from my eight-hour day at the construction site.

I thought about our chance encounter; it seemed to be something like out of a movie. I felt Laurent and I were bound to meet. I was sure of it!.

I wanted so desperately to hear Laurent's voice, and in his own words reassuring me he's out of harm's way.

I looked at my watch; the time was eight-thirty; I jumped a bit as the phone rang. I felt as if I were sitting on pins and needles.

"Hello?" I answered. "Jack?" the voice asked "Yes!" I said excitedly—instantly recognizing it as Laurent's. "Jack, this is Laurent. Thank you ever so much for being in the right place at the right time! I owe you a world of gratitude! I would very much like to see you again as soon as possible. Are you free tomorrow evening—say, eight-thirty for dinner at my place?" he asked tenderly.

"Yes, of course! I haven't thought of anything—or anyone, since we last saw each other!" I said unabashedly.

"Neither have I, Jack. Well, then it is settled. Barthelme will pick you up at eight o'clock tomorrow evening.

Bring your appetite Jack, as the food will be plentiful," Laurent instructed.

"Yes, okay—I will. I'm so relieved that you're okay, Laurent!" I said breathlessly.

"Jack, I cannot thank you enough! I'll look forward to our wonderful evening together," he said.

I blushed a bit. "Thank you, Laurent; I'll look forward to seeing you as well," I said.

"I'm counting down the hours, Jack! Until tomorrow evening—sleep well," he said, tenderly.

The next day at work was a blur; I felt much like a robot, preoccupied with thoughts of Laurent. I finished my shift and raced back to the Stardust to shower and get dressed in my Sunday finest— which included: a sport jacket, dress shirt, dress slacks, and dress shoes—I even ditched my white cotton socks and traded them in for some dress nylon socks from that fancy designer, Pierre Cardin. I thought, *I'm sure a gentleman of Laurent's standings would notice even the socks a man wore, however insignificant that might sound. I wanted to look perfect and look the part—someone like me, fortunate enough to call a man like Laurent—my boyfriend.*

These thoughts I was having seemed so strange. I had never been comfortable around other gay men; I looked at them as mere physical conquests. Laurent was different. Was I hoping for a future together? Could I even imagine one with another man? My Catholic upbringing said, No, instead, I decided to go with my gut instinct for once and not base my decision on my faith.

Barthelme arrived with the Rolls. He got out of the car and opened my door. I entered the passenger door in the back of the large vehicle and enjoyed the showiness of it all. I wanted to better myself, become more refined, like Laurent. I was determined to develop manners, to challenge myself quite literally to be anything but the lower-middle-class guy I grew up and identified with all my life. Laurent made me want to be more like him. I enjoyed this roleplaying—at least I could pretend? And maybe—I would be able to change?

***

(Laurent narrates)

As Barthelme arrived with Jack, I felt like I was awaiting some important government representative. How strange that I should be feeling this way? A two hundred and fifty-year-old vampire anxiously awaiting someone?

I made sure everything was perfect. Barthelme had been preparing the estate for Jack's arrival all day, everything from polishing the silver— to cleaning the crystal and creating making what was sure to be an exquisite feast—for Jack.

I could hear the car approaching, and walked towards the window to gaze out briefly— I didn't want Jack to catch me as I peered out of the window. The front door swung upon, and there before me stood the most handsome man—even more so than he had appeared the night we met at the Jazz bar.

Jack had cleaned himself up rather nicely! Gone was the start of a three-day-old beard which Jack had worn at our first encounter. He had gotten his hair cut and styled and was dressed in a sports jacket with a dress shirt, pants, and dress shoes; he had made quite an effort. I couldn't have been any happier than I was at that moment; my smile conveyed that.

"Jack! How handsome you look!" I said approvingly.

"Thank you, Laurent—as do you! It's a pleasure to see you and to be back here under much more pleasant circumstances! I'm so glad that you're okay and feeling better! —I guess I saved your life!" he said as he let out a faint laugh.

For a moment I became confused by what he meant, my expression gave that away— then quickly remembering Jack had found me in my undead slumber— where no sign of "life" could be detected, which included a lack of a heartbeat. The color of my skin would have also resembled a corpse. Jack truly felt as if he had intervened and rescued me from a near-certain death—not yet knowing my secret! I offered up my thanks.

"Yes, Jack, you are a lifesaver!" I said and looked at him intensely. "Shall we move into the drawing before adjourning to dinner?"

I suggested.

"Yes—that would be lovely!" Jack said, which I felt was very uncommon for him to be using these words? I thought, *is Jack putting on airs, or is he genuinely making a conscious effort to become the gentleman I know is buried deep inside? Which is all to be a part of Jack's transformation?*

We sat on the sofa near the roaring fireplace, gazing into each other's eyes.

I had two of the windows open, a cool summer night's breeze had blown in—it smelled of jasmine and honeysuckle; the aroma was overpowering; it was almost hypnotic.

"Ah! Just smell that Jack! Isn't that heavenly?" I asked while closing my eyes.

"Yes, Laurent, it's heavenly."

At that point, I looked over at Jack and found him laughing a bit. "Are you amused by something Jack?" I asked, sounding confused.

He looked at me, as he stopped laughing and said, "I'm sorry Laurent, but this is all so out of my element, I'm just trying to impress you, I guess I'm putting on airs."

I thought, *Aha! As I had suspected.* I looked at him and shook my head as I said "Jack, you are quite an enigma." "Enigma?" he asked, looking confused.

"It means you are something special—as if you were the chosen one."

"Chosen one?" he asked, looking even more confused. Barthelme called us into the dining room, announcing dinner was about to be served. Our festive evening was about to begin.

We walked into the dining room, seeing the candelabras lit, and the dining table, which seated twenty, was set with Wedgewood china— crystal glasses added to the already elegantly decorated table. A lovely bouquet of freshly cut flowers filled the crystal flower vase. It had been a long time since I had entertained anyone; mostly, the table sat empty.

"Jack, please sit next to me; I will sit at the table's head," I instructed.

Shortly after being seated, the wine began to be poured. Barthelme came over to offer Jack a glass. "Yes, please!" Jack said.

Barthelme came over to me out of courtesy, as he knew I did not drink alcohol—knowing the only thing to sustain my existence was blood. I indicated to Barthelme that I would not partake.

"You don't drink, Laurent? Jack asked, sounding confused. "No! I can't handle the stuff Jack if you know what I mean?" I said.

"I understand," he said as a nervous smile appeared.

Barthelme announced the first course was a chicken consume, with herb baked croutons and French bread and butter.

I thought about how long it had been since I had eaten any mortal food— the thought of it sickened me.

"Aren't you eating, Laurent?" he asked innocently. Jack noticed that I was drinking but not eating— Barthelme had poured me some blood earlier which he served me in a silver goblet— hoping Jack wouldn't notice precisely what I was drinking.

"No, Jack I hope you don't mind, but I will not be dining this evening. I had a very late lunch this afternoon, I'll simply enjoy my tomato juice—I didn't want my lack of an appetite to interfere with our wonderful evening together," I said rather apologetically.

"That's okay; it's just nice to be here and have the pleasure of your company Laurent," he said as Barthelme offered him another slice of homemade French bread with butter.

I looked at him longingly and smiled, as I picked up my wine goblet containing blood and took a sip—it washed down my throat, which felt good.

Barthelme returned and cleared Jack's bowl and bread plate. He served Jack his main course—which consisted of petit filet mignon with roasted red potatoes and white asparagus drenched in a Béarnaise sauce. "Wow!" Jack said excitedly. I merely sat there and observed my new love interest.

I desperately wanted to believe that Fabien—soulmate and maker—had returned to me in the form of Jack. As if by some miracle! I wasn't about to let **ANYTHING or ANYONE** interfere in this process.

I would wine and dine and win over Jack's heart. At the right time—I would reveal my secret to him and allow him to decide if he wishes to accept the dark gift I would offer him. It would, however, be entirely Jack's decision whether to accept or not.

Once we finished dinner—we adjourned to the drawing-room to let Jack's dinner settle. Barthelme replenished my goblet with more blood and poured Jack's more wine.

"Let's leave the French doors open to the garden; it's such a lovely evening out Barthelme; there's no need to close them."

"As you wish, Master Laurent. Will there be anything else?" Barthelme asked in a hushed voice.

"No, Barthelme, thank you, that will be all."

"Excellent Sir!" With that, Barthelme retired to his room.

***

(Jack narrates)

I had to take it all in, I asked myself; this *was like something out of a movie. This refined European gentleman, is he that into you? It didn't make sense. We're so different! As if we're from two other worlds! What does he see in me? This mysterious, cultured man could have any man or woman he chose to have; why me?* The pressure I was putting on myself to maintain this well-mannered individual's interest seemed too much; it wasn't me! All I wanted was to grab a beer with some guy— screw his brains out, and leave. No! That was the old me—the lonely, empty, pathetic soul I used to be— before I met this amazing man. Did I think, *maybe I was never really living before, but merely existing? I needed him — and something told me, he needed me, for whatever reason—perhaps I would find out soon enough?*

"Jack!" Laurent said. His words suddenly pulled me out of my thoughts as Laurent spoke my name.

"Is everything alright?" he asked.

"Yes! I'm sorry. I'm so grateful to be with you here tonight!" I said.

Laurent gazed at me affectionately and leaned over and kissed me. It was soft and romantic.

"Jack, you have no idea how happy I am that you are here with me!" Laurent said breathlessly as he tenderly touched my face; however, his hand's iciness broke the romantic moment as I began to shudder a bit. For the first time, I was noticed how white his complexion was.

"What's the matter, Jack?" Laurent asked me.

"I just noticed how pale you are. You're not a fan of the sun, Laurent?"

He looked at me strangely, apparently disturbed by my question. "No, I'm not, I have a rare skin disorder, and so I try to avoid any contact with the sun, which could lead to a disfiguring burn." Abruptly he stood up from where we were both seated and walked over to the French doors. Somewhere, dogs began howling.

"Why do you think those dogs are howling, Laurent? Does that happen often?" I asked. He turned and looked at me with a mysterious grin on his face and said in an eerie way,

"Perhaps they sense danger Jack, or perhaps they're just hungry?" His response made me a bit uncomfortable. I wasn't used to feeling intimidated by other men—I was sure of myself, could take care of myself physically— but this man was different. He had such self-confidence; at times, he almost came across as invincible.

I thought, *Laurent made me rethink everything I've ever known, and for the first time in my life, he had me doubt myself! Who is this man? — Why do I feel so helpless and weak, as if I'm not myself, as if I'm supposed to be someone else? Listen to yourself, Jack; this is starting to sound like crazy talk!* I needed to get away to think things through.

"Laurent, if you don't mind, I'd like to go to sleep; I suddenly feel exhausted," I said.

"Of course, Jack, I understand; perhaps you have had a long day?" "Yes, that must be it," I said as I made up an excuse for suddenly wanting to end our evening together.

"Thank you for the wonderful dinner Laurent; it was exceptional!" "Jack, I hope you don't mind—but I'll be staying up a bit, you see I'm rather nocturnal—perhaps you are more of a morning person? If you would like, you're welcome to stay in the same guest bedroom as your last visit? It is the room closest to mine," he said assuredly.

"Good night Laurent."

"Good night Jack, pleasant dreams—one other thing, I won't be around when you awaken; I have some business to attend to in Atlanta," he said.

"When can I see you again, Laurent?" I asked in a shy way. "Soon, Jack—very soon!" he said as he gave me a warm and tender smile. I returned his smile with one of my own and headed towards the staircase.

I made my way up the long stairway, and walked down the semi darkened hallway— a wide passage illuminated with a lit candelabra placed every few feet. As I walked along, I passed statues and oil paintings that looked old and very expensive. I've never been much of an art lover, so I couldn't tell who the artists were—but no doubt they were European.

I entered my room and flung myself on the bed. All at once, exhaustion swept over me. I knew deep sleep would set in soon.

I began to undress and thought, *How strange that there isn't a single mirror to be seen anywhere?* I slipped on the silk pajamas I had on from my previous stayover and smelled the fabric; they appeared freshly laundered.

I could still hear the dogs howling outside as I climbed into the canopy bed. *It reminded me of a horror movie I had watched once; what was the name?* I asked myself but was too tired to continue thinking of anything.

A cool breeze blew over my entire body from the open window in the bedroom; it felt good, caressing my body as a lover might.

I managed to fall asleep quite suddenly; I hadn't reached a deep sleep and began to stir a bit in bed, wrapping myself up in the silken sheets and goose down comforter, laying in a fetal position in the direction of the window.

I opened my eyes and saw what appeared to be the outline of a man, simply standing there observing me! Thinking, *I must be hallucinating, or maybe I am asleep—which is all part of a dream? This vision can't be real? I'm on the second story of Laurent's mansion; how could there be anyone in my room?*

I continued to stare at the dark figure hidden in the shadows—the image starting to become more transparent and more apparent.

What was it I was seeing? It appeared to be two red eyes glaring at me. They looked like two rubies on fire, as I yelled out,

"Laurent!"

There was no reply—I figured perhaps Laurent had decided to go outside for a stroll and couldn't hear me.

"Who are you?" I demanded of the shadowy figure; there was no reply.

I climbed out of bed and slowly started to approach the figure—just before I could get close enough to see its face, the character vanished into a mist that seemed to exit out the open window. I pinched myself to make sure I wasn't still asleep having a nightmare, and much to my amazement felt the pain from my self-inflicted pinch telling me this hadn't been a dream, but rather a living nightmare! How was it possible that someone got into my room, and something with two red eyes?

I saw something I thought I would never see in my life, a ghost! That's what it must have been—the thought of it had me cry out again, only this time much louder!

"Laurent!" I screamed at the top of my lungs. Instantly, the door to my bedroom sprang open as Laurent appeared.

"Jack! What's wrong? You must have been having a nightmare!" he said, trying desperately to comfort me. *Perhaps I had dreamt it? No! —I hadn't; I was fully awake!* I began to tremble.

"Laurent, I saw someone, just now, glaring at me with two red eyes; it just stood there staring at me!" I said, nearly hysterical.

"What do you think it was, Jack?" Laurent asked with a look of doubt in his eyes.

"I don't know, a ghost? Or something—it had two red eyes that glared at me," I said, immediately feeling ashamed as I heard my answer.

"Two red eyes glaring at you?" Laurent replied as he began to laugh.

"I know what I saw, Laurent; I didn't imagine it," I said with a bit of resentment in my voice.

"Jack, you admitted how tired you were. When a person is in a state of exhaustion, the mind can play terrible tricks on the eyes, Laurent said, trying to reassure me.

"This happened, Laurent!" I said as I raised my voice.

"Perhaps it was a nightmare? You were dreaming." Laurent replied. I thought, *Dreaming? Maybe I did; otherwise, how could anyone enter my bedroom two floors up? It didn't make sense.*

"You're right Laurent, maybe it was just a nightmare, and either that or I'm losing my sanity!" I said.

"Jack, I must go back to bed—I have to be up in a few hours to leave for my business trip," Laurent said apologetically.

We said our goodnights, or what was left of it, as Laurent left my room.

CHAPTER 11

A Slow Descent Into Hell

I looked at my watch; the time read four o›clock in the morning. It seemed every time I agreed to spend the night at Laurent's—I never get laid and end up having the strangest nightmares, that and staining his soft pajamas—twice now. I took them off and decided to sleep in the nude, not wanting to feel the sweaty material stick to my skin as I fell back into a deep sleep and began to dream.

I found myself wandering down a darkened hallway, passing by horrific paintings depicting scenes of bloodletting, burning buildings— portraits of ravenous dogs and wolves snarling; as I passed each picture, they seemed to come to life.

The blood spilled down from the pictures onto the wood floor— the hungry dogs and wolves snarling, biting, reaching for me, yet somehow I managed to continue my journey. I walked down the darkened hallway where I noticed clock after clock, but none of them were running; they appeared to have stopped. I finally reached the end of the hall, seeing a portrait shaded partially by the hallway's darkness.

Finding a nearby candle, I held the flame up to the portrait, but before I could make out the face in the picture, I awoke yelling, "Let me see!"

This time it was Barthelme who came to my rescue, knocking on my door.

"Master Jack—may I enter?" he asked with concern in his voice. "Yes," I replied.

"Are you alright, Master Jack?" Barthelme looked at me with a puzzled expression on his face.

"Yes, just another one of my nightmares; I guess this place inspires them," I said as I feigned a smile.

Barthelme being the cultured servant he was, ignored my remark and began to explain that the Master had already left for Atlanta and asked me if there was something he could bring me to help calm my nerves. I asked for a shot of something, anything containing alcohol.

"Right away, Master Jack," Barthelme answered.

Why did he refer to me as "Master Jack"? I didn't live here, nor was I his master? And why did he call Laurent "Master Laurent" like back in the slave days? I may be from the South, but the thought of a black person calling me "Master" made me uncomfortable.

After what seemed an eternity, Barthelme returned with a glass of bourbon—I took the glass from him and took one big gulp, feeling it burn my throat as it made its way down into my stomach, anything to help calm my nerves. He stared at me for a brief moment. I felt the deafening silence; it was awkward.

After a long pause, Barthelme asked, "Will there be anything else, Master Jack?"

"No, Barthelme, thank you!" I said, feeling embarrassed as if I were a child that a parent had just given a glass of warm milk.

I decided at that moment that I needed a break from my budding relationship with Laurent. We had gotten together twice, and nothing even remotely physical happened, and all these strange occurrences. I was unconvinced the figure with the red eyes was just a dream, but who or what was it? I was starting to wonder what kind of game Laurent was playing, or simply that his house was haunted?

Thinking, *Perhaps he's a virgin?* I chuckled to myself softly, hoping not to awaken Barthelme.

A few hours later, I was driven into town by Barthelme.

"I hope Master Laurent and I see you again soon, Master Jack," he said.

"Thanks," I offered up awkwardly as I shrugged. I needed time to think—to sort things out. Since meeting Laurent, I hadn't thought of anyone else; he was all-consuming; it was one of the most amazing things to happen to me. Yet, at the same time, it strangely was one of the most disturbing things to happen to me as well. Perhaps my imagination was more vivid than I thought? I tried reassuring myself, *How could there have been someone in my room, and what could explain the red, glaring eyes? Monsters don't exist; except in fiction. I must have dreamt the whole thing!*

Laurent must have thought I was a fool for mentioning what I had seen. There was one thing that puzzled me.

The expression on his face when I described my experience, it almost appeared to be an acknowledgment—did he believe my story? As I climbed the stairs of the motel, I felt exhaustion hit every inch of my body. I needed to rest—having had a sleepless night at Laurent's. I undressed—keeping only my underwear and socks on. As soon as I laid down on the bed, I fell into a deep sleep.

I slept a few hours and awoke from hearing my growling stomach— it was time I found a place for a late breakfast or early lunch. I looked at my watch.

"Holy shit!" I said as the face of my watch read eleven-thirty in the morning.

I quickly showered and got dressed, and made my way to the "Ruby Slipper," a diner-type restaurant that served all-day breakfasts for those who tend to sleep late.

Walking along, I passed a newsstand and decided to pick up a paper. I glanced at it quickly—to the front pages left a headline about President Reagan's meeting with the Soviet leader in some country called Iceland—the other article was about a local girl being attacked and nearly left for dead. I decided it would provide me with exciting reading material while I enjoyed my breakfast.

I was practically starving as I arrived at the "Ruby Slipper" at twelve-thirty—as I made my way in and was seated, I ordered a full breakfast including two eggs, bacon, toast, home fries, and coffee. The article about the girl being attacked captured my interest.

As I read the story—I felt the hairs on the back of my neck standing up. It sent shivers up and down my spine. "Mary Margaux, age thirty-two—found half alive with two puncture wounds in her neck, nearly drained of her blood."

While interviewing the victim sent to Ochsner medical center, she described the assailant as having two red eyes—a hypnotic glare and a thick European accent, read the article.

It sounded like fiction! Like something from a scene out of "Dracula," especially the part about the red eyes and two puncture wounds and draining the victim of her blood? I was shaken and thought *I had the same vision while staying in Laurent's guest room. Was that a dream, or had the attacker somehow gotten into Laurent's mansion where I was staying? Perhaps it was the same attacker?.*

I thought, *Listen to yourself, Jack, that's crazy thinking! Your imagination is running on overtime—vampires don't exist, only in fiction.*

But what would explain the same red eyes seen in my encounter—as the victim had reported about her attacker? I was starting to feel that however bizarre my encounter was at Laurent's was not a dream!

I decided to visit the young woman at Ochsner medical center and play detective to ask her some questions. Maybe she could provide me some information I was seeking, which didn't appear in the newspaper article. I was hoping whoever was standing guard outside her room would let me in, and if not, I could come up with a reason why I was coming to see her.

I walked over to the hospital. The head nurse greeted me at the nurse's station, a plain sort of uptight woman who hated what she was doing, as she directed me to room three hundred and two.

I made my way to the elevator and walked down the hallway until I reached the entry to Mary Margaux's room. As suspected —a policeman was seated outside of Mary's room; little good did it do as he appeared to be asleep.

Some protection, I thought! —I fought hard not to laugh out loud. As I cleared my throat loudly, "Ahem, Hi!" I said to the policeman, who promptly awoke and stood up startled.

"I'm Mary's cousin—I heard about what happened to her and wondered if I might visit with her for a few minutes," I asked.

He looked me over. "You related to the young lady?" he asked in a strong southern drawl.

"Yes, officer—I'm Mary's cousin Sam from Baton Rouge. I've come all this way after hearing about what happened to dear Mary; we almost lost her! We're all so relieved to hear she survived!" I said, trying my best to sound convincing and not blow my cover.

He looked me over suspiciously and finally said, "Alright, go on in—but just for five minutes."

"Yes, of course, thank you, officer," I said as I reached for the door handle.

I opened the door and discovered Mary asleep. I quietly crept over to her bed and put my hand over her mouth before she could wake and scream for help. She instinctively reached for my hand—her eyes wide and wild looking.

"Hush! I'm not going to harm you; I just wanted to meet you and ask you some questions. I said, trying to reassure her. You won't scream, will you?" I asked her.

Mary shook her head, agreeing not to make a sound, and looked at me with her pale green eyes, which began to soften a bit—appearing less wild. I took my hand off her mouth. She asked if I was a reporter, thinking to myself, *Thank you, Mary, for giving me a cover.*

"Yes, I'm a reporter," I said as I nodded my head and told her my name was Sam and that I worked for the *Advocate* in Baton Rouge and that her attack had made a newsworthy read in all the state of Louisiana—as far away as Baton Rouge and that I had just a few questions for her.

She blushed at hearing the news. "What can I answer for you, Mister?" she asked.

"Mr. Thompson, I said (quickly thinking of my high school football coach's name back in Baton Rouge). Listen, the policeman outside your door keeping watch has given me a time limit of five minutes—we've already used up two minutes. So, I'll make this short and sweet," I said.

"Do you have any idea what your attacker looked like?" I asked. She seemed to struggle with her response as she turned away from me and started to cry.

"He had dark hair, a slender pointy nose, and two red eyes. He had some accent; he didn't sound like he came from around here," Mary said, struggling to tell her story without crying once again. "He approached me down by the Café DuMond and asked me if he could bum a cigarette off me—I told him I didn't smoke. Then he asked if I lived here locally," she reported.

She told me he was looking for someone local to show him around town—show him the sights as he was new to town.

"He made it clear that he was not interested in women in a romantic way," she said with a smile as she stopped crying.

I became even more intrigued as Mary continued telling me her story. They had walked down towards the waterfront when suddenly he went for her neck. She realized the attacker lied and was interested in women after all—otherwise, why would the attacker be going for her neck? Mary told him to stop; he said it wasn't what it appeared to be, that he had a hunger and proceeded to try and bite her. That's the last thing she could remember.

I had brought a notebook and a pencil with me and was jotting down notes—looking professional.

At that moment, the door opened—the policeman told me my five minutes were up.

I thanked Mary for the information, concealing my notebook inside the newspaper I had brought, so the policeman still thought I was Mary's cousin.

"Thank you, Cousin Mary!" I said as I quickly left the room and down the hallway and into an elevator that was just about to close. I heard the cop's footsteps come running behind.

Mary must have told him I was a reporter when I had introduced myself to him as her cousin from Baton Rouge. I reached the street and ran as quickly as I could and hid down an alleyway—I saw the policeman come out of the hospital's main entrance as he stood there looking for me.

I waited until I saw the cop leave, undoubtedly heading back to the hospital to "stand guard over Mary."

I heard my heart beating wildly, knowing I could have been taken in for questioning, masquerading myself as her cousin and a reporter.

It was well worth the effort. Mary had provided me with enough information regarding the attacker's features, particularly his red eyes! I went back to the motel, feeling satisfied with my undercover work. —but what did it all mean? An attacker claiming not to have a romantic interest? Was he looking to lure her into something? And telling her he had a hunger and then attacked her neck? Then the same red eyes she described, like what I had seen in Laurent's guestroom! My head was swimming; I had to take in all these details.

After returning to the motel, I kicked off my shoes and opened up a beer I had picked up at a nearby convenience store. The beer felt good as it hit the back of my throat; as I looked over my notes and read how Mary had described her attacker.

Dark hair, a sharp pointy nose, a strange accent, and ruby red eyes— it sounded like a character right out of a horror movie.

I thought, *was it Dracula himself that had returned from the grave? But didn't that fictional character live in Transylvania? Then moving to England, but that was fiction! Vampires don't exist! —Or do they?* I felt the hairs on the back of my neck raise.

Honestly, who wouldn't want to live forever and not grow old and die? Who wouldn't want to stay up all night and sleep the day away? I would sign up for that!

I decided another way to clear my head of all this talk about vampires was to go out to a club. I had saved up a little money and I was going to quit my construction job anyway; I could go out on a "school night." Perhaps I'll find another job that was more respectable and refined —as Laurent would want. He disapproved of my doing manual labor anyway and had expressed that thought to me over dinner we had together—where he never joined me in eating. I thought about how odd that seemed!

I left the motel and walked over to The Rawhide—maybe I could hook up with someone to forget about all the strangeness going on all around me.

Laurent never made any moves on me —which also seemed weird? I thought, *He doesn't eat, and he isn't into sex, so precisely what does he enjoy?* The good news was, I was becoming a little more comfortable with my being gay; I have Laurent to thank for that; at least I owed him that.

He made me feel that being gay wasn't just the sex part, but the other things everyone wants—companionship and a closeness similar to friendship. I became a little sad thinking about him. I barely noticed the dark figure that appeared beside a tree in the park across from the bar. I thought someone was following me, or more accurately— stalked. My thoughts returned to Laurent.

If he's so perfect, Jack, what the hell are you doing going out on him and behind his back, and why aren't you with him instead? —Surely, he must be back from his business trip to Atlanta by now. I should call him. But then again, maybe I should wait for him to call me. Laurent is a bit odd. He doesn't even have electricity at his mansion. He told me he wanted to preserve the estate in its historical context or bullshit like that. I thought, feeling frustrated.

I entered the bar feeling guilty going out on Laurent. Why did I feel as if I was cheating on him? —maybe it was the connection I felt with him—for the first time in my miserable life?

I walked over to the bar and decided to order anything but a Jack Daniels—my old staple. I wanted to break that pattern and decided to order a gin and tonic in Laurent's honor.

The bartender recognized me as a regular from the past when he heard my drink order—he looked at me as if I had two heads.

"Hey man, did you join a country club for queers or something?" he asked.

Now the old me would have taken offense at his comment and told him to "go fuck himself" — but this was the new Jack—I laughed it off and told him, "Yeah, I'm moving on up in the world, like "The Jeffersons," you know that TV show? Even they got tired of being poor!" And I started to laugh.

He gave me a look—shook his head, and said, "One gin and tonic coming up," which turned some heads, I must admit, this was a beer drinking bar.

My tough exterior didn't quite match my insecurity inside. I thought *I'll show all of them! From now on—it's the new Jack Devereux! But then again, why am I out at a gay bar, a leather bar at that? And why aren't I with Laurent instead?*

Before I could think about anything else, in walked this strikingly handsome man with dark hair and deep-set eyes, he caught my eye as he entered the bar and nodded his head—as he walked over to where I was standing.

"I couldn't help but notice you as I entered the bar," he said.

He stood slightly taller than me, broad shoulders, dark hair, with a distinctive nose. He had an accent I couldn't place. I noticed his skin was as white as milk; the only thing missing were the red eyes, as in Mary's description.

I asked him where he was from.

"I'm from Europe," he said with a grin.

I looked at him closely; perhaps he thought I was some sort of red neck from Louisiana. As I said sarcastically, "Well, that's a bit vague—I know Europe is a continent, not a country. Which country in Europe are you from?" My geographical knowledge seemed to please him.

"I'm from the land of the Eiffel Tower and champagne," he said, looking me over.

"Let me guess, France!"

"Very good! So, you're familiar with France?" he asked.

"I have a friend who's from France as well—perhaps the two of you can meet sometime, provided we get to know each other better first?" I said with a grin —as I began to flirt with this mysterious Frenchman.

I thought *if Laurent was going to play hard to get, then perhaps my new friend would give him a little competition.*

"Forgive my rudeness, allow me to introduce myself; my name is Stefan, and you are?" he asked with one raised eyebrow.

"My name's Jack Devereux," I answered.

"Ah, so you are French as well? As he spoke, I noticed the slightest trace of what appeared to be blood on his shirt collar, *which* distracted me.

"No, I'm Cajun, born and raised in Louisiana; I have French blood in me. Speaking of blood—I hope you don't mind me mentioning this—you have a tiny stain right there on your shirt collar," I said, feeling awkward for having mentioned it.

Our conversation came to an abrupt end. It appeared my new friend, and hopefully my possible hook up for the night, had suddenly become uncomfortable with the mention of blood as he turned away from me.

"I'm sorry! Did I say something to upset you?" I asked.

His reply with a hearty laugh left me at ease. He told me to forget about it—admitting to me that he must have cut himself while shaving, and that he felt embarrassed for going out in public with a stained shirt.

"Let me buy you a drink, Jack," he offered up as an icebreaker.

"Sure, what the hell— I've only had one, and somehow I feel like it's going to be a long night," I said as I winked at him with one eye. He responded by giving me a grin, an evil sort of look that gave me the creeps, yet oddly enticed me all simultaneously.

"What's your pleasure, Jack?" he asked.

"Jack Daniels," I said, thinking, *how soon the old ways return, so much for my short-lived attempt at becoming more refined for Laurent.*

Unlike my other Frenchman, Laurent, I sensed this man to be more of a dominant type. He struck me as someone who realized how powerful he is and is used to getting everything and anything he wants; I was intrigued by this show of force and physically attracted to him.

Usually, I was always the dominant one, but I decided to go with the flow and allow someone else the pleasure of this role, after all—wasn't that what being gay meant, not to be limited to one role? Despite both men being from the same country—they couldn't be more different from each other.

As Stefan walked back from the bar with our drinks, I couldn't help but notice how tight his jeans fit him and how muscular his thighs were.

The swagger in which he moved had me transfixed and imagining all sorts of sexual acts.

Stefan buying me a drink was a good sign; it meant he was interested—and getting laid was possibly going to happen this evening. As he handed me my glass, I asked him what he was drinking, "A Bloody Mary," came his reply.

"Isn't it a little late in the day to be drinking one of those?"

"It's never too late to have a Bloody Mary!" he said sarcastically with a hearty laugh—I began to laugh as well. All this talk about Bloody Mary had me think about the poor girl who had been attacked. Oddly her name was Mary, and she was found bloody. I decided to bring up the subject about the girl— undoubtedly, he would have heard or read about it to gauge his reaction.

"Did you hear about the attack down by the waterfront the other day?" I asked carefully, observing him see his reaction as I took a big gulp of my Jack Daniels.

"Yes, I did, although I didn't finish reading the article. Poor girl— who would do such a thing? He said calmly.

The more I thought about the attacker's description, the more suspicious I had grown about this guy. Either he was a hell of a good actor, or it wasn't him. I needed to dig a little deeper and described the attacker to Stefan— that the attacker had dark hair, a distinctive nose, and had a European accent.

He looked at me and said, "The description fits me perfectly, but where are my red eyes? Are you honestly implying that I'm the attacker? If I were the attacker, why wouldn't I be out looking for another victim instead of in this bar talking to you?"

I just looked at him with a blank look on my face.

"Such a shame about the victim; what was her name?" he asked. "Mary," I replied.

"Such a shame Mary didn't survive, isn't it?" he said, sounding almost victorious when talking about her supposed death.

"If you had continued reading the article, you would have known that she survived," I said, noticing at once how quickly his mood changed; there was a look of concern on his face, which struck me as suspicious.

Was this man the attacker? What could explain the red eyes seen by Mary as described in the article?

"Jack, do you want to spend all night talking about some random woman that was attacked, however tragic—or are we going to talk about getting to know each other a little better?" he said with a wink of his eye.

"I don't know you tell me," I replied, challenging him as I licked my lips.

He looked at me and said, "Rarely, if ever, have I been challenged, Jack. Can we go back to being physically drawn to one another" he said, as I took a drink from my Jack Daniels and noticed he never once took a sip from his cocktail.

I thought briefly that *perhaps I could overpower him and hand him over to the police if he was the attacker. They would offer up some reward money, plus I would be doing Mary and other potential female victims a favor by getting this guy off the street. The thing that puzzled me was, he genuinely came across as being interested in men, or more to the point—me.*

So why would he have attacked a female? It just didn't piece together.

Instantly I heard one of my favorite songs begin to play, "Forever Young;" the DJ must have been reading my mind.

Attempting to break the tension that was developing between us, I asked him, "Hey, do you want to dance?"

"Sure, "let's go for it, as you Americans say!" he said as we hit the dance floor and freestyled to the music, our dancing seemed to continue nonstop—partly because the DJ played the extended version of the song.

As we moved around each other, Stefan shot me these intense looks as the music continued to play, as I listened to the words, *"do you really want to live forever, forever, and ever!"* thinking about that gave me a momentary chill. I wondered if this were a mere coincidence, this song the DJ had decided to play for my dance with Stefan? I thought, *how crazy this all seemed!* As I began swooning to the music, it enticed Stefan, who was quite a distance away from me and at once by my side, locking himself around me. I tried to get him off me, maintaining some distance. It was no use; he was too strong, unnaturally so!

I could do nothing other than allow myself to be embraced by Stefan—dancing in almost a bear-hug manner. I felt powerless to resist him, and I'm sure this spectacle looked odd to the other bar patrons. I looked deep into his eyes, which seemed to say—*I have you exactly where I want you, and you have no control of anything!*

His blue eyes seemed to display a hint of red in them; I wondered if I imagined that, or was it from the lighting displayed out on the dance floor?

For the first time in my life, I must admit I felt physically intimidated by another man. I wrote it off as a case of my imagination running rampant. All this talk about Mary and her attacker—trying desperately to put that all behind me and focus on this incredibly sexy man interested in me physically.

Stefan leaned over and whispered in my ear—suggestively, "I think we should go back to your place Jack, as I do unspeakable things to you!"

I felt conflicted; on the one hand, it had been a long time since I had any physical contact with anyone—on the other hand, I felt intimidated—I reluctantly agreed.

"I'm staying at a motel not far from here; we could walk there— it's called the Stardust. Is that okay with you?" I asked Stefan.

"Anywhere is fine, Jack—as long as you and I are alone," he replied intensely. He released me from his powerful embrace—as we exited the dance floor.

I thought, *How many men I have dominated physically over the years—did they think the same thing about me?* The irony had me chuckle a bit.

We left the bar as the steamy, humid summer night's air, which hung heavy and thick, hit us like a lead weight.

We walked under multiple gas lamps as we passed building after building with wrought-iron balconies; I had never really appreciated the city's beauty until this evening. I wondered if I saw the city through different eyes.

We finally reached the Stardust Motel; I admit, I was embarrassed for taking Stefan to such a dump. My emotions ranged from asking myself how my life would end up after tonight—to feeling the need for sex as we walked up the stairs to the second floor of the Stardust. I felt his eyes—as if they were burning into my back.

As soon as I unlocked the door to my room and opened it, Stefan paused and asked if he could enter the room, which I thought was a strange question.

"Yes, of course, Stefan—it's why I invited you back here," I said sarcastically.

"I was brought up with manners, Jack—forgive me, I'm a bit old-fashioned," he said, as he waited for me to lead the way.

As soon as we entered my room, and the door was closed, I wondered what would come next.

I had taken a seat on the bed as he walked over and leaned over me; I thought, *Did I hear him growling a bit?*

I began to shiver.

"You're shivering, Jack? I must admit something; you remind me of someone I knew a long, long time ago—someone very special to me—I realized that the moment I saw your face as our eyes locked while I entered the bar. You and he could have been twins!"

He said with a raised eyebrow. "What happened to him, Stefan?" I asked with a bit of apprehension, as he turned away from me.

"He died, he was taken from me, Jack, we never got to live together for very long. I regret that," he said, as I noticed his mood change to sadness.

I could sense he was softening up a bit; perhaps our conversation of his deceased love interest would ruin the idea of sex?

"Perhaps I should go, Jack—you seem a bit disinterested in me", he said as he appeared to look right through me with his gaze.

"No, that couldn't be farther from the truth, Stefan—I find you very interesting and damn sexy and a bit mysterious. I want to learn more about you. I would love to see you again. Could I?" I asked, holding my breath slightly as he thought about his reply.

"Perhaps—you intrigue me; you are so much like him, Jack," he said, not being able to shake his melancholy mood.

"What was his name, Stefan?" I asked, feeling poorly about asking such a sensitive question.

"His name was Fabien; we lived together for a brief period.

We were thrilled in the beginning—the world was our oyster! We had wealth, power—all of that was not enough!" He said as his mood switched to anger.

"Fabien told me he couldn't be with me—that he wanted to leave me that he didn't love me — that nearly destroyed me. So, I let him go; he left me for another—and that was his mistake, his mood changing from anger to sadness once more. He turned away from my gaze and wiped his eyes.

When he faced me—I noticed smeared blood near his eyes. "Stefan! Are you ok? You're bleeding!" I said, sounding alarmed. "I'm fine, Jack; I merely cut myself shaving this morning; that was the spot of blood you saw on my shirt collar earlier. I'm afraid I have reopened the cut, which appeared to have blood running down my face— my apologies Jack! I need to go; I think the mood for sex has been ruined. I find you very interesting— I'm very attracted to you Jack. Yes I would like to see you again if you're interested? But for now, I must go," he explained, sounding distant.

"But how will I reach you? —where can I find you?" I asked, practically pleading.

"I know where you live, Jack; if you're not here, I will leave a message with the front desk on how you can reach me. Are we in agreement?" he asked me in a way, I couldn't refuse.

"Better yet—why don't we say next week, Saturday evening? I can pick you up here—and we'll go to dinner and a movie?" he asked.

Stefan seemed to display many sides of his personality. In an instant—he could switch from being the brute that had put me in a bear-hug while dancing at the club to someone who still seemed to be mourning his dead lover. There was so much about Stefan I was dying to find out—not to mention having another guy interested in me when Laurent couldn't make himself available to me. I suddenly didn't feel so guilty going out on Laurent.

"Sure, great! I said excitedly.

"Wonderful, I'll pick you up here at six in the evening!"

"Yes, Stefan, I'm very much looking forward to our date together."

He leaned towards me to kiss me, careful not to smear the blood on the side of his face on mine; it was a tender kiss, his lips, however, felt like ice, reminding me of Laurent's lips, which seemed to have the same coldness to them.

"Until Saturday, Jack."

"Yes, until Saturday, Stefan."

He got up and began to walk towards the door—stopping and turning in my direction and smiled at me as he left.

The door was left open—I got up from the bed and closed it, throwing myself on the bed thinking, with a bit of doubt: *What happened here? Lately, every guy I meet stopped short of any physical contact, unloads their past on me, and suddenly, the mood is gone!*

Damn it! —Maybe it's me? Perhaps I'm losing my touch?

I tore my shirt off and stood in front of the bathroom mirror—examining my chiseled chest and arms from all my years at the construction site. Looking more closely, I noticed hand imprints on my sides, which began to bruise! Thinking, *Man, this Stefan is powerful! That must have been where he held me in that vise-like grip back at the bar while we were dancing?*

I began to think about Laurent, the other mysterious Frenchman, as I anxiously awaited his return from whatever business trip he was on. I started to feel conflicted about being torn between two lovers.

Laurent had a certain air of sophistication—which didn't correctly transfer over to my new love interest Stefan, despite them both being from France. I guess even over there, you have your upper-crust white collars and your blue collars. Laurent was white-collar for sure—with his estate, a servant, a Rolls Royce, and his love of the arts.

Whereas Stefan goes out to gay bars—isn't exactly clean-shaven, and his hair isn't perfect. I'm certain Laurent wouldn't be caught dead looking like that in public!

Thinking about these two men—and how different they were, made me laugh. How is it that a plain Louisiana Cajun boy should be dating not one but two guys from France? I thought about the irony of all of that.

I decided I needed to shower after lifting my arm and smelling my armpit, having forgotten to wear deodorant before going out to the club and working up quite a sweat dancing with Stefan.

I entered the bathroom thinking, *I've already been in this dump a month! One month since I left my wife and straight life behind—leaving everything that had become familiar to me. Having met Laurent changed my world. I felt like a different person when I was with Laurent—I knew there was so much he was willing to show me, educate and refine me, and perhaps change me into something more like himself.*

Compared to Stefan, who liked me—yet something about him made me uneasy. He was a complete mystery to me. Whether it was his strength and manliness—yet feeling threatened by that and completely drawn to him. I was deep in thought as I stepped into the shower. The hot water hitting my face and running down my hair onto my shoulders and towards my aching sides.

The water felt good—almost healing. I listened as the water hit the tiled floor, splashing—making an almost hypnotic sound.

I got out, toweled myself off, and slipped into bed. In minutes, I was fast asleep.

I started to dream; of being in a castle, dressed in period clothing. I couldn't tell what period exactly as I walked down a long hallway— lit only with candelabras when suddenly the image of a man appeared in the fog at the end of the hall. Everything about this man seemed normal—all except two gleaming red piercing eyes, which seemed as if they were looking right through me, directly to my soul.

I kept moving closer and closer to the man's image—the face became more evident and more apparent; it was Laurent! His eyes were ablaze and hypnotic—when suddenly another embodiment of a man appeared, with the same red eyes.

The two were staring at me when suddenly an unearthly guttural growl from both of them followed by hissing, it appeared as if the two were claiming their prize—which was me!

Unexpectedly each one was upon me when waves of red came crashing down around all three of us. It seemed to be streaming through the walls, I thought, *But what were these waves of red? — Was it blood?* I tried to swim in the pool of red, which was trying its best to pull me under—trying to drown me. I resisted, trying desperately to keep my head above water, but it was no use— it was too powerful, losing the last of my strength, the red sea finally managed to take me under.

Once below, both swam towards me, opening each one's mouth— and appeared to be drinking the liquid. I tried desperately to swim away from each of them, but they surrounded me, one from either side. I looked at each in the red haze of the liquid and screamed out loud, "No!" I awakened with a jolt and found myself drenched in a cold sweat; I felt comforted to find myself in my bed at the Stardust Motel. This old dump never looked so good.

I began to shake, my breathing became heavy; I couldn't tell the difference between dreams or reality for a while. I couldn't remember the last time I felt so frightened and unsure of myself. What did it all mean? Why were Laurent and Stefan trying to hurt me? It seemed as if each one was trying to claim me for their own as if they were locked in a battle.

I better not bring this up to them; I don't want to risk sounding crazy and losing either of them; they would surely question my mental state.

Finally, I have two good-looking, interesting yet mysterious men interested in me after all these years. Jack Devereaux, an ex-high school football star, a blue-collar boy from Baton Rouge, who just so happens to be a closeted gay guy, and admittedly self-loathing as well!

I wondered how Laurent and Stefan felt about their sexuality— and whether the two of them should meet each other.

I thought, *What the hell,* deciding at that moment that they should meet. *I'm sure the two of them would have a lot in common, both from France, who knows? Perhaps even from the same town? Maybe we could all become best friends, what was there to lose,* I thought

CHAPTER 12

The Dinner Invitation

J ack returned to bed, wondering whether the bad dreams would return or if he would enjoy a restful, uninterrupted sleep. The following day Jack checked with the front desk manager to see if he had received any calls—as luck would have it; there was one, it was from Barthelme, asking that Jack return his call with a number included in the message.

Jack sprinted back to his room and called Barthelme, anxious to find out whether Laurent had returned—He picked up after the third ring.

"Hello, Barthelme, it's Jack. Has Laurent returned from his business trip?"

"Yes, he has; the master would like to see if you are free this Saturday night to join him for dinner?", Barthelme asked.

"Gosh, I already made plans," Jack said apologetically.

"I'm certain the master will be very disappointed," Barthelme said in a concerned way.

"I know this may seem rude, but do you think Laurent would mind if I brought a friend along? As luck would have it, my friend is from France as well—maybe they'll become friends? I would hate to turn down Laurent's dinner invitation and disappoint him," Jack said, almost apologetically.

There was an awkward pause, then finally, Barthelme

answered—"I'm certain Master Laurent would not mind you're bringing a friend along."

Jack felt awkward and knew that it was bad manners to invite someone along—especially knowing Laurent wanted to have Jack all to himself. But the fact that both men were from the same country could be an icebreaker, and perhaps Laurent would enjoy Stefan's company as much as Jack was beginning to.

At long last, Saturday arrived, and Jack began to get ready. Before leaving for the store—he took an inventory of his clothes, which included mostly denim jeans, flannel shirts and maybe a polo shirt or two, these types of clothing would not work for someone as formal as Laurent who was hosting dinner. Jack decided he needed to buy a complete wardrobe, even those fancy nylon dress socks; he figured his white cotton crew socks would not work so well with dress clothes.

He made his way to a fancy Men's boutique on St Charles called *"George Bass."* And with the help of the salesman, he purchased a sports jacket, a designer shirt, pants, along with the fancy nylon socks and more formal shoes—he was certain Laurent would approve.

Jack had put aside some money to buy his now ex-wife, Lisa, something Jack would now use to buy something for himself.

Jack looked at himself in the mirror from head to toe and whistled. Saying to himself, *Jack Ol' Boy, how could these two men NOT be into you? —You look like a male model!* As soon as the sun had set, Jack looked out the window, wondering when Stefan would arrive. Sure, enough there, he was walking up the stairs to my room on the second floor. A strange thought occurred to Jack: *We never agreed on an exact time; it was merely as soon as the sun had set.*

Stefan had cleaned himself up rather nicely as well, he had even shaved off his five o'clock shadow he had worn the last time they saw each other at the bar. Now both would appear respectable enough to join Laurent at his estate for dinner.

Naturally Jack couldn't resist thinking about the possibility of sex, *Who knows?—Maybe Laurent will find Stefan equally attractive enough so it might end up in a three way?* The thought of that caused Jack to laugh out loud, as soon as he thought that, another idea entered his mind, *Good luck!—Laurent is way too refined for that kind of activity!*

A knock at the door, it must be Stefan. Jack opened the door and said, "Hello fine Sir, how handsome you look!" as he reached his face towards Stefan to kiss him, Stefan returned the favor—and once again that stinging, biting cold came from his lips.

"So, change of plans Stefan, I have a dinner invitation from a friend I just couldn't turn down—I asked if it would be alright if I brought you along with me—my friend is from France as well, so you two should get along just fine," Jack said proudly "From France?" Stefan said. Jack noticed that Stefan seemed intrigued by this bit of news. After a brief pause, Stefan answered, "Well, if he's from France, how can I resist?— Besides that will spare me the money on taking you out for dinner as my guest," Stefan said kiddingly.

"Great! His driver should be here any minute to pick us up," "His driver? Well! He does sound like a fine Frenchman of means; I'm very much looking forward to meeting him," Stefan said. Jack thought he detected a hint of jealousy but wasn't sure. No sooner had those remarks been uttered—Barthelme arrived as planned. Barthelme always appeared right at the exact moment—as if he had some kind of homing device, it was uncanny.

Stefan and Jack left the motel room and headed down the stairs. "Barthelme! I would like you to meet my good friend Stefan." "A pleasure," replied Barthelme.

"The pleasure is all mine, Barthelme," answered Stefan. Barthelme held the door open for both men, closed each passenger door, and stepped into the Rolls Royce.

Jack could tell by the look on Stefan's face that he was impressed. As both men sat in the back seat—each gazed out of the window, chatting about various subjects, and giggling with a bit of handholding—which drew Barthelme's attention knowing his Master had romantic feelings for Jack.

As Barthelme looked in the mirror—expecting to see both men, and instead only seeing the reflection of only Jack, Barthelme looked horrified—as if he had seen a ghost, unbeknownst to Jack.

Barthelme knew enough about the undead to realize they did not cast a reflection and became alarmed.

Upon arriving, Stefan commented on how lovely the estate looked and that he was looking forward to meeting this mysterious fellow Frenchmen Jack had spoken so highly about, which was a lie—as Jack had shared very little with Stefan in regards to Laurent.

Barthelme asked Stefan his last name, to which Stefan replied, "Baron Vitré."

As Barthelme opened the large double front door to find his Master walking down the grand staircase—he proceeded to announce the uninvited guest, "Master Laurent, may I introduce to you Stefan Baron Vitré?

Laurent was nearly to the bottom of the staircase when he abruptly stopped after casting his gaze upon the uninvited guest, instantly recognizing Jack's friend to be Stefan—the very same creature who had destroyed his beloved Fabien over two hundred years ago.

Laurent looked sternly at Stefan, avoiding Jack's eyes altogether; Laurent's gaze became increasingly more and more intense—there was a momentary uncomfortable silence between all present. Stefan returned Laurent's gaze equally as intensely.

Until the host finally spoke breaking the uncomfortable silence. "A pleasure to meet you, Monsieur? Laurent said coldly, not addressing Stefan by his last name, which Barthelme had just given him.

"Baron Vitré, Monsieur Baron Stefan Vitré, if you will, kind Sir," Stefan said equally coldly.

"May we enter?" Stefan asked in an equally cold manner. "Where are my manners, yes of course" came the cold reply from Laurent.

Jack thought, Am I seeing a bit of jealousy—or is it something else? It almost appeared as if these two men have known each other before, but that's impossible!

"Shall we adjourn to the drawing-room?" Laurent suggested. Once inside the drawing room, a roaring fire greeted all three—

which seemed to cozy up the atmosphere, despite the frosty encounter between the two Frenchmen seconds earlier.

"What an exquisite estate you have, Monsieur, my apologies—I did not get your last name", Stefan said, appearing to try to break the ice between them with seemingly little to no success.

"Monsieur Richelieu. If you'll both kindly have a seat—I must address something with my servant Barthelme, if you'll excuse me, gentlemen," Laurent replied coldly.

Laurent exited the drawing-room with haste heading into the kitchen—leaving both Stefan and Jack alone. Stefan, who was seated next to Jack, began to nuzzle Jack's neck.

"Stop Stefan! Behave yourself— I'm sure Laurent wouldn't approve," Jack said and began to laugh.

In the kitchen, another scene was playing out—Barthelme was busy preparing a delicious dinner consisting of, duck with a cranberry orange glaze, whipped potatoes, sautéed cabbage, and onions. To humans who eat food, the aroma was heavenly. To those like Laurent and Stefan, the smell would induce nausea.

Laurent held back his nausea, upon entering the kitchen smelling the food as it was being prepared —confronting his trusted servant, Barthelme. Laurent approached his servant in a menacing manner.

"What is he doing here, Barthelme? Laurent demanded in a hushed whisper.

"What do you mean, Master?" Barthelme replied innocently. Upon hearing that, Laurent became enraged, taking both hands and proceeding to strangle Barthelme.

"How dare you invite this miserable creature into my home, the same monster who destroyed my beloved?" Laurent asked in an angry whisper.

Barthelme struggled to free himself from the iron grips of Laurent, but it was no use, his Master was too powerful.

"I don't know what you're talking about!" Barthelme said as he made a choking sound as he struggled to breathe.

Upon hearing those words, Laurent released his trusty servant from his powerful grasp.

"You mean to tell me, you have no idea who Jack brought along?" Laurent said as his anger subsided a bit.

"Master Laurent, I have no idea who he is; the only thing I do know is that as the two of them were sitting in the back of the car—I looked in my mirror and only saw Master Jack's reflection.

"I guess I cannot blame you—Barthelme; you never met Stefan before this evening; it was Jack who invited this miserable creature to join us for dinner," Laurent said as he began regaining his composure.

Suddenly, the kitchen door opened as both Jack and Stefan appeared, standing at the entry to the kitchen.

"Is everything alright in here, Laurent? You've been gone quite a while," Jack asked with a concerned look on his face.

"Yes, Jack—I thought I smelled something burning and decided to check in with Barthelme; it appeared everything was under control. Please, gentlemen, let's return to the dining table; I'm certain Barthelme will be able to salvage our dinner," Laurent suggested.

Jack returned to his chair while Stefan remained standing near the entry to the kitchen.

"May I borrow a moment of your time to speak with you in private, Monsieur Richelieu?" Stefan asked.

"If you insist, Monsieur Vitré, Barthelme leave the room, do not return until I ask you to," Laurent commanded as Barthelme quickly exited the kitchen.

"To what do I owe the pleasure of your visit Baron Vitré? Laurent asked sarcastically.

"You may call me Stefan; may I call you Laurent?" Laurent ignores his question.

"Well, it appears you and I have someone in common, your friend Jack—or is his name Fabien?" Stefan says as he starts to laugh.

"Let's stop this charade, Stefan! Surely you remember me? I will never forget you or what you did to my beloved! How dare you enter my home—my sanctuary?" Laurent said, filled with rage, as he slapped the other vampire across the face.

"For your sake—I will ignore that; you are incorrect Laurent, it was Jack who invited me along as his guest—I had no idea of where I was to have dinner. I would never have suspected in a thousand years you and I would once again come into contact, much less invited to dine at your estate. Yes, I do remember you, it was, after all, you who I was coming to destroy!" Stefan replied, sounding smug.

"I want you to leave here immediately! You are not welcome here!" Laurent snarls his face twisting with rage as he bears his fangs at Stefan.

"But that would be so rude of me, to leave so suddenly when the night has just begun—isn't it Jack's decision whether I stay or go? Wasn't it he that extended the invitation to me? Shall we ask him, if he would like me to leave Laurent, it was you after all who told me I could enter?" Stefan asked mockingly, knowing he has the upper hand.

"You know that's impossible! He knows nothing about what we are—or our past, you miserable creature!" Laurent said defiantly.

"Well then, it is settled, I shall stay— on a good note, I won't be dining, as I have certain dietary requirements, as do you, so please tell your servant I shall not need a place setting. I shall dine later— as I suspect you will. Now, shall we join Jack at the dining table, Laurent?" Stefan said, sensing he has the upper hand as he held the door open for Laurent as both vampires return to the dining table.

"I was beginning to wonder what happened." Jack said with concern.

"Yes, Stefan and I recalled how our paths had crossed years ago in our home country— neither one of us made that connection shortly after your arrival, Jack," Laurent said sounding slightly unconvincing.

This sounded strange to Jack, as he wondered, *why they would have needed to speak to each other in private regarding that?*

Barthelme arrived, announcing dinner is being served; Laurent asked that everyone take their seats as a silence descended upon the dining room.

Jack is served a generous portion, as Laurent and Stefan are served a very minimal amount. Laurent asked his servant to prepare food for both vampires so as to not draw any suspicion from Jack.

"So, how is it that you two guys know each other?" Jack asked, forgetting his manners as he started to eat, not waiting for the others to join him, not knowing that neither desired nor required food.

Laurent and Stefan appear to be playing with their food, never once consuming any of the delicious dinner Barthelme had so painstakingly prepared.

"I believe we met once briefly in Paris—wasn't it Laurent?" Stefan asked sarcastically.

"Yes, briefly," Laurent answered coldly as he shoots Stefan a disapproving look.

"Man! This duck is incredible! Why aren't you guys eating?" Jacks asked oblivious to the underlying tension between the two vampires.

Both Laurent and Stefan seemed to be ignoring Jack's question— as both appear to be staring the other one down.

"Hey! Guys!" Jack said, trying to get the attention of Laurent and Stefan. Each appeared to be consumed by the other— until Laurent finally broke the silence and said, "I'm afraid I don't have much of an appetite for duck, Barthelme seemed to forget this, so there will be that much more for you to enjoy, Jack."

"I dined very late this afternoon—so I'm afraid I'm not that hungry either, Jack, but I am rather thirsty," Stefan said mockingly, displaying a devilish grin as he looked over at Laurent and winked.

It appeared Laurent had decided to drink rather than eat— holding a glass with what seemed to be a very thick red liquid in his glass, which he relished with every sip.

"Monsieur Richelieu, may I sample a glass of whatever it is you're drinking? — I'm certain it will be very fulfilling?" Stefan asked. "Barthelme, pour Monsieur Vitré a glass from my finest collection." "Right away Master Laurent," Barthelme replied, knowing the code words "finest collection" to mean blood, as he pours Stefan the same dog's blood that his master is drinking.

"Merci, Monsieur Richelieu," Stefan said as he thanked their host. "Hey! The two of you are making me envious; I want to sample some of that!" Jack said—not realizing it is blood, not wine, that Laurent and Stefan were drinking.

"I don't think you're quite ready for that, Jack; it's very potent— perhaps in due time," Laurent said uncomfortably as he looked at Jack rather intensely then switched his gaze to Stefan as if to challenge him. "Jack, how did you meet Stefan?" Laurent asked seeming disinterested on hearing the answer.

"We met at a club called the Rawhide!" Jack answered his speech, becoming slightly slurred—as he appeared to be amused with his answer; it was apparent to both vampires that Jack was becoming a bit intoxicated from all of the wine being drunk— which seemed to be Jack's standard practice.

"The Rawhide?" Laurent asked, raising an eyebrow that appeared to show disdain while looking for an explanation.

"Yeah, Laurent, it's a club where men go to meet each other; I've asked you a few times to join me—but you always turned me down, so I decided to go out on my own to clear my head and have a bit of fun," Jack replied defiantly, his courage aided by his alcohol consumption.

"I see; I had no idea you were looking to meet other men, Jack?" Laurent replied, causing Jack to react forcefully.

"Look, you were out of town on business or something like that; what was I supposed to do until you got back—sit around and wait for you?"

"I was under the impression that we were dating; apparently I was wrong," Laurent said, his tone sounding hurt by Jack's admittance of going out on him.

"Laurent, it's all very innocent; that's where I met Stefan. He bought me a drink—we danced together a little, and we had a few laughs; he told me I reminded him of someone he knew a long time ago, besides that—we didn't make out if that's what you're wondering, " Jack replied, appearing to offer up a confession of sorts.

The mood inside the dining room had taken on a dramatically cold atmosphere. Laurent's facial expression was one of loathing for Stefan and outright contempt for Jack. To Laurent, it appeared that both Jack and Stefan were challenging him.

"Excuse me, but am I to assume that the two of you are seeing each other romantically?" Stefan asked in a thinly veiled attempt to sound genuinely concerned.

"Yes," Laurent replied. "No," Jack replied.

At that moment, Stefan began to laugh and said: "Well, which is it? —Yes or no?" As Laurent can barely control his seething anger. At the same time, Jack appeared to be consuming more and more of his wine, oblivious to Laurent's reaction. Laurent knew he had to take control of the situation.

"Jack, I think it would be best if your friend were to leave at once! As far as you're concerned, I think it's best if you were to lay down in one of the guest rooms as you seem to be getting intoxicated. Barthelme will show you to your room," Laurent said, struggling to remain calm.

"I agree with Monsieur Richelieu, I shall leave—I feel I'm not welcome here!" Stefan announces, his tone sounding agitated and indignant.

"Good!—Then it is settled," Laurent replied, reacting triumphantly, sensing that it is he who has the upper hand now.

"For the record, Monsieur Richelieu, you cannot prevent me from seeing Jack; that is entirely his decision to make. I suspect our paths will cross again—with that; I wish you both a delightful rest of the evening. Until we meet again, Monsieur," Stefan said, appearing as if to challenge Laurent.

"I trust you can see yourself out Monsieur?" Laurent replied coldly.

"Yes, by all means Monsieur— don't bother escorting me to the door—I can tell that you and Jack require some time alone to sort through some of your issues. Good night" as Stefan walked out of the dining room into the long hallway and out the front door, his footsteps fading in the distance.

Outside the estate, the sound of dogs howling can be heard, as a late-night fog had developed, making it impossible to make out any of the large oak trees that lined the pathway on either side, leading to the massive estate, as Laurent turned to face Jack.

"Jack! I forbid you to see Stefan ever again. If you and I are to be together—there is to be no third, do you understand?" Laurent said commandingly.

"What? Am I missing something, Laurent? Since when did you and I ever finalize anything about not seeing other people?" Jack answered back defiantly, continuing to slur some of his words.

Laurent grew increasingly more and more impatient with Jack's condition and said, "You're drunk, Jack! —go to bed and sleep it off; there is no point in discussing this now. We will talk more about this tomorrow evening; once I have returned from a day business trip, I'll be back tomorrow evening. I welcome you to stay here and collect your thoughts and dry out a bit before I return. There is a lot to discuss, Jack, but it is pointless to discuss anything with you while you're like this in this condition—do we understand each other, Jack?" Laurent said, sounding angry and dominant.

"I guess I have no choice Laurent" Jack replied resentfully and sounding like his ego has become a bit deflated.

"Right this way, Master Jack," Barthelme said as he quickly assisted Jack. At this point, Jack is barely able to walk on his own— as he mutters something under his breath followed by a display of staggering, as Barthelme locks his arm around Jack's.

"Master Jack!" Jack said mockingly as he broke down with drunken laughter.

The beautifully ornate wooden grandfather clock struck midnight as Jack and Barthelme struggled to walk up the grand staircase to the guestroom, which awaited him.

Upon entering the guestroom, Jack flung himself onto the bed. Jack was unaware of Barthelme helping to undress him so that he would be more comfortable. Soon, Jack was stripped of all his clothes except for his underwear and the fancy black nylon dress socks he had worn to dinner.

Barthelme opened the bedding for Jack, having rolled Jack to one side of the bed, "Your bed is ready for you, Master Jack," Barthelme said as Jack crawls carefully under the luxurious comforter and exquisite bed linens—no sooner had his head hit the pillow, Jack passed out before Barthelme could even leave the room.

Barthelme observed Jack sleeping for a brief moment and thought, *How much Jack looked like the man in the painting in Laurent's bedroom. Perhaps his Master was right—that this blue collar, uncultured man was indeed the reincarnated Fabien as impossible as that may seem?*

Barthelme suspected what the Master planned regarding Jack— offering him the dark gift, Jack, the man resembling his master's beloved lover Fabien, would be able to gain eternal life, cheat death, and recreate the past in the present.

Perhaps that plan would be challenged due to Stefan's arrival—as he had been the one that ended Laurent and Fabien's dreams of eternal existence together, according to Master Laurent.

Barthelme quietly slipped out the door, gently closing the heavy wooden door behind him so as not to disturb Jack's sleep.

Outside, the howling of the dogs had started up, only this time, more intensely than before. Barthelme knew what that meant, that another one of his Master's kind must be nearby, as only the undead caused the dogs to howl sounding tortured, he suspected Stefan might be nearby.

The window to Jack's bedroom was left open, as a thick mist of fog had begun swirling outside Jack's window.

Suddenly trails of a thick fog had begun, spilling over the windowsill and onto the floor. It started to form an image of a man—or what appeared to be a man.

The deep-set red eyes stared at Jack intensely. A telepathic voice command, which entered Jack's mind telling him to awaken and rise and come towards the image—still enshrouded with fog, so intensely thick, that it seemed to fill the entire bedroom spilling out of the bottom of the bedroom door and into the hallway.

Jack tossed and turned in bed, unable to fight the commanding voice in his head—which over and over told him to rise and walk over to it.

"Come to me, Jack!" the figure commanded.

The voice sounded familiar, but Jack couldn't instantly identify it. He felt powerless—unable to deny the figure's command. As Jack answered, "Yes—I hear you, and I shall obey."

Jack made his way out of bed, walking in a hypnotic trance closer to the figure—the voice which was heard telepathically by Jack seemed to hypnotize him, struggling to regain consciousness, though still struggling to form words in his mouth. After a few agonizing seconds, Jack was finally able to cry out "Laurent!"

In the neighboring bedroom, Laurent, who had just begun his undead slumber once the sun had started to rise, sprang up and out of his blackened bedroom, hearing Jack's cries for help.

Laurent ripped open Jack's bedroom and saw firsthand what had frightened and disturbed Jack; seeing the image enshrouded in fog—able to see the figure using his vampire vision, he recognized it to be Stefan. He hissed at Jack and Laurent, bearing his incisors. To a mere human, anyone other than a vampire, this display of rage would strike fear into the heart of any man. Laurent was unafraid, feeling rather possessive when it came to Jack— hoping that he would soon accept the dark gift Laurent would offer Jack once he revealed the secret. A gift transforming Jack into a vampire—with Laurent convinced Fabien had returned to him through reincarnation, returning to his immortal lover in a different time and place and a different body.

Summoning all of his vampiric rages, Laurent screamed out in a powerfully supernatural voice— which echoed and reverberated throughout the grand estate, "Get out! I command you! You are not welcome here!"

Jack covered his ears as his knees began to buckle for shaking so badly, finally collapsing on the floor as his legs gave out.

CHAPTER 13

Confession Time

Instantly, the vampire known as Stefan disappeared into the night air. "You saw him too! Didn't you?" Jack asked, his voice trembling with fear.

"Yes, Jack, I commanded him to leave. I am your protector, Jack; it is me who you should trust, not Stefan!" Laurent said in a passionate tone.

"I have to leave, Laurent—I can't think clearly!" Jack said as he struggled to stand up, still visibly shaken from what he had just witnessed.

"But it's late, Jack, and you're not safe out there without me!" Laurent pleaded, but it was no use; Jack had made his mind up—he had quite clearly sobered up from last night's drunkenness.

"No, I can't stay! I need some sleep, Laurent! Every time I stay over at your place, something strange happens, and I never get laid! Plus tonight's spectacle took the cake! What did I witness in the bedroom just now? How did Stefan get into my bedroom, and why would he want to harm me, and what was with that mighty opera-like voice you have?" Jack asked, sounding frustrated and scared.

It was clear to Laurent Jack hadn't been able to see Stefan's long incisors—it was quite dark in the room, Laurent with his vampire ability, was able to make out Stefan's twisted and rage-filled face, complete with his fangs bared.

Jack, I think you had better sit back down on the bed," Laurent said in a commanding tone.

"What is it, Laurent? Jack asked, glancing up at him with concern in his eyes. Laurent returned Jack's gaze lovingly.

"Jack, I have something to tell you; this goes against everything in my being to say to you what I am about to share with you—you better sit on the bed" Laurent confessed, as he hesitated, which felt like an eternity to Jack.

As Jack sat down on the bed preparing for whatever Laurent was about to share with him. "Please, Laurent! For Christ's sake, just come out and say it!" Jack shouted as he was clearly becoming agitated and anxious.

"Jack, I am not who I appear to be. To you— I appear to look like you, a human; but I'm not. I am one of the living dead—in other words, a vampire," Laurent confessed his voice sounding full of agony and despair.

What followed was a long silence, then Jack rose from the bed, and began to walk over to the window, pulling the curtain open ever so slightly, as he glanced out at the approaching dawn in the sky.

"Really Laurent? Vampires don't exist; that's just fiction!" Jack said, sounding as if he didn't believe Laurent's confession.

"Why would I lie to you Jack?"

"Well, if this really is true, give me some proof?" Jack asked dismissively.

"Jack, please! Don't make this any more difficult than it already is, please! Alright, if you insist, but I warn you, Jack, prepare yourself for what you are about to witness, it may come as quite a shock!" Laurent said in an ominous tone.

Instantly, faster than any mortal eye could detect, Laurent moved across the room to where Jack was standing near the window, now face to face, separated only by inches. Jack could feel Laurent's warm breathe on his face.

Laurent's face began to contort, his eyes turning from their pleasingly alluring blue color into blood-red, Jack instantly recognizing that same red color that had stared at him in the bedroom earlier. The vampire, known as Laurent, opened his mouth to reveal two large incisors. He reached his arms towards the ceiling— commanding the weather to turn instantly violent, followed by a spectacular display of thunder and lightning, as the wind began to moan. As quickly as the weather turned violent it began to calm as Laurent lowered his arms.

"Would you like any other proof? Or does that satisfy you?" Laurent's voice sounded exhausted and filled with despair.

Jack was visibly shaken by Laurent's display of immortal abilities, which he possessed as a vampire.

"It's late; you had better return to your bedroom Laurent," Jack said as his voice began to tremble.

"Jack, did you hear what I asked? You witnessed everything I showed you as proof of what I am," Laurent said, starting to sound irritated.

"Yes, I believe you—I find it incredible that creatures like you, and apparently, Stefan, exist! How could I not believe you after what you showed me? But why me, Laurent, I don't understand?" Jack asked, pleading for an answer.

"Jack, if you would follow me to my bedroom, there is something I need to show you; it will hopefully answer your question," Laurent said, sounding mysterious, as Laurent glanced at Jack, as he nodded and took Laurent's hand.

Jack thought, *Now it's all beginning to make sense, why Laurent never ate food, why he was never able to be seen during the daylight hours, and why his touch always seemed to remind Jack of touching ice or what it must be like to touch a dead body.*

As Jack entered Laurent's bedroom, pushing past the heavy wooden doors, becoming consumed by darkness—with the heavy burgundy velvet drapes drawn to prevent any trace of sunlight from entering the bedroom, just a single candelabra burning on a dresser.

Laurent released his hand from Jack's and walked over towards the candelabra that burned brightly, picked it up and shone it towards the wall. There, hanging on the wall—the light from the candelabra revealing a portrait of Laurent's beloved Fabien, Jack's counterpart.

Jack couldn't contain his shock as he gazed upon the portrait and let out an audible gasp, "Oh my God! — He looked just like me!" Jack shouted as the color left his face.

"Yes, he does, he was my love and eternal soulmate; he was taken from me. To this day, I mourn the loss of him," Laurent confided as a single tear of blood ran down his cheek.

"So you're trying to turn me into him, is that it?" Jack asked innocently.

"Don't you see, Jack? From the moment I met you at the jazz club, I knew that my love Fabien had returned to me, in another body, your body—we are destined to be together, and don't you feel that as well? " Laurent asked, almost pleading with Jack.

"I need to leave here. I can't think clearly; none of this made sense to me!" Jack says, growing angry.

"Doesn't any of this mean anything to you, Jack? Even now as I bear my soul as well as my dark secret to you?" Laurent said, sounding weak, wiping away another blood tear that began to run down his cheek.

"Not exactly, I didn't say that, Laurent. As I told you, I need to leave; I have a lot of thinking to do about Stefan and the two of us," Jack said as he tried to get past Laurent.

Jack had difficulty getting past Laurent when, Laurent took ahold of his arm in a vise-like grip.

"We haven't finished this discussion yet, Jack!" Laurent commanded as Laurent's sadness turned to anger.

"Let go of my arm, Laurent; you're hurting me!" Jack said, as Laurent reluctantly released his arm as Jack made a mad dash to the bedroom window to rip open a panel of the burgundy velvet drapes, hoping that the sun, which had risen, would stream through the window, causing Laurent to back off. He rips open the heavy velvet drape exposing the rays of the sun.

A bloodcurdling scream is heard from Laurent, "Argh! Close it! I command you to close it!" Laurent commands in a loud tone.

"I will—under one condition, Laurent," Jack says, feeling as if he has the upper hand.

"Yes, anything, just do it!" Laurent replied angrily.

"That you let me leave safely, Laurent. I need some time away from you to sort out my feelings—not to mention the bombshell you dropped on me about being a vampire," Jack said calmly, despite feeling shaken.

"Alright, I shall let you leave in peace, Jack. Understand this, it has taken me over two-hundred-fifty years to find you, I cannot lose you ever again! I feel it's our destiny to be together for all eternity, Jack; I need you to realize this," Laurent said, pleading.

Jack closed the heavy burgundy velvet drape panel, once again filling the room with darkness—except for the light coming from the candelabra sitting on the dresser as he left Laurent's bedroom.

"When will I see you again, Jack?" Laurent asked timidly.

"I'll be in touch, Laurent; give me some time," Jack answered.

"Jack, one word of caution before you leave," Laurent said, sounding mysterious.

"What's that?" Jack asked coldly.

"Stay as far away from Stefan as possible, Jack! I don't have time to tell you the entire story at this time—I need my rest with the daylight outside; Stefan is evil. There are those vampires that cling desperately to any ounce of humanness—to remember and cherish what it felt like to love and be loved, and who long for companionship. Yet some have chosen to ignore their former human traits—becoming more like wild, bloodthirsty and diabolical animals; Stefan possesses all of these undesirable characteristics!" Laurent warned.

Jack hesitated before answering and then said, "Thanks for the warning, Laurent—I'll take it under advisement," as he left the bedroom, hearing the door slam shut.

Laurent laid down on his canopy bed draped with the finest silks and remained motionless—he knew the sun was out with full-force, diminishing a vampire's powers significantly. Before entering his undead slumber—the thought of Jack's reaction left Laurent feeling hurt and demoralized, as a single blood tear forms in his eye running down his cheek, as he wipes it away. No sooner had Laurent entered the realm of deep slumber than he started to dream. Stefan appeared— but he was not alone; there was another, Jack, and both seemed to be laughing, locked hand in hand.

Meanwhile, downstairs, Jack approached the last few remaining steps of the long staircase leading to the foyer; Barthelme greeted him. "Where would you like me to take you, Master Jack?" Barthelme asked sounding surprised to see Jack leaving so early in the morning. "I would like you to take me to the City Park, Barthelme; I need to do some thinking," Jack said politely.

"Right away, Master Jack, I will fetch the car and meet you in the front." Barthelme headed towards the garage to retrieve the car.

Jack was left alone briefly, to process all that he witnessed, as he looked up at the sun, as it nearly blinded his eyesight, thinking, how good the warmth of the sun felt on his face, and how nice to hear the birds singing their morning song as if they were serenading him. What a pity that Laurent, and Stefan for that matter—cannot enjoy the daylight, the gloriousness of the sun, hearing birds chirping, Jack wondered if he were to accept Laurent's dark offering—whether he would miss any of this? He would become a creature of the night, much like Laurent and Stefan.

Jack had a lot of thinking to do. He had a difficult decision to make, either accept Laurent's offer or live as one of the living dead or to stay as he was, rejecting Laurent and continuing along a path of unhappiness and loneliness just as before. Jack thought, *Laurent must love me; otherwise, why would he be giving me a choice? He could have attacked me and turned me; why did he give me a choice?* Jack wondered.

But before Jack could continue his thoughts, the Rolls Royce pulled up, as Barthelme stepped out of the car to open Jack's back passenger door as Jack entered—giving him a polite smile as he shut the door as the car sped off. Jack remained silent for much of the ride—trying desperately to comprehend the secret Laurent revealed to him. Barthelme didn't initiate any conversation, Barthelme knew; Jack was told the truth about his Master; he had been standing outside Laurent's bedroom door overhearing their entire conversation.

The silence between both men became increasingly uncomfortable until Barthelme finally broke the silence and said, "You know Master Laurent cares for you very deeply, Master Jack. It's not easy, my saying this—I don't understand two men together in that way, but I do understand love—he seemed to have fallen for you, with his entire being. I've seen the way he looked at you; he believes you to be his long-lost soulmate, Fabien," as Barthelme continued to look at Jack in the mirror, trying to gauge his reaction, as Jack sat in the back looking out the window, thinking about what Barthelme had just shared with him.

"You know what he is, don't you?" Jack asked, their eyes locked on one another in the driver's mirror.

"Yes, of course, I know what Master Laurent is; I've known that for a very long time—since the beginning I was there for Master Laurent, you might say I am the master's gatekeeper," Barthelme said as he continues,

"How do you know all of this, Barthelme?" Jack asked while squinting, his eyes locked on Barthelme's eyes in the driver's mirror.

"The Master has shared some of his past with me—

You saw the portrait of Master Laurent's dead lover, didn't you?
—I'm sure you noticed the uncanny resemblance between you and
Fabien?" Barthelme asked.

After a considerable pause, Jack replied, "Yes, I did. But I'm not
Fabien; at least I don't think I am."

"There are many mysteries, Master Jack; we don't know all there
is to know—there are many unanswered questions that lay ahead of us
on our journey in life," Barthelme said.

"I don't know; perhaps I have been reincarnated? All I know is that
my head is swimming; I need time to think," Jack said, pleading.

The Rolls made its way into the city limits of New Orleans and soon
arrived at its destination, The City Park.

"Thank you, Barthelme," Jack said humbly. "For what, Master Jack?
Barthelme asked. "For listening and being the voice of reason."

"All in a day's work, Master Jack—bear this in mind, you are two
souls that are bound to be together; Master Laurent loves you very much
and will always be there as your protector and companion— now is that
so bad?" Barthelme asked as Jack exited the Rolls, as it drove off.

Jack felt the sun's warmth and heard the birds singing their morning
songs; he was struck by the wonder of the early morning hours as he
glanced down at his watch; the time was seven-thirty.

For a moment, his thoughts involve the sun—if he were to accept
Laurent's dark gift, he, like Laurent, would never be able to experience
it ever again, in fact, it would destroy him.

Jack walked into the City Park, seeking a park bench to sit and
collect his thoughts, quickly spotting a park bench with someone seated
there. He wanted to find a park bench all to himself—unable to find one;
he reluctantly walked over to the park bench with a woman seated there,
located directly across from a pond with magnificent old oak trees with
hanging moss; the trees line the banks of the pond.

CHAPTER 14

A Queen Intervenes

An elegantly dressed black woman with a head wrap sat on the park bench reading a newspaper as Jack approached her.

"Excuse me—do you mind if I sit here?" Jack asked politely with a smile. The woman looked up at Jack, seeing a vision of another standing beside him; the image looks identical to Jack, except that his hair is longer—and his clothing appeared to be from a different period. She couldn't hide the astonishment on her face; as her eyes become squinted, she continued to stare at Jack.

"Excuse me?" She asked

This time Jack didn't sound so polite, feeling annoyed that he needed to ask her the question again, "I said, do you mind if I sit here as well?"

"No, I don't mind, please join me; there is certainly enough room for the two of us. I'm sorry I was lost in my thoughts." She confides.

"Yeah, I know the feeling," Jack replied with a sigh. He focused his attention on the pond and the trees in the distance, hoping that the beauty of it would distract him from his troubled thoughts. An awkward silence ensued.

Finally, the woman puts down her newspaper and sighs loudly. Jack looked over at her; she returned his gaze with a smile. "We both appear to be troubled by something," she offered up as an icebreaker opening the way for a conversation.

"Yes, I've just become aware of something—which is beyond belief."

She stared at him in amazement. "Would you like to share your thoughts with me?" she asked, seeming to help.

"Why? Are you a shrink of some sort?" Jack asked sarcastically "Heaven's no, my child! As the woman laughs almost uncontrollably.

"What's so funny?" Jack asked, feeling confused.

"Everything and nothing at all, forgive me—allow me to introduce myself to you, my name is Queen Raphaella, I own a Voodoo shop on St Ann just inside the French quarter," she said proudly.

"Nice to meet you. I'm Jack Devereux, hmm—a queen who runs a Voodoo shop? Are you really royalty?" Jack asks timidly, feeling stupid for asking such a question.

The mysterious black woman let out a boisterous laugh, "No, my parents gave me that nickname when I was young; they said I acted as if I came from royalty!" As she continues to laugh.

"Are you a psychic?" Jack asked; the woman ended her laughing abruptly.

"Not only am I a psychic, but I am a medium as well!" she confided. "A medium?" Jack asked.

"It means I can speak with ghosts—dead people," she said proudly. This time it's Jack who laughs.

"Excuse me! You doubt me?" Raphaella retorts.

"No, not at the rate I'm going; anything is possible!" Jack said as he shook his head.

"So, you, believe me, Jack?" Raphaella asked sternly.

"Yeah! At this point, I'm pretty open to anything; maybe you can see into the future?" Jack says apologetically, feeling poorly that he seemed to offend her.

"Do you want to know why I looked at you so oddly when you approached me to ask if you could join me on the park bench?" Raphaella asked with a sense of urgency.

"I was kind of wondering that myself," Jack said.

"I'll take that as a yes, Jack," Raphaella looked back at him, sounding annoyed.

"I apologize, yes, please tell me more," Jacks said.

As she looked him over and said, "First, let me tell you a little bit about myself. I'm originally from Haiti—I've experienced all sorts of phenomena in my life, from raising a corpse to seeing and conversing with the dearly departed—more commonly known as ghosts. When I saw you for the first time—I also saw another standing beside you; he appeared to look just like you—only he was dressed differently than you and wore period clothing—his hair was tied back in a ponytail," Raphaella confided.

"You mean I have a doppelganger?" Jack asked as he immediately thought of the portrait hanging in Laurent's bedroom.

"Yes, Jack," Raphaella replied.

"You say this twin looked identical to me, except for his clothing?" Jack asked.

"Yes, identical in every way" Raphaella confirmed.

Jack suddenly felt a rush of coldness wash over him as all of the color left his face. He thought back to being escorted into Laurent's bedroom, seeing the portrait of his beloved Fabien— Laurent's destroyed vampire maker, and soulmate. Could this be his doppelganger?

"What's wrong, Jack? You look like you've seen a ghost!" Raphaella said as she starts to laugh.

"This is no laughing matter," Jack scolds her.

"I'm sorry—please tell me what's troubling you?" Raphaella asked, trying to regain Jack's trust.

"I've met someone; I've been seeing him romantically for a little over a month," Jack confided.

"Go on," Raphaella said, obviously very interested in hearing all the details.

"At first, I didn't know what was going on; his hand was icy every time we touched. I never was able to see him during the daylight hours; he told me he traveled a lot on business.

"Whenever we got together for dinner, I never once saw him eat anything; usually—he would drink a glass of some red substance, which I knew wasn't wine; he even admitted that he couldn't drink alcohol. At first, I thought it was a protein shake, or something else. Then finally, he came out and admitted he was a vampire; he even demonstrated his powers when I asked for proof! —Now it all makes sense!"

"I see; go on," Raphaella said.

"There is another vampire, far more dangerous one than the one I have been dating; I met him recently at a club—the two of them have known each other for a very long time; they strike me as enemies. I believe they are each trying to turn me into a vampire", Jack said, feeling scared and confused.

"Jack, I want you to come to see me at my shop; I can perform an in-depth reading for you and perhaps call on the spirit of your counterpart—and get him to confirm your suspicions. I believe everything you've told me, I think you are in great danger! Are you available this evening, say seven?" "Yes, I am, Jack replied.

"Excellent! My address is 709 St Ann; it is located in the French quarter; do you know where that is?" Raphaella asked.

"Yes, I've lived in New Orleans a little over ten years; I know exactly the street; I will find your shop," Jack assured her.

"Good! Until this evening Jack, I must go now, but before I go, I want to give you something—this was given to me by my late parents, it's always provided me with comfort and good luck, she said as she hands him a crucifix.

"Doesn't that just work in vampire movies and on television?" Jack asked defiantly?

"Don't be a fool, Jack, take it! It symbolizes goodness and purity and love; it is a powerful weapon to guard against evil!" Raphaella warns him.

"Jack reached out his hand as she gently placed the crucifix in his hand, as she stood up to leave, and rushed off.

"Wait! What's the name of your shop?" Jack asked in a panic. "Why, the Queen's Voodoo Shop!" She answers him with another boisterous laugh.

"Of course! I should have guessed that", Jack said flatly.

"Until this evening Jack Devereux! Be safe and walk with the light, Jack, and don't let that crucifix out of your sight! She said as she rushed off.

Jack watched her as she made her way across the park. As she exited—feeling a little safer since meeting this mysterious Voodoo queen, as he continued to sit, staring at the crucifix, touching and examining it—lost in thought, finally looking down at his watch. It occurs to Jack that he must have lost all track of time, realizing it's been an entire hour since Raphaella left him.

A wave of exhaustion suddenly consumed Jack. He struggles to stand up and staggers—thinking back to the night before, seeing Laurent's incredible abilities and how the vampire's face transformed itself. With blood-red eyes and two large fangs. *Is that what I am to become?* Jack thought.

Jack couldn't tell right away why he suddenly seemed to have very little energy—other than he hadn't had much to eat the night before and the shock of what Laurent had confessed to him. Not to mention having just met a woman claiming to be able to communicate with the dead!

Was it any wonder why he struggled to find the strength to walk? Somehow Jack managed to get himself out of the park and there at the entrance, appearing to him as a knight in shining armor, sitting there, a taxicab! Jack, using all his remaining strength, quickly walked over to the cab.

Jack opened the car door, "Are you available?" He asked.

"Get in, Mac! Where, to?" The cab driver asked with a northeastern accent.

"Take me to the Stardust motel, and stop calling me Mac; that's not my name, Jack said, annoyed.

The cab driver shot him a dirty look in the driver's mirror—"whatever you say," he replied rudely, as the cab bobs and weaves its way through the rush hour downtown traffic, arriving at the motel in a little under fifteen minutes.

"Five bucks," the cab driver tells Jack.

"I'm impressed; no one else has been able to get me around town as quickly!" Jack said.

"Yeah, you can probably tell I'm not from around here; I learned to maneuver much harder streets than these back in New York!" the cab driver said proudly.

Jack, seeming disinterested, paid the cab driver.

"Thanks, Mac!" the driver said one last time as he pulled away, speeding down the road.

In the past someone calling him "Mac" would have gotten a violent reaction from Jack; he was known to have quite a temper— but Jack felt as if he had mellowed out a bit after meeting Laurent, in some way, he thought, *Laurent must have rubbed off on me.*

Does becoming more refined really matter—Jack would become more than just that, he would turn into what Laurent and Stefan were as well. Jack thought *it was all a part of Laurent's plan to turn him into Fabien; only Jack would still be himself?*

As long as I have my trusted crucifix with me, Laurent and Stefan are powerless over me; Jack thought as he climbed the Stardust motel's staircase to the second floor where a comfortable bed would await his weary body.

Jack opened the door to his room and had only enough strength to remove his shoes before throwing himself onto the bed.

Jack was so exhausted that sleep soon followed. Although Jack felt that the nightmares would haunt him again—knowing quite well, who his dreams would involve, both vampires.

Jack slept the entire day away, waking up only a couple of times. Sure enough, the nightmares returned with a vengeance— especially as night approached. He tossed and turned in bed, dreaming that he was in a wide-open field with someone that Jack couldn't make out at first, as there was a thick layer of fog that enveloped the figure.

As he made his way over to the figure—its facial features became more apparent to Jack. The man's hair was dark—his eyes were deep-set and cruel-looking.

He realized at once it was Stefan! Somehow he had managed to invade Jack's dream! *But what did he want from me?* Jack wondered. Suddenly, a loud, almost eardrum bursting tone of laughter from the mouth of the vampire known as Stefan, then his hand reaching out to Jack—drawing him closer and closer to him with a vise-like grip, with at least the strength of fifty men.

"Did you think you could escape me, Fabien?" Stefan asked as he released a boisterous laugh, and as sudden as the laughter began, it ended. The face that had appeared to be laughing at once becoming a menacing grimace twisted and contorting the facial features of this handsome creature into the bloodthirsty animal—with his mouth open to reveal two large incisors and blood-red eyes

"I'm not Fabien! I'm Jack!" Then a bloodcurdling scream from Jack's mouth awakened him as his entire body drenched in sweat. Jack wondered if his dream was perhaps an omen—a warning of sorts.

Jack sat up, still feeling sluggish from the night before, looking out the window only to find out—that daytime had turned to nighttime.

"My God! How long have I been asleep?" Jack said out loud as he looked down at his watch; it was seven in the evening. Jack had slept the entire day away and was late for his reading with the Voodoo queen. He quickly got out of bed and decided he needed to shower, thinking that would re-energize him.

Jack quickly undressed and showered in record time; he didn't want to be later than he already was—running half an hour late. As he dressed, Jack heard a scratching sound coming from his window.

Jack froze, becoming motionless with fear, thinking it was an unusual sound, almost as if an animal were making the scratching sound.

Instinctively, Jack picked up the crucifix Raphaella had given him earlier that morning and cautiously walked over to the window. He was met with a horrific sight—as he saw the levitating figure of a man cloaked in darkness scratching at his window, it was Stefan!

"Leave here Stefan, you're not welcome here!" Jack shouted defiantly.

Stefan ignored him and repeated, "I command you to open this window at once and welcome me in!" Stefan's booming voice was heard echoing in the night. A voice so overpowering and commanding—it felt as if he were going into a trance; Jack thought he had little choice but to do Stefan's bidding—as he began to lose his will to resist Stefan.

Jack reached for the window latch unlocking it, and opened the window; Stefan asked, "I didn't hear you invite me in, Jack? Do you invite me in?" —as Jack conceals the crucifix he is holding tightly in the palm of his left hand.

"Yes! I hear you, and I obey you, Stefan—you may enter," Jack replied, his voice sounding emotionless and flat.

Instantly and without warning—Stefan made his way through the window and is standing just a few feet away from Jack. A look of scorn displayed across Stefan's face as he spoke, "Did you think you could escape me, Jack?" Jack thought; briefly, *those were the exact words*

Stefan's said in my nightmare; the only difference was the name he called me.

As Stefan uttered those words, it temporarily jolted Jack out of Stefan's trance and back to a clearer mind—though Jack continued to act as if he were still in Stefan's hypnotic spell.

"Jack, I hope you realize you are the chosen one; you know what I am and what Laurent is—we both want the same thing, for you to return to us as Fabien. Your special friend Laurent most likely failed to mention to you, that it was me that transformed Fabien into what he was—it was not Laurent! Fabien was to be mine for all eternity; instead — he left me, and worse than that, he disobeyed me and created one of his own—you're beloved Laurent. So, it appeared as if history is trying to repeat itself; however, this time—you will be mine, and will stay with me for all eternity!" Stefan said in a guttural growl.

For a split second, Jack remembers all the vampire movies he has seen in his lifetime—never dreaming it really existed, not to mention finding himself in this sort of unbelievable predicament!

He remembers that a crucifix helped defend the victim from the vampire. He prayed from his innermost being that this was going to work!

Jack took a step towards Stefan slowly, as Jack clutched the crucifix tightly in his palm, trying desperately to conceal it as he stood face to face with Stefan, as Jack quickly thrust the cross directly into one of Stefan's eyes. A blood-chilling scream erupts from Stefan. The crucifix was embedded deeply in Stefan's eye as smoke and fire erupted—causing Stefan to stagger back towards the window, instantly disappearing in a trail of smoke, as screams followed Stefan's departure into the night.

Feeling a bit of relief, at least for the moment, Jack thought this was not the last time he would encounter Stefan. Jack knew the vampire was older and much more potent than Laurent, making him much harder—if not impossible to destroy.

Jack decided he needed the Voodoo queen's help now more than ever, looking down at his watch, which read, eight o'clock. *I'm an hour late!* Jack thought, *she probably has given up on me—I'll prove her wrong, and allow her to show me, beyond just a crucifix, how she plans to help me.*

At Raphaella's shop, a sense of dread had come over her, she had a vision in her mind involving a struggle but couldn't quite make out who they were—her vision had become blurred. She hoped that if one of the figures was Jack, and if he were struggling with either vampire, that he remember to use the crucifix.

Raphaella had been cleaning her shop all afternoon— dusting and mopping the floor, and arranging various artifacts that adorned her shop, awaiting Jack. She owned her shop for a little over a year. Despite owning her shop that long—there was a lot of competition due to the numerous Voodoo shops in New Orleans.

How exactly would the public be able to tell the difference between a legitimate shop and a tourist attraction? She hated calling her shop a Voodoo shop; she felt it diminished her natural born talents in being able to communicate with dead people.

She had experimented with actual Voodoo, only once, with some other friends' help—managing to raise a corpse in her hometown of Port Au Prince, Haiti. But shortly after that, she lost interest in that; she was much more than simply a "Voodoo queen." First and foremost— she was a psychic and medium, quite possibly a direct link between the world of the living and the dead.

Now how many others who ran "Voodoo shops" in this area, or any area for that matter, could attest to those credentials? She thought. While Raphaella truly was a psychic, her talents did not reflect so well on her own life or fortune—the visions usually involved others.

Had that been the case—she would have been able to foresee the future as it related to her own business and how dismal the return upon her investment would have been.

While she certainly wanted to help Jack—he would also have to pay her handsomely for her insight; after all, she had a mortgage payment to make to the bank—along with feeding and caring for herself. Despite the apartment being directly above the shop, which meant no commuting costs, the rent was pricey for being in the heart of New Orleans, in the desirable and famed "French quarter."

At eight-thirty, an hour and a half after the scheduled appointment reading with Jack, Raphaella had given up hope he would show. Perhaps Jack was one of the figures she had seen in her blurred vision struggling with the other—thinking *maybe he's injured or worse? If he's dead, he will come to her in spirit, just like all other ghosts that came to her.*

No, she knew deep inside, he wasn't dead, injured perhaps, but not destroyed; at least with that comforting thought, she decided to break open a bottle of vintage rum that she had brought with her from Haiti, perhaps the entire evening wouldn't be a total loss.

Raphaella enjoyed spirits that came in a bottle—almost as much as the spirits that came to her once she summoned them.

As she walked over to the kitchenette, which was adjacent to the private medium reading room in her shop, she heard footsteps outside but quickly decided it must be some tourists walking by. She thought, *doubtful they would stop in, as the window looked too ominously decorated, potentially scaring some potential customers away.*

Opening the bottle of rum, she toasted herself in the process to soothe her nerves a bit. The rum hit the back of her throat—out came an audible "Ah!" as her front door opened, triggering her entry bell to ring.

"I'm closed!" Raphaella yelled in protest

Now that she was finally getting a customer to visit her, she felt uninspired and wanted nothing more than to enjoy the rest of her bottle of rum.

Raphaella walked out towards the front of her shop and repeated what she had said: "I'm closed—come back another day!"

"I hope not—I had a lot of trouble getting here!" she heard the voice of the man say as he walked in her front door. Much to her astonishment, it was Jack standing there—breathing heavily, as if he had run over.

"Jack! You made it!" She said, nearly coming close to tears; she seemed delighted to see him, then suddenly turning severe and saying sternly, "Let's get started."

As they both walked through the shop, Jack noticed the shrunken heads, the many candles, and books that dealt in various subjects such as witchcraft, Santeria, and Voodoo until they reached the back.

"I'm impressed," he said, noticing all her merchandise for sale. "Thanks, Jack, but let's skip the small talk; we need to start right away!" she said with a sense of urgency.

They walked to a small cozy room containing a round table, covered by a tablecloth and a candelabra in the center of the table, the candles not yet lighted.

As Jack gazed at the candelabra, it reminded him of the one in Laurent's bedroom, which instantly gave him a chill, which quickly ran up his spine.

CHAPTER 15

Calling Long Distance

Raphaella tells Jack to sit at the table opposite her; clear all his thoughts from his mind and join hands with her. "It is important that whatever you experience, you must not break the bond, do not let go of my hands at any cost Jack, do you understand?" She asked intensely.

Yes, I understand," Jack replied.

"Give me the crucifix Jack," she asked. "I don't have it," he answered back.

"What do you mean—you don't have it?" Raphaella said, becoming increasingly irritated.

"I used it against Stefan in a life-or-death struggle before I came over here. The last time I saw it—I used it to fight him off; by sticking it in one of his eyes. If I didn't have that crucifix—I wouldn't be with you right now. I'd be one of the many spirits that come to visit you telling you I've just been murdered!" Jack says sarcastically.

"Look, let's get something straight here Jack, I'm here to help you— what I don't need is your bullshit sarcasm in my shop; do I make myself clear?" Raphaella said in a commanding tone.

"Sorry!" Jack said, trying to offer up a half-attempted apology. "Apology accepted, now, please! Let's concentrate on the candles and clear your thoughts out of your head so that you are open to receiving the spirits."

Jack wondered *whether the spirits Raphaella was referring to had anything to do with the alcohol she had drunk before he arrived at her shop; the* thought of that made Jack grin. The voodoo queen shot him a dirty look; it was as if she could read his mind as Jack quickly composed himself.

Jack had his doubts about Raphaella's ability to contact any spirits— much less Jack's counterpart ghost; he was open to just about anything or anyone who offered their help against the two vampires.

Jack thought, *well, why not? If vampires exist, ghosts must indeed exist as well. It was like Barthelme said that we don't know all there is to know in life.*

"Now, before we begin, please give me the full names of the two vampires looking to turn you" Raphaella asked as Jack struggled for their exact names.

"The one I have been dating, his name is Laurent Richelieu, the other's name is Stefan, damn it! —why can't I think of his last name? It's very French sounding, Vita?" Jack answered sounding frustrated. "Alright, calm down! Focus and concentrate, in French, it would be Vitré—does that ring a bell?" Raphaella asked.

"Yes! That's it! Vitré!" Jack answered her excitedly.

Instantly, the voodoo queen slipped into a trance, with eyes tightly shut.

"If there are any from the spirit world who had any associations, either romantic or not —with either of the two known as Laurent Richelieu and Stefan Vitré, please come to us and let your presence be known" Raphaella pleads.

Suddenly, the flames of the candles began to flicker as Raphaella started to moan. "Oh, oh," in a voice that sounds differently from hers. "Why have you called me here out of my slumber?" It was the voice of another. "Who are you?" Jack said, thinking Raphaella can't speak for herself—as this spirit has overtaken her, it was up to him to find out which entity had come to them.

"I repeat, who are you?" as he raises his voice.

"My name is Anne; I died over three hundred years ago."

"Why have you come to us?! Why have you come back?" Jack demanded.

"I was summoned by the one seated across from you. Some are attempting to remake the past! —One more sinister than the other; he will stop at nothing to achieve this! He can be defeated— but it will be difficult!" the spirit said, offering very little insight.

Raphaella started to come out of her trance, moaning aloud, only for her and Jack to see the spirit.

The female spirit known as Anne is in the corner of the room with a hand outstretched; she appeared gaunt and dressed in period clothing. Somehow the ghost no longer needs Raphaella to speak through as the spirit began to speak independently.

"There is one who only seeks power over others, who has rarely if ever, felt love for someone. The other is also looking to recreate the past—yet who feels he met someone that can take the place of his long-destroyed lover? Only you can decide who the real evil is between both vampires, as the spirit known as Anne fades away.

Both Jack and Raphaella are stunned at what they have just witnessed. However, to Jack, this warning is not new, as he remembers what Laurent had said about Stefan.

Jack is the first to speak amongst them, almost uncontrollably, "Laurent was right about Stefan; he tried to warn me about him—but I wouldn't listen! Stefan is pure evil, and he tried to destroy me before I came over here this evening!" Jack shared with Raphaella. "That was the struggle that I saw in my mind", Raphaella adds.

"Struggle?" Jack asked, "Yes, your struggle with Stefan— where you took the crucifix I gave you and rammed it into one of his eyes; I had a vision of that in my mind!" She said excitedly.

No sooner had she shared this with Jack; she noticed a shadowy figure in the corner of the room—it's the spirit of Jack's doppelganger! "Spirit speak, tell me what your name is?" Raphaella commanded.

"The spirit answered Raphaella, "my name is Fabien.

"Tell us, Fabien, why have you come to us—what is it you want?" Raphaella asked. The spirit of Fabien once again answered her, "I want him!" As the ghost of Fabien appeared alongside Jack; it was nearly impossible for her to tell the difference between Jack and Fabien; they are almost indistinguishable, except for their clothing.

Jack's outfit, contemporary in style, and Fabien clearly from another period, perhaps eighteenth century?

"You will never take over my body Fabien!" Jack shouted.

"We shall see about that, Jack Devereux!" The spirit warned Jack. Suddenly, towards the front end of the shop, various objects begin falling off the shelves.

"Stop it! I command you to stop this destructive behavior!" Raphaella demands as the spirit continues to wreak havoc, smashing items on shelves. Books were thrown on the floor by an unseen angry entity named Fabien until it finally appears again, much to the shock of Jack and Raphaella.

As soon as the destruction began, it ended as the spirit said, "I need a body to inhabit, and you, Jack, shall provide me a vessel in this world," Fabien threatened, as the entity came face to face with Jack.

To Jack, the spirit of Fabien's face has become as distorted as Laurent had been able to distort his, as a vampire.

"Laurent offered you a gift, one that is sacred, and that many have not been able to experience, and you dare to contemplate this? Look at yourself, Jack, your pathetic existence; you were a lost, desperate soul—not comfortable amongst men or women; in fact, you hate what you are! My beloved saved you from your agonizing loneliness and despair!" Fabien retorted.

"Don't listen to him, Jack!" Raphaella screamed.

"Do you think I haven't observed your visits with my beloved? How awkward you always felt, feeling inferior, drinking yourself nearly drunk every time you two were together?"

"Give me your body, and I shall reunite with my beloved and gladly receive his dark gift so that we can be together once more for all eternity!" Fabien says.

"Stop it!" Raphaella shouted to the entity, as he turned his attention to Raphaella.

"You're a poor excuse for a woman—you're nothing more than a drunk! You who claim to be a psychic; although had you truly been— you would have foreseen how miserable your life and business were going to turn out! Not to mention your parents ending up with a fatal disease—killing them!" the spirit said cruelly.

Suddenly the spirit of Anne once more appeared and directed her attention to the entity known as Fabien.

"You must leave! —go back to your eternal resting place!" she said, which caused the spirit of Fabien to disappear, as Anne fades away as well.

"That was close! It's nice to know we have an ally in Anne, whoever she might be," Raphaella said as she breathed a sigh of relief. "Yes, but exactly who is she? And what does she want in return?"

Jack asked.

"What do you mean, Jack?" Raphaella asked.

"Well, clearly she has some connection to either Laurent or Stefan; otherwise, she would not have appeared when you called out to all who crossed paths with either vampire. But to whom is she connected to?" Jack asks.

"Only time will tell Jack, only time will tell", Raphaella said calmly.

"Well, I guess we're done here for the evening? Unless, of course, you want to try and conjure up some other spirits tonight?" Jack said, trying desperately to lighten the mood, breaking into a grin, as he appeared to be leaving.

The voodoo queen did not return his grin but instead has a stern look on her face as the conversation turned from light-hearted to more serious.

"Jack, aren't you forgetting something?" Raphaella asked. "What?" Jack asked sounding annoyed.

"Payment for tonight's session," She said.

"Payment? For what? Endangering my life this evening?" Jack replied angrily.

"Endangering your life? Why, you ungrateful bastard! How dare you! —I reached out to the spirits to see if any of them would be willing to help us, and Anne, whoever she is, answered!" Raphaella answered him angrily.

"Yeah, well, another spirit answered your call as well— one who is trying to take over my body so he can be bitten by his long-lost lover Laurent so they can be reunited again as vampires, and where does that leave me?" Jack shouted at her as he paced the shop back and forth.

Jack finally looks up, saying, "Alright—how much do I owe you?" "One hundred-and fifty-dollars Jack," she said defiantly.

"You think I carry that much cash around with me?" Jack said with resentment.

"I accept credit cards as well," Raphaella answered him back coldly.

"Send me a bill!" Jack said as he walked towards the door. "Jack! Come back! Don't leave; it's not safe for you; ok, we can negotiate the price!" Raphaella shouted.

But it was no use; Jack had already left her shop—the bell over her door announcing his departure.

She thought, *That man will get himself killed; well, I guess the evening won't be a total waste, I could finish that bottle of rum I have in the cabinet?* As she walked over to the cabinet to get herself a highball glass, as she pours the rum to the top, "Here's to you, Jack!" she said sarcastically, angered by his very sudden departure, and thinking, *Guess the only other spirits I'll be dealing with tonight are the spirits in this bottle* as she shrugs and lets out a boisterous laugh.

Jack walked the darkened streets of the city, wondering where to go? His mind is racing after the series of events that happened this evening. *Let's see, I fought off a vampire stabbing him with a crucifix. I went to a crazy woman's voodoo shop, only for her to conjure up two ghosts. One whose motivations are questionable, and the other one who is trying to possess me and steal my body so he can reunite with his vampire lover!* He thought.

Jack decides; perhaps he could use a drink and maybe a little company after all. He thought; *it's been a while since I've had sex with anyone. Thinking that he was going to be with the mysterious man known as Stefan, Stefan had to ruin everything only to reveal his true self, a monster, an even worse one than Laurent! Why must things be so complicated?!* He shook his head as Jack enters the Rawhide.

Right away, after entering the bar—Jack sensed something wasn't right; he had a feeling he would probably run into Stefan here.

Sure enough, there he was. Jack spotted him from across the bar wearing an eye patch over one of his eyes; the same one Jack thrust the crucifix in.

His one eye met Jack's gaze—in an instant, Stefan appeared right beside Jack. "Do you like my eye patch Jack? It was a gift from you! That wasn't a very nice thing you did to me back at your motel Jack! —I thought you liked me, Jack? You even invited me to have dinner with your friend Laurent—not that he or I ever eat food," he said sarcastically, with a tone of anger.

"So, I guess the old crucifix does work and not just in all of the vampire movies?" Jack answered back coldly while looking away from Stefan.

Stefan began to laugh; instantly his mood turned from laughter to anger with a warning. "You are funny, understand this—I could kill you, right here and right now, and there wouldn't be anyone that could prevent me from doing this!" Stefan said in an angry yet whispery tone. "So why don't you, Stefan? Why don't you kill me and end this torture?" Jack said, challenging Stefan as he looked right into the vampire's one eye.

"Because much like your friend Laurent, I believe you are the reincarnation of Fabien, my vampire minion—who centuries ago disobeyed me and left me to create his vampire fledgling, which would be your special friend Laurent."

"I destroyed Fabien by accident, it was Laurent I was coming to destroy—and now that I have found you, I have my second chance, and this time, you will be mine—you will stay mine for all eternity. I will let you think about that. I'm in no rush; I have all the time in the world. One more important note—if you think you can run to your friend Laurent for help, realize there's nothing he can do—I'm much older and more powerful than your friend Laurent. This time, I will destroy Laurent— as I meant to do over two hundred and fifty years ago," Stefan threatens Jack as Bauhaus "Lugosi's dead" began to play in the background.

Jack thought, *how ironic that this song should be playing preciously at this moment, here I am talking to a vampire, and the music is about the famous actor that played Dracula?* "God, I need a drink!" Jack said out loud.

"Stefan, I'm going to go to the bar and get a drink—I would offer you one, but they don't serve blood here" Jack said sarcastically as he shot Stefan a grin and a wink; Stefan merely scowled back at Jack.

Jack walked over to the bar and couldn't help noticing the oddly dressed bartender, a very young man, perhaps in his early twenties, dressed entirely in Goth style clothing, including eyeliner and wearing a leather bar. He stuck out like a sore thumb!

The bartender had the blackest hair Jack had ever seen; its color was like a raven's. His dark hair seemed to make his skin color stand out even more; it was milk-white, like Laurent and Stefan's. Jack thought *if I didn't know any better?* It was as if, suddenly, Jack's thoughts were interrupted by Stefan's commanding voice, "Say hello to the bartender from me," as Jack looked back at Stefan—catching a wink from Stefan's one eye.

Jack refocused his attention on the young bartender dressed in black. The bartender did not speak but merely looked at Jack with a scowl.

"Thanks for asking; I'll have a Jack and coke and make it double, will ya?" Jack asked sarcastically, examining the bartender closely, only to see what appeared to be two minor puncture wounds on the side of the young bartender's neck. As the bartender returned with Jack's drink and noticed Jack staring at his bite marks, saying, "You like them? I could give you the same if you'd like?" the bartender asked as he began to smile, revealing his two sharp incisors

"That's okay; I'll take my drink for now. By the way—I'm supposed to tell you hello from Stefan," Jack said nervously.

"Cool! He sure is a mighty fine man. His eye patch made him that much hotter? Don't you agree? —I heard some asshole attacked him" as the bartender shoots Jack a scowl, knowing it was Jack who had injured Stefan.

"Yeah! Cool! gave him a bit of character, wouldn't you say? — In fact the only thing missing from your cool look is an eye patch like your friends—I'm sure we could work something out!" Jack replied. The young man dressed in black slams down Jack's drink almost spilling most of it and shot Jack a dirty look.

"There you go, Jack," as he addresses him by name—much to Jack's surprise.

"How do you know my name?" Jack asked as his eyes squint at the young bartender.

"I'm a friend of Stefan's; he's told me all about you; frankly, I don't see what he saw in you!" The young Goth-dressed bartender said sarcastically as he walked away to serve another patron at the bar. Jack looked over across the bar to where Stefan had been only minutes before and who was now nowhere to be seen.

Jack downed his drink, and in one fell swoop, drinking every drop, with the blink of an eye, the bartender in black is standing right in front of Jack.

"Pour you another? Somehow—I feel you're going to need it, Jack; you have a very long night ahead of you", the young man in black said, sounding threatening.

"No, thanks, I'm good; besides, you never know who I might have to fend off tonight! —oh, and by the way, fuck off, kid!" Jack said commandingly.

Instantly, the young man's face began to contort into a snarl with teeth barred—eyes turning red. Jack thought, *are those teeth real or fake and are his eyes turning red? No—it must be one of the lights from the ceiling, coloring the young man's eyes. He's just another punk-ass kid trying to be cool looking like someone would on Halloween; he can't possibly be what Laurent and Stefan are, or could he? —perhaps Stefan turned him?*

Jack felt uneasy as he walked away from the bar as the song, "Like a virgin," started playing. Listening to some of the song's words "touched for the very first time," Jack cringes a bit. *Maybe I will take that other drink, Jack thought. Jack returned to the bar looking for the goth-punk bartender, only he is nowhere to be seen*— but rather a guy dressed as most of the patrons in the bar, complete with a flannel shirt, tight jeans, and cowboy boots. "What will you have?" asked the normal-looking bartender.

"Jack and coke, and make it a double," Jack replied. "Coming right up," the bartender answered back.

Jack thought, *where did this cocky Punk go? Maybe he's with Stefan; if that's the case, then that was an actual vampire, made to look like he's into Punk; how brilliant! No one would ever suspect someone like that of being one of the living dead. Clever! I got to hand it to you, Stefan; that is plain fucking brilliant!* Jack downed his drink in a couple of gulps, quickly finishing his double. *Well, this ought to help me sleep tonight, provided I don't have any unexpected company! Jack thought. It's time to* leave this place; after having seen Stefan and his Punk vampire minion, I'm hardly in the mood to try and score with anyone tonight; I might as well walk back to the motel and turn in.

As he made his way through the crowd, he thought he saw the punk vampire—but it was merely another bar patron dressed similarly after a second glance. *"Is everybody going nuts around here, or is it just me?"* Jack said out loud as he shook his head in disgust and threw the door open.

The humid Louisiana night air hit Jack like a slap across the face. He checks his wallet, thinking, *guess I did have the money to pay Raphaella—as he decides to stop off at the shop to pay her for the commanding performance earlier in the evening.*

Jack thought, *it appeared she does possess a talent in communicating with ghosts. Besides—if I go back to my motel room without any protection from these bloodsuckers, I'm screwed; maybe she'll have something else I can use to help guard against them, which now includes Laurent and Stefan; but the Punk vampire as well!!.*

Unbeknownst to Jack, someone is not only watching him but following him as well.

A few minutes later, Jack found himself in front of the Voodoo queen's shop. Jack began to knock on the door; after a couple of minutes with no response—he began to pound his fists, yelling, let me in. I need to talk to you!

"Go away. I'm closed for the night!" Raphaella yells back from inside.

"Please! It's urgent!" Jack screamed.

Suddenly, the door opened with a creaking sound, "back so soon, Jack? —are you here for another reading without paying?" She said bitterly.

"No, I'm here to apologize and pay you for earlier in the evening; I'm sorry—here!" As he takes out his wallet to reveal two crisp one hundred-dollar bills—there's a little extra there for you," he said, handing her the money, sounding embarrassed.

She looked at him as if he's mad. Suddenly her demeanor changes altogether as she reflects on his words—Jack sounding almost sincere. "Jack, what's gotten into you? —what changed your mind?"

She asked.

"I've just come from The Rawhide; I thought I would stop in and have a nightcap before returning to the motel—and guess who I should run into?" He asked, sounding mysterious.

She merely shrugs her shoulders. "Stefan! That's where I met him originally about a month or so ago—guess what he was wearing?" She shrugs once more. "An eye patch, that's where I stabbed him with the crucifix you gave me! —and that's not all; Stefan made a vampire minion of his own, the kid, pretended to be a bartender at the bar— now I have not only two vampires after me, but three! So, I thought I would come back to you for your help", he said, sounding desperate for help.

She looked at him as if he has lost his mind. "My help?" She said, stunned.

Jack could smell that Raphaella has been drinking—but then again, so has he—thinking, *perhaps this is why she's loosened up a bit?* As he began to chuckle.

"What are you laughing at?" as her mood started to sour, growing defensive.

"It doesn't matter! It's all so unbelievable!—I never dreamed any of this could be possible!" He said, sounding almost amused.

"Jack! You must accept what is happening—I know it's terrifying, but you and I must have a clear head if we're going to deal with these creatures," She said, encouraging him to remain strong.

"We?" Jack asked with a surprised look on his face. She held out her hand.

"What?" He asked absurdly.

"The money Jack, if I am going to offer you any more of my time— then you need to pay me!" She retorts.

"Of course, I don't expect you to do this for free. I need some other form of protection; I used the crucifix you gave me— which took out one of Stefan's eyes, but that's gone, and I have nothing else to ward off these bloodthirsty monsters," Jack explains.

"I have just the thing! Follow me, Jack," as they walk to the back of the shop where the readings performed. The Voodoo queen opened a drawer to display a glass vial containing what appeared to be a clear liquid.

"What is it?" Jack asked, looking confused.

"Ain't you never seen any holy water before? What kind of Catholic are you, Jack?" She said, sounding as if she's scolding a child.

"I thought you were supposed to be some Voodoo queen or something?" He said.

"Jack! I was brought up a Roman Catholic on the island of Haiti. Do you even know where Haiti is, boy?" giving him a look of disapproval as she shook her head.

"Would you even believe me if I said I did?" He answered. "Never mind, Jack! We don't have time for this. I thought you were in trouble with just the two vampires—now there's a third?" She said excitedly.

At that precise moment, the Voodoo shop door opened as a cold breeze rushed in—as the young man dressed in black made his entrance. The man asked if he may enter. Raphaella made the mistake of saying yes and said she will be right out.

Raphaella and Jack walked towards the shop's front to greet the unexpected guest and were stopped dead in their tracks; as there standing before them is the Goth bartender, Jack recognized him instantly as a look of shock came over his face.

"Well, Jack, fancy meeting you here in a place like this; nice to see you again!" The Goth Punk said sarcastically.

"I wish I could say the same." Jack said equally sarcastically. The young Punk appears amused by Jack's cockiness and utters a laugh. "Jack, is that any way to speak to a new friend? —and who do we have here?" The Goth Punk asked, as he looked at the Voodoo queen with an air of cockiness.

My name is Raphaella; I own this store—not that it's any of your damn business!" She said defiantly.

"Ah! A lively one! I like that!—what does one do in a Voodoo shop if you don't mind my asking —are you going to turn me into a Zombie? Or perhaps cast a spell on me, turning me into an animal— perhaps a rabbit? Or are you just a sorry ass phony like every other Voodoo shop in this wretched city!" The Goth Punk asked taunting her.

"Don't mess with me, Boy! I can summon any number of spirits willing to assist me at any time!" Raphaella replied, challenging the Goth Punk known as Seth.

"Is that right? Now just who might that be?"

He asked, challenging her equally, as he began to walk towards them, leaving one of his arms outstretched as he started knocking item after item off bookshelves and display cabinets. A single book dropped at his feet, displaying the title "Vampires, the Myth, and the Reality."

"Oh, look! One of my favorite subjects!" he said as he kicked the book away from his feet, laughing and displayed his fangs at both, instantly lunging towards Jack.

The Voodoo queen reacts quickly, despite having drunk a bit of her Haitian rum before Jack's return. She reached for the glass vial containing the holy water and tosses the water into the face of the encroaching Punk vampire.

"Take that demon spawn! Be gone from here! —you are not welcome here in my shop!" She shouted, only to be outmatched by the young Punk vampires scream! "Bitch, you'll pay for this!" The holy water burns the young vampire's face, turning his milk-white complexion into a red, burning, smoldering spectacle.

"You haven't seen the last of me, Jack or you Voodoo queen!" he threatens and is gone instantly in a trail of smoke.

CHAPTER 16

Possession

Laurent appeared to be transfixed by the flames dancing and flickering in the fireplace in the drawing-room of his estate. He seemed to be disturbed by many of his thoughts that have occupied his mind ever since meeting Jack. *Has Stefan finally tracked down me down—only to fulfill his vision of restoring the past and making Jack his Fabien? Will Stefan attempt to make good on his promise and destroy me, as he had intended to do over two hundred and fifty years ago? Is Jack the reincarnated version of Fabien? If not—how will I transform Jack from a blue-collar, uncultured man with many bad habits into the romantic, witty, and well-spoken beloved Fabien? Or is it enough that Jack could pass as Fabien's counterpart?*

Laurent is so engrossed in his thoughts that he is unaware of Barthelme, who has entered the room—and began to say, "Is there something on your mind Master Laurent?"

His question went unanswered, "Master Laurent?" Barthelme asked once more, trying desperately to capture the attention of his master, who appeared to be rooted in thought.

"Yes?" Laurent asked softly.

"Did you hear what I asked you, Master Laurent?"

"Yes, I heard you, Barthelme. I would rather not discuss that with you. I feel the hunger coming on—bring me a glass of nourishment", as Laurent's face turned to meet Barthelme's gaze, his face has taken on a ghostly shade of white, and eyes that have turned from blue to red.

"Right away, Master Laurent Barthelme," he replied as he quickly exits the drawing-room.

While Laurent ponders his many thoughts, he was unaware that a translucent figure appeared to be coming through the drawing-room wall, its image becoming more precise and more apparent; it was the spirit of his beloved Fabien.

"Laurent, I'm here!" The spirit of Fabien's said as he extends both arms out—gaining the attention of the vampire. Laurent is mesmerized and overcome with emotions, just as he was the first time, seeing Fabien's ghost in the crypt in Paris so many centuries ago.

"Fabien! It is you! You have come back to me!" Laurent saidys as he extended both of his arms out towards the spirit of his beloved, sensing nothing but air, as the ghost of Fabien has no solid vessel.

"Yes, I have returned, and with a proposal—if you are willing to consider it?"

"Yes, please share your thoughts with me; I am listening," Laurent pleaded.

"The one known as Jack Devereaux is not my reincarnated self; I can assure you that I am stuck here in existence known as the spirit world; I am a ghost."

"What do you mean, Fabien?" Laurent asked innocently.

"It's quite simple, I am without a body to host my soul—as you can see, I am translucent. You cannot touch me, nor can you feel me. I shall get right to the point; you have experienced many feelings since meeting Jack, have you not?" The ghost asked Laurent.

"Yes," he said, turning away from Fabien as a single drop of blood runs from Laurent's eye.

"I have been observing you for quite some time now, even though you could not see me, nor did I reveal myself to you, I was here the entire time to witness your budding romance with Jack and your disappointment in him. He is, how shall I say this, a bit of a challenge, is he not?" Fabien asked.

"Yes, candidly, I must admit, Jack has been a bit of a disappointment. He certainly doesn't have the refinement, such as you have Fabien. Despite my efforts," Laurent admits, almost sounding embarrassed upon hearing his own words.

"Well, I have a solution for that."

"What would that involve?" Laurent asked.

"It would mean that you would agree to have my soul possess the body of Jack. Once I have taken over Jack's body, and you have bitten me—we will then be together for all eternity. I observed the two of you when you offered Jack the dark gift and his reaction of shock and needing to ponder your generous offer of immortality.

Do you think if Jack were me, reincarnated, that I would have given it even a second to consider? I want to be together with you again—only this time, for the rest of eternity, and nothing will stop us, not even Stefan!" the spirit of Fabien proudly proclaimed.

"Stefan?"

"Yes, not even Stefan, like you and me—along with the other ghosts of those whose lives he ended, will destroy him, with the help of one that has the power to command the spirits! All I need is your agreement to lure Jack back to your home, and I shall take care of the rest. Are we in agreement?" Fabien asked.

"But how? Jack told me that he needed time to think things over; how I can get him to come back so soon against his own will?" Laurent asked innocently.

"You have the ability, the gifts I gave to you so very long ago— are you perhaps reluctant to use them?" Fabien asked Laurent tenderly.

"Do you mean through hypnotism?"

"Your voice will carry through the wind—he will hear you, and he must obey your voice", Fabien said.

"I wanted it to be Jack's choice; unlike many of our kind that simply does not allow the individual to choose between their mortal existence and ours," as Laurent walked over to the large window of the drawing-room peering out into the night.

Barthelme suddenly returned with a glass of blood.

"Your drink Master, pardon the long wait; however, the kill was a bit dificult" as he hands Laurent the glass, seeming to be unaware of the presence of Fabien's spirit in the room with him and Laurent.

"Thank you, Barthelme, that will be all for this evening." "Excellent Sir, I bid you a pleasant evening, Master."

As Barthelme moved past his master, Laurent gently reached for his arm—immediately offering his appreciation, "And to you, my trusted servant." A smile is shared between them as Barthelme left the room.

"How touching; you have maintained many of your humanlike emotions—haven't you, Laurent?" Fabien asked tenderly.

"Barthelme is a good man, extremely loyal—and has been with me for over two hundred years. He has provided me a bit of companionship, however not in an intimate way, and that is what I most long for, intimacy!" Laurent confides.

"As do I, that is why you must agree to and follow through with my plan!"

"What would happen if Jack decided to reject you and tells you he does not wish to become what you are? Would you then take him against his will?" Fabien asked, leaving Laurent to ponder deeply.

"I don't know, most likely not," Laurent replied.

"Well, then? What are we waiting for?" Fabien asked sternly. Back at Raphaella's Voodoo shop, Jack thanked and wished her a good night after both having fought off the vampire fledgling known as Seth. The victory felt bittersweet, as Jack somehow felt he had not seen the last of the punk vampire and made a silent vow to himself that he would destroy the young vampire at any cost.

"Before I go, do you have any more of that holy water? —it seemed you used quite a bit of it on that punk." Jacks asks Raphaella. "Yes, you might need it, Jack; he may wait for the right opportunity and ambush you out of nowhere—you best have some more protection, let me go get it," she walked over to a chest of drawers and opened a drawer to reveal another glass vial containing the blessed water known as holy water.

"Here, this will take the rest of that young vampire's face-off should you need to use it!" She said proudly.

"You sure are well supplied!" Jack says as the two of them break into laughter, providing a break of the tension left in the room.

"Oh, Jack! You can always get me to laugh; I guess that's one of your endearing qualities," she said as she shot him a tender glance. Jack notices the look she is giving him, returns her gaze, and said, "You're a good woman, Raphaella; I appreciate all your help!" She returned his compliment with a big smile as a single teardrop rolled down her cheek.

"Be safe, my friend," she said with concern—handing him the glass vial filled with the holy water as he left her store.

Once outside, Jack had an unsettling feeling as if he were being stalked as he clasped the glass vial of holy water close to his chest. He began to walk from St. Ann, crossing Dauphine heading deeper towards the center of the French quarter—thinking that perhaps the Punk vampire may not attack him with a lot of other people around.

Like lightning Seth appeared, his face distorted, showing redness and decay where only moments before Raphaella had used the holy water against him.

"Hello again, Jack! Look what that bitch did to my face! She will pay with her life! —but not before I take yours!" Seth hisses as he lunges towards Jack's neck, as he opened his mouth to reveal two large fangs that appear to be as sharp as razors—with red eyes ablaze.

He is instantly upon Jack, knocking him to the ground, as the young vampire struggles to reach Jack's jugular vein.

"Unlike your two other vampire lovers—I have no interest in turning you into what I am; no! That would be too good for you; instead—I think I'll drain you dry and watch your pathetic life-force run out of your pathetic body!" Seth said sarcastically. Jack managed to land a punch right to the young punk vampire's nose, stunning the young undead creature a bit.

"Not so fast, Seth; it's not up to you to decide who lives or who dies!" Jack heard a voice, instantly recognizing it as Stefan's—as he witnessed the Punk vampire being violently pulled from on top of him and being lifted high in the air with Stefan's hand, as it wrapped itself tightly around the fledgling's neck.

Seth struggled and was instantly released from Stefan's vise-like grasp. "Master, I thought you loved me?" Stefan asked as he regained his composure.

"You are nothing to me, other than a play thing" Stefan said sternly as Seth issued a threat. "You'll regret this Jack! As he took to flight disappearing in an instant.

"Guess you owe me one, Jack—or should I say Fabien? I could have let him kill you, but how could I ever reclaim you and remake the past?" Stefan admits.

"What do you mean?" Jack answered, visibly shaken by his near-death encounter.

"Ah, Jack! There is so much you still must learn. Still, I consider it a challenge—and unlike your vampire lover Laurent, I have more patience and see you for what you really are; you're nothing like Fabien; however, I shall see to it; I will transform you in more ways than you can ever imagine! I have the patience—and I'm in this for the long haul— as you American's say." He shot Jack a devilish grin, which caused Jack to shutter a bit. Jack thought *since when have you turned into such a coward?* It was always Jack that held the upper hand, who had seduced both men and women with his self-confidence and swagger, practically making those that met him swoon in his presence.

"Go forth, Jack, and think about what your mortal existence is like presently. Take a good long last look at what the sun felt like, its warmth—as it washes over your body, and to hear birds chirping—unfortunately there are no birds that sing their song at night; there will be no light, no warmth, only the darkness and the creatures who dwell at night."

"What a meager existence Stefan" Jack replied candidly. "Meager? Not on your miserable mortal life, Jack! Think about once you have been changed into what I am—the thrill of the hunt. How every human will be a part of your food chain, and that you will never fear illness or death! —now how can that be a meager existence, Jack?" Stefan asked sarcastically. "You and I shall be kings of our kind—we shall be together again as it was meant to be. This time Laurent will not interfere with that plan!" Stefan warned.

"What do you mean, Stefan?" Jack asked innocently.

"Is it not obvious, Jack? I intend to destroy Laurent—as I should have over two hundred and fifty years ago!"

"Stefan, you can't!" Jack pleads.

"My, my! What are you saying? —are you admitting something to me? —could it be that you have feelings for Laurent?"

"Speak, Jack!" Stefan commanded as his face becomes angry and started to contort.

"Perhaps," Jack admitted.

"Perhaps?" Either you do, or you don't, Jack! —you will be mine at last! I have waited too long for this! Now leave here, Jack! When the time is right—I shall come for you; I will give you my dark gift—which will change every aspect of your being!" Stefan said commandingly.

Jack doesn't return Stefan's gaze, which transformed into a twisted and inhuman monster. He started to run back towards his motel; he thought to himself, *I must contact Laurent and share Stefan's diabolical plan; perhaps Laurent can help save me?*

In the distance, Jack can hear Stefan's laugh growing fainter and fainter with each passing city block until he finally reached the Stardust motel, the place he called home for nearly a year.

As Jack enters the motel room, he immediately began to undress, thinking that *perhaps a hot shower might help clear my head?* Jack removed his clothing piece by piece until he was completely naked as he entered the bathroom. Looking at himself in the mirror, he cannot help but say aloud, *My God! You've aged, old boy!* As he noticed a perfect white streak that appeared alongside his left temple— "most likely due to all the stress I've had lately,"

Jack said, as he reaches to turn on the water and steps into the shower stall.

The hot water immediately started to splash across his back, leading down Jack's muscular torso, as he lost all track of time, seduced by the warmth of the water. He finally reached for the soap and began to lather his entire body, feeling dirty for merely having been in Stefan's presence. Finally feeling clean enough, he turned the water off and stepped out of the shower stall, reaching for a towel, as he began to dry himself off, trying to avoid glancing at his reflection in the bathroom mirror.

Jack walked over to the bed, which appeared inviting and heaven-sent, as he lays across the bed naked, not bothering with a t-shirt or underwear, as the humid, uncomfortably hot Louisiana night has him drenched in sweat so soon after his shower.

Just as Jack began to go to sleep, he is awakened by the sound of someone's voice, beckoning and calling his name from the open window.

"Jack! I want you to come to me," the voice commands in an eerie sounding whisper. At once, Jack recognized the voice; it is the voice of Laurent.

"Is that you, Laurent?" Jack yelled as the voice continued, "you must come to me, Jack, I need you, Jack!"

"Yes, I hear you, and I will obey!" Jack replied as he hypnotically rises from his bed; as he reached for his clothes, he is dressed within an instant and is out the door and down the stairs, hailing the nearest cab at the street corner.

He gave the cab driver the address in Vacherie, and the cab sped away—arriving just over an hour as the taxi made its way down the long driveway.

"Wow! Whoever lives here must have some money! This mansion is some swanky place!" The cab driver said as if mesmerized by the size of the looming mansion. Jack ignored his remark and paid him as the cab pulled up to the massive estate.

Without uttering a word, Jack paid the cab driver and exits the taxi as it pulled away. Suddenly, the massive front door opened as Barthelme appeared, greeted Jack and motioned him to come in.

"Right this way, Master Jack—we have been expecting you" Jack walked in and saw Laurent coming down the staircase dressed in an elegant smoking jacket and dark trousers.

Immediately Jack felt he was underdressed.

"Jack! How good it is to see you again! —I have missed you", Laurent admitted as he leaned over to kiss Jack directly on the mouth, which made Jack flinch ever so slightly as if he were trying to avoid Laurent's advances.

"Jack! What's the matter?" Laurent asked innocently with a look of bewilderment on his face.

"Laurent, you summoned me here—I heard your voice, you called me here, I had no choice but to come—don't act so surprised to see me, but now that I'm here, there is something I could use your help with Laurent," Jack replied.

"Really? What is that, Jack? —before we go any further, please, Jack, have a seat," Laurent said as he motions his arm towards the chaise lounge as Jack walked over and sat down.

"May I offer you something? Would you care for a drink?" Laurent asked.

"No, thanks—I didn't come here for a romantic interlude Laurent, I came because you summoned me here, but while I'm here, I need your help with Stefan."

"Stefan?" Laurent asked, sneering the name as he turned to walk over to the window gazing out at the blackened night.

"Yes, you heard me correctly. You're not alone in your desire to remake the past, Laurent; Stefan has sworn that his blood will unite him with me—that he will turn me into what both of you are, after which he intends on destroying you—most likely forcing me to help him!" Jack said excitedly.

"But what can I do? —Stefan is so much older, and his powers are much greater than mine", Laurent said sounding defeated.

"You forget Laurent; I have the help of a powerful medium. At first, when I met Raphaella, or as I call her, the voodoo queen—I thought she was a phony, but then I saw her in action, Laurent! She conjured up a ghost!" Jack admits as he began shouting.

"How can this Voodoo queen help us, Jack?" Laurent asked as his eyes begin to squint in seriousness.

"Perhaps she can command the spirits to help us somehow?" Jack said excitedly.

"Us?" Laurent asked while reaching his hand to touch Jack's hand, "Does that mean you are willing to accept my dark gift and become my beloved for all time and reject Stefan?" Laurent asked tenderly.

"Yes, I reject Stefan and all that he stood for; he is the very definition of evil. But I haven't decided whether to accept your offer Laurent; I still need some more time to think about that; it's a huge decision," he said as he visibly recoiled and removed his hand from Laurent's hand.

"We need to pull together all of our resources to destroy Stefan before it's too late!" Jack said as he once again raised his voice.

"What do you propose, Jack?" Laurent asked as a trace of doubt appeared on the vampire's face as Jack began to share his plan.

"I will lure Stefan to Raphaella's shop on a date, saying that we have a reading and that it's just for entertainment. You will get to her shop before we arrive and hide; once he and I are there, she will conjure up every spirit that has fallen victim to Stefan over the centuries, of which I'm sure are endless! With all that energy and with you at the shop, combined with Raphaella's powers, together—we can defeat Stefan!" Jack said with an air of confidence.

"I'm afraid it won't be that easy, Jack—let me make you a drink," Laurent offered as he appeared to grimace.

"Thanks! I could use one—are you going to join me?"

Jack said without thinking—as he stopped to think about the words he just uttered. "Never mind!" Jack said as he gave Laurent a glance and chuckled to himself. Laurent poured Jack his favorite drink—a Jack Daniels and coke as he handed Jack his beverage.

"How will you lure Stefan to your friend's shop, Jack"? Laurent asked innocently.

"Well, first, I need to run into Stefan again; other than that, I have no way of getting in touch with him. He seemed to be fond of a bar called The Rawhide—in fact so fond that he turned one of the bartenders into his vampire minion—that's who my friend and I had to deal with when he decided to show up at her shop unexpectedly— she was very helpful in fighting him off me!" ! Jack boasted about his newfound friend, who he had grown to respect.

"She provided me with several things that you and your kind aren't particularly fond of—for example, a crucifix—handed down from generation to generation, and some holy water." As Jack described the weapons used on Stefan and his fledgling Seth, he noticed Laurent wince as if he were in pain.

All at once, Laurent didn't appear to be the all-powerful vampire he prefaced to be, as Jack looked at Laurent tenderly and said, "Of course, I would never use those weapons on you, Laurent."

At that moment, Laurent is overcome with emotion; a single tear of blood forms in one of his eyes and runs down his cheek. Laurent's reply sends shivers up and down Jack's spine.

"Never say never, Jack," Laurent uttered almost in a whisper— wiping the single tear of blood from his face as he sees Jack consume his drink in a couple of large gulps.

"Do you mind?" Jack asked Laurent sheepishly while holding his glass up, which revealed the glasses empty contents and suggested that Laurent pour him another drink.

"Not at all, Jack," Laurent flashed Jack a broad smile which revealed his two large incisors.

"You don't mind if I join you, do you, Jack?" Laurent lifted the glass of blood and emptied the glass with two gulps to match Jack's— with only a tiny trace of blood which trickled down his lips and onto his chin. With the blood that Laurent consumed, suddenly, his deathly white pallor was replaced with a rosy-colored complexion and eyes that turned from their fiery red color, and returned to their beautifully azure blue color.

As Laurent handed Jack another drink, Jack quickly drinks, which leads to a third and a fourth. Was it a case of nerves, Laurent wondered, or something else?

"Wow! I just realized I hadn't eaten anything since lunchtime; these drinks are going to my head! Don't you have any food in this place, but then again, why would you?" Jack said rudely and started to laugh uncontrollably. Jack's rudeness and lack of self-control were beginning to annoy Laurent.

"Barthelme!" Laurent shouted to his trusty servant in a commanding voice. At once—Barthelme appeared dressed in a robe and pajamas, thinking he had completed his Master's tasks for the day. "Prepare Master Jack something to eat, anything he desires,"

Laurent instructed.

"What be your pleasure, Master Jack?"

Barthelme respectfully asked Jack as he bows his head with respect.

For a moment, Jack thought about the entire process of eating— of needing food to sustain himself. He thought about what it would be like to only drink blood—as his love interest Laurent, Stefan, and other vampires exist on. How much he would miss food.

"What shall it be, Jack?" Laurent asked.

"How about a hamburger, cooked medium rare?" Jack suggested. "Right away, Master Jack"—Barthelme replied as he headed from the drawing-room towards the kitchen to prepare Jack's snack request.

"I wouldn't mind another one of these while I'm waiting for my snack," he again held up his glass, which revealed its emptiness.

"Ah, Jack! You are quite fond of your drink—I only had one, to your four drinks—but then again, who's counting?" Laurent said sarcastically.

Laurent recalled what the spirit of Fabien shared with him. Jack is not the reincarnated Fabien—but merely an identical twin in every sense of the word, except for the all-important mannerisms of refinement and elegance that bespoke Laurent's only love, Fabien.

And with that thought, Jack gave Laurent a drunken look before he staggers and falls onto the couch—passing out, Laurent merely shook his head in disgust.

Laurent pondered this thought, *Ah Jack, you have once again proven to me that you are not my reincarnated lover— your actions leave a lot to be desired. I shall have no choice but to carry you to the bed where you will encounter nightmares, which may prove to be true!"* As he bent over, picking up Jack effortlessly—as if he were light as a feather, despite Jack's six foot two inches, two-hundred-and thirty-pound frame.

As Laurent carried Jack up the long staircase, he heard Jack mumbling in his half-asleep—drunken state, something about being "a no-good bloodsucker," which Laurent ignored.

Laurent gently laid Jack down on top of the guestroom bed, where Jack had stayed in on more than one occasion. But this night might prove to be very different from Jack's previous visits.

"Now try and get some rest Jack," Laurent offered up, knowing Jack will do anything but rest this evening. Laurent decided he should stay with him until the task is complete—in case there were any complications, and Jack decided to sober up and try to escape.

Laurent had hoped that Jack was his reincarnated love Fabien; still, the distinction was made clear—with Fabien's spirit appearing before him to say that Jack was not his reincarnated counterpart— and proposed a plan to spirit possess Jack's body using it as a vessel so that Fabien—once inside of Jack's body, would receive Laurent's dark gift transforming him into a vampire so that both he and Fabien would be reunited after so many centuries of emptiness and loneliness.

Laurent sat in a chair—awaiting the arrival of his beloved's spirit calling out to Fabien. "I did what you have instructed me to do; Jack is fast asleep and is yours for the taking—please come to me and take over Jack's body so that you and I can be together for all eternity!" Laurent emphatically called out.

Just then, a mist started to filter out of walls as an image began to take shape—it was the image of Fabien who was smiling, clearly pleased at Laurent's efforts to lure Jack back to his mansion so that the possession may start.

"You have done well; my love—my what a fine specimen he is, he will do rather nicely!" Fabien said, sounding pleased.

"But one thing escaped me?" Laurent asked rather timidly.

"What is that?" the spirit of Fabien asked.

"If Jack is not you reincarnated, then how and why did we meet at all? —was it just by chance?

"No, I spotted Jack on this earthly plane—I'm the one who led you to the jazz club on the night that you met Jack. It hurt me to see you fall for such a pathetic man," Fabien said as his facial features become more precise and transparent, which showed a look of disapproval on his face—for the body lying on the bed known as Jack.

Suddenly, Jack's body began to stir.

"Don't be alarmed, my love, that is merely Jack in yet another drunken state—I have witnessed it countless times," Laurent admits.

"I see, well then, are you ready to sacrifice this man to me— so that you and I can be together for all eternity?" the spirit of Fabien asked. "Yes! Take him! —take him now!" Laurent replied.

The spirit smiled tenderly and levitated in the air moving ever closer to the sleeping drunken Jack—at once; the ghost was inches away from Jack's face.

It is dificult for Laurent to tell the difference between Jack and Fabien's spirit as the entity seemed to be covering Jack's body, becoming one. Jack instantly awakened and started thrashing about as he opened his eyes and saw his counterpart's spirit hovering over him—he felt a burning sensation like something attempting to bore its way into his body physically.

Jack screamed, but only for a moment—images of his life flashed before his eyes—at once, it all made sense as Jack was given a moment of clarity.

That he was only ever a vessel for Fabien, his sole purpose in life had become defined in this very moment in time, and upon the realization of that, Jack's eyes closed.

The body which lay on the bed opened its eyes with wonder and amazement. The awkward drunkenness which had annoyed and disappointed Laurent so many times was gone.

The person formerly known as Jack sat up and glanced at his hands in wonder and amazement.

"It worked! —I have a body once again!" Fabien said with excitement. Instantly Laurent recognized the voice of Fabien and was overcome with emotion.

"You have returned! You truly have returned to me!" as blood tears run down Laurent's face, while mortal salt tears run down the cheeks of Fabien's face.

They touched and embraced as memories of their time together in Paris came flooding over each of them— finally, they kissed, a long and passionate kiss—two hundred and fifty years in the making.

"Take me now—give me your dark gift so that we can become one," Fabien pleaded. Laurent smiled upon hearing this as he removed Fabien's shirt worn by Jack. Fabien looked at his beloved's handsome face—instantly transforming into a twisted snarl, the eyes of blue turning violently red as Laurent's mouth opened to reveal two razor-sharp and elongated incisors.

Fabien felt a searing pain as Laurent's fangs penetrated deep into his neck—the rich red blood ran down as Laurent lapped up the blood looking more like a wild animal.

"Yes, Yes!" Fabien yelled as Laurent continued to feast on his blood. At once, Laurent stopped sucking the blood from Fabien's neck and turned to bite his wrist, which began to bleed and released the vampire's rich lifeblood.

"Fabien?" Laurent asked, filled with tenderness, "Yes?" Fabien replied with barely a whisper; as he was close to unconsciousness.

"Drink my blood, which will be your resurrection to eternal life!" Laurent instructed.

Fabien followed Laurent's instructions and feasted on the crimson life-force known as vampire blood, which would cause rebirth as one of the living dead. Fabien, finally feeling satisfied, started to have seizures known as "the transformation" from mortal to immortal.

Fabien's body started to convulse as he started to heave, mouth opened— gasping for air until finally looking at his beloved Laurent. The lover that Fabien had given the same dark gift of eternal life to over two hundred and fifty years ago, before he was destroyed by Stefan.

Outside, the wind began to moan— followed by thunder and lightning, illuminating the sky.

Fabien ceased all motion and laid entirely still—no shallow gasps for air; it appeared he had died a mortal death. Suddenly, a violent jolt of Fabien's body and eyes which opened at lightning speed.

The transformation had worked as Fabien began to speak. "I felt your blood course through my veins—I have been reborn, and to that I am eternally grateful; what now?" Fabien asked Laurent innocently. "The crucial task at hand is defeating Stefan and ending his miserable existence once and for all—you will help set a trap for him,"

Laurent instructed in a confident tone "But how do I lure him here? —I don't think he'll come back here—each of you recognized the other when Jack brought him to dinner," Fabien says in a panicked voice.

"No, you shall not bring him here— rather, you will lure him to the voodoo shop! First, you must go to her and convince her you are Jack and get her agreement to help. Once you have her commitment to helping—she will use her mystical psychic powers to call on the spirits of those that perished at the hands of Stefan. You will go back to the bar—seek out Stefan, convince him you are Jack and get his agreement to accompany you to the Voodoo shop where you will introduce Stefan as one of Jack's friends. Before all of this—you shall bring me along with you to the voodoo shop where you will introduce me as another one of Jack's friends.

I will hypnotize her—so she is under my control; I will hide in the shop until you return. Once you have lured Stefan back to the shop, there, along with the summoned spirits and the Voodoo queen's help— we will overpower Stefan and end his existence once and for all!" Laurent said as he laid out his plan step by step.

CHAPTER 17

The Plot

Once Fabien received his instructions from Laurent, he was off to seek out Stefan. As Laurent instructed—he would masquerade himself as Jack so that Stefan is lured to the voodoo shop where the showdown would start.

Fabien asked the still present Jack deep inside to help Fabien disguise his voice and instead use Jack's voice and slight southern drawl—something that Fabien would have found nearly impossible to imitate despite his unearthly abilities. Jack had no choice but to assist as he was utterly and entirely under Fabien's command.

Fabien took flight from "Le Petit Fleur" and appeared at the Rawhide's front door within minutes; apparently, he was not alone; another vampire was nearby.

The young vampire, Seth, approached Fabien, thinking it was Jack—not realizing he was buried deep inside Fabien and that he had come into contact with another vampire.

"Hey, Pretty Boy! Where do you think you're going?"

"Why I thought I would stop in for a drink and see if my old friend Stefan were here and ask him to join me," Fabien replied, duplicating Jack's slight southern drawl as Fabien turned to face Seth.

"Wait! There's something different about you," the young vampire fledgling said as he approached Fabien and took him by the arm.

Fabien incensed that this younger vampire known as Seth would dare lay his hand upon his arm—ripped his arm away from the young fledgling in lightning speed.

"What the hell? Hey, you're not, Jack!" Seth said in total disbelief. "That's correct!" Fabien hissed as he bared his fangs and clutched Seth's throat—as the young vampire choked and coughed up blood, but somehow managed to escape Fabien's powerful grasp as he staggered backward.

"What a pathetic excuse for a vampire you are!"

Fabien said as he leapt onto the young vampire's chest, as Fabien's nails grew sharp as razors, "I will end your meager existence—it will give me great pleasure to take from Stefan what he created and turn it to dust! Fabien said.

The young vampire made a valiant attempt to defend himself by hitting Fabien with a clean left hook—the punch landed square on Fabien's jaw, which caused Fabien to stagger backward, as he rubbed his mouth.

"So, you fancy yourself a boxer, eh?" Fabien teased the young vampire as he massaged his jaw a couple of times.

"Yeah, before I became this way—I studied self-defense, and it's come in handy," the young vampire said defiantly.

"Well, fledgling—you'll need a lot more to defeat me than your boxing skills!" Fabien threatened as he leapt and tackled the young fledgling, instantly standing above the novice with his foot on the fledgling's neck—as the young vampire squirmed and gasped for air.

"Not feeling so mighty now, are you?" Fabien said in a mocking tone as he took his foot and crushed the young vampire's skull. The rich blackened blood was released from the crushed skull, which soaked the pavement as the body convulsed uncontrollably—finally going entirely still.

"Now for that drink!" Fabien said in a sarcastic tone as he entered the Rawhide.

Fabien entered the bar with the swagger that the regular bar patrons knew Jack to have. He moved through the crowd of men, each one flirting with the vision of inhuman masculinity moving in front of them. He moved with the grace and the agility of a panther—moving from one end of the bar to another. Fabien finally stepped up to the bar.

"What can I get you, good-looking?" The ruggedly handsome bartender asked Fabien.

"A jack and coke," Fabien said as he studied the bar anxiously, hoping to spot Stefan.

Despite the many hot men gathered—Stefan was nowhere to be seen.

"What's going on, good-looking?" A nearby patron said suggestively.

"Not now; I'm here to meet someone!" Fabien answered back, seeming disinterested.

"Well, now you have met someone, me!" As the patron placed his hand firmly on Fabien's ass. Fabien turned to the man, who was approaching fifty, balding with a slight beer gut—and hissed at him and bared his two large incisors and ruby red eyes that glared and said in a threatening tone—"I told you, not now!"

The man staggered back in horror and disbelief, nearly falling over a table—and unto a couple of men seated at the table, he quickly ran out of the bar for his life.

Fabien spotted the elusive Stefan as he entered the bar. Stefan searched the room and spotted Fabien; their eyes met, and each acknowledged the other with a slight nod. Stefan didn't suspect a thing and assumed it was Jack who entered the bar and approached the bar— he drew nearer and nearer until Stefan is standing next to Fabien.

"Well, well—look what the cat dragged in!" Stefan said in a sarcastic tone.

"You don't sound happy to see me, Stefan," Fabien said.

"Quite the opposite, Jack; I've thought of no one else since we last saw each other—but I must admit, I'm surprised not to see you half-drunk already?" Stefan said rudely.

"Yeah, I've had a few already—I don't want to get too drunk tonight; I'm on a mission—call it the new Jack!" Fabien said teasingly. "A new Jack? —I'm intrigued! Tell me more!" Stefan began to laugh a little as Fabien turned to Stefan to study his face. He saw the same old cruel soulless eyes Stefan always had. For now—Fabien felt that Stefan truly thought he's seeing Jack.

He decided at that moment to make his move on Stefan.

"You know Stefan; I could be persuaded to spend a little more time with you if you play your cards right!" as Fabien nuzzled up to Stefan, as he took Stefan's arm wrapping it around his shoulder.

"You have my full attention; go on, Jack! Stefan said, which intrigued the ancient vampire.

"Well, lately, I've been fascinated by astrology—I've located someone here in town; she is truly gifted. It's my friend, Raphaella; she could tell us if we were meant to be together," Fabien said, as Stefan looked at Fabien and shook his head in a disapproving way.

"Oh, come on, Stefan! I would never have dreamt that you and Laurent and others of your kind could exist! —I heard that vampires were a legend—having grown up listening to and watching vampires in movies and television, and here you are—in the flesh and blood, quite literally, might I add! Who knows? It may just open your mind to other possibilities; you may be surprised at the results!" Fabien said, he hoped to entice Stefan to visit the Voodoo queen's shop—unaware that his ultimate demise would await him there.

"I doubt it!" Stefan said with a grimace. "So, will you?" Fabien asked innocently.

"Will I what?" Stefan answered back, he sounded annoyed. "Will you come and do a reading with me and my friend Raphaella? —she runs the Voodoo shop here in town. Sure, she has plenty of competition—but this woman is truly gifted, unlike all others who scheme and lie to get their money. I think you'll be amazed at the results; you'll never believe what she's capable of conjuring up!" Fabien explained, sounding excited.

"Let me think about it," Stefan replied, sounding skeptical. Fabien once again nuzzled up to Stefan.

"Alright! If it's that important to you—but just so you know, I remain a skeptic," Stefan said, as he laughed and shook his head.

"Keep an open mind, Stefan; that's all I ask of you, simply show up—and keep an open mind," Fabien said excitedly, he knew he had just laid the trap.

Reluctantly Stefan replied, "Alright if it's that important to you, I'll do it," as he shrugged.

"It is, it is!" Fabien replied with a grin.

"Now you have to do me a favor, Jack," Stefan said "What's that?" Fabien asked guardedly.

"I want you to dance with me, as we did the first time we met," Stefan says, determined to get back out on the dance floor.

In the background, a pop artist was singing about wondering whether she should take someone home. This sort of music may have appealed to Jack—but Fabien disapproved of current music. It was so very different from his time, where beautiful music was created by playing the harpsichord. Back then, ladies were dressed elegantly and not like prostitutes, and gentlemen wore their finest silks—not flannel shirts and blue jeans so tight; it revealed specific male anatomy attributes—it all seemed so ridiculous.

"Alright, Stefan, just one dance, and then I should get going; I still need to stop by my friend Raphaella's store to arrange for the reading, shall we say tomorrow night at eight? Fabien asked.

"Of course, but how do you know if she is available for this so-called reading?" Stefan asked, as he appeared to look puzzled.

"You forget, I know her; she's a friend of mine. She has no customers, or should I say—I am her only one? She's very talented psychically, but she's also a bit of an alcoholic; I think she's scared most of her customer base away—her taste for alcohol discredits her." Fabien said.

"Okay, I'll meet you tomorrow at eight in the evening" Fabien smiled that brilliant smile and gave Stefan the address—they proceeded onto the dance floor, as Stefan said, "I know someone else who has a fondness for alcohol!" A comment that Fabien chose to ignore as it didn't apply to him, that slight was meant for Jack.

Stefan extended his hand, which Fabien declined, fearing Stefan might become suspicious if he felt the same deathly cold touch that he possessed; he needed an excuse and fast!

"Stefan, we're not doing the Viennese waltz!" Fabien said sarcastically; Stefan replied with a robust laugh. *Stefan hadn't changed a bit in over two hundred and fifty years,* Fabien thought. Fabien searched his innermost soul for any lingering feelings that may still be around, given Stefan was his vampire maker.

The answer came into Fabien's mind in less than a blink of an eye, a resounding *no.*

How could Fabien possess any emotions for the monster that destroyed him and who had come to destroy the only man Fabien loved, his beloved Laurent? No! Stefan must be led to Raphaella's store, held down by all the spirits commanded by Raphaella to appear, each who had suffered at Stefan's hands and then destroyed by both he and Laurent, once and for all!. Fabien smiled at the thought of this, then he and Laurent would finally be together for all eternity; the past will reclaim itself, only slightly different this time; the one destroyed and now reborn, would become the destroyer of Stefan. This evil deserved to be wiped off this planet for the betterment of all humanity, and vampires.

As they danced, side by side, Stefan had his gaze fixed on Fabien.

He could detect some of the redness in Stefan's pupils; Fabien wondered if Stefan could see any trace of redness in his? —perhaps it was just the lights on the dance floor? Feeling a bit paranoid, Fabien told Stefan he'd had enough and that he was growing tired.

"Stefan, I need to take a rest—you have limitless energy, which is sadly not the case for me," he offered up as a lie, now; as a vampire in Jack's body, Fabien had the strength of more than fifty men. Clearly, no match for Stefan alone, but most certainly more energy than an average mortal like Jack has—both agreed to end their dance as the dance floor became crowded with men.

As they left the dance floor and headed back to the bar, Fabien saw and heard the pulsating jugular vein in one of the nearby bar patron's necks. It took extreme concentration as he fought the bloodlust as the person walked slowly by, as they returned to their table.

As they sat down, Fabien reached for the Jack Daniels and coke which had always been Jack's signature drink. Fabien knew he would be sickened later by consuming anything but blood—still, feeling the need to act as naturally as possible, which unfortunately included drinking alcohol, was a sacrifice Fabien had to make.

As Fabien put the glass to his mouth and smelled the putrid mixture—he paused slightly then took a big gulp of the alcohol and the soft drink combination. As it hit the back of his throat, as it shot down his esophagus and into his stomach, it immediately caused Fabien to feel sick to his stomach.

"Stefan, please excuse me. I'll be right back," as Fabien made his way into the men's bathroom and began to vomit up the drink into a nearby sink.

Well, it was a decent enough attempt. This way, Stefan will not suspect I'm anyone other than Jack—who regularly drank too much, to the point of being ill. Why should this evening be any different than any other? Fabien thought as he rinses his mouth using water to swirl

248

around his mouth—careful not to consume any of it either, looking into the bathroom mirror, seeing no reflection, only the bathroom toilets behind him.

Fabien finally returned to the table after having been away for nearly ten minutes, where he found Stefan eagerly awaiting the return for someone he thought was Jack.

"Are you feeling okay, Jack?" Stefan asked as a smile came over his face.

"Oh, you know me, I guess I misspoke; I think I did have too much to drink this evening, Fabien confessed, not knowing whether Jack would ever have admitted something like this.

"I better say good night Stefan, I still need to stop in to see Raphaella and make arrangements for our reading tomorrow night, which I am excited about!" Fabien said with a gleam in his eye.

"Are you sure you're okay? —you look a bit pale, Jack," Stefan asked, sounding concerned.

"Yes, I'm fine," Fabien replied.

"Yes, it should prove to be an interesting evening if you're into that sort of thing," Stefan said, sounding doubtful.

"Good night Stefan!" Fabien said as he leaned over to kiss Stefan on the cheek, as Stefan suddenly grabs Fabien by the arm; he had forgotten how strong Stefan was, nearly the strength of a hundred men.

Fabien looked at Stefan and panicked for a moment, with a thought that Stefan may be suspecting something, as he gave Stefan a nervous smile.

"That's my, Jack!" Stefan said with a devilish grin as he released Fabien's arm.

Stefan's vise-like grip would have severely bruised or injured a human's arm, but Fabien is no mere mortal—he is left unscathed. Only now, he is Laurent's fledgling creation released from Stefan's control, as Fabien gave him the address.

"My friend's Voodoo shop is 709 St Ann; see you there tomorrow evening at eight, Fabien said as he waved to Stefan as he turned to leave.

"I'm certain I'll find it," Stefan replied as he watched Fabien leave the bar.

Once outside, Fabien took to flight; flying high over the French quarter and landing in front of Raphaella's shop in a matter of seconds. Fabien felt a bit anxious; in spite of Stefan believing Fabien to be Jack—would Raphaella believe him as well? A thought came to Fabien; *what if, somehow, Queen Raphaella can tell that I'm not honestly Jack? With her psychic insight, is it possible for her to know that I've overtaken Jack's body?*

Fabien decided to put all his doubts aside as he entered the shop. A bell rang indicating someone has entered the shop—then she appeared; she had been drinking as Fabien's keen vampire smell could detect the alcohol stench from across the room.

"Jack!" She shouted from across the shop as she came running towards Fabien—almost knocked into a table displaying the many books she had for sale on various occult subjects.

"I've missed you! How have you been?—I've been worried about you!" She said, as she slurred her words.

"It's good to see you, Raphaella," Fabien said as he offered her a hug; at once, she detected his coldness.

"Jack! Why are you so cold? It's a hot and humid night out!" She said, sounding alarmed.

"I think I may be coming down with a cold or something. I'm here to arrange a reading for my friend Stefan and me tomorrow evening at eight—of course; I'll pay you handsomely; there may be an additional guest here as well," Fabien said with confidence, knowing she will accept his proposal because of the additional fee involved. She seemed delighted at the offer.

"Well, let me check my appointment calendar to see if I have any availability," she said as she strolled across the room— as she bumped into a chair and made her way to her desk. After a minute or so, she said, as she sounded more and more intoxicated, "What time was it you were looking for?" The rum, she had drunk earlier—started to take effect.

"Eight in the evening," Fabien answered, sounding annoyed; as Fabien thought, *I cannot understand how mortals consume this liquid called alcohol? A substance that disables and affects an individual in such unflattering ways it made them lose all control over their senses, making downright idiots of themselves!* As he thought back to when he was a human—before meeting Stefan—did alcohol so consume him? *No, it must be an American phenomenon—including a Haitian Voodoo Queen.*

"Yes, I have availability at that time." She answered excitedly.

"Wonderful! With that, I need to bid you a good night— I want to be well-rested for what will prove to be a big day tomorrow," Fabien offered up because of his abruptness and having to leave so soon after arrival.

As he turned to leave, she shouted, "Wait!" As he turned around cautiously, as panic enveloped Fabien thinking that perhaps she detected an imposter.

Instead, Fabien was relieved to hear her invitation to join her for a drink and nothing more—"Why don't you join me?" she motioned towards the bottle of rum sitting on the counter across the room. The thought of him drinking any more alcohol, and anything other than blood nauseated Fabien.

"I hate to be rude, Raphaella—I need to leave, "Good night!" Fabien said as he exited the store without as much as a glance back.

"Good night!" She replied as she heard the door close.

"You know, if I didn't know any better—I would say that Jack seemed different tonight, he didn't seem like himself—it's as if someone else had taken over Jack's body? —No, that's ridiculous!" she said to herself, as she laughed and poured herself another glass of Haitian rum.

"Here's to you, Jack!" she said as she gulped down the rum, the taste of it burned her throat as she let out a sigh of relief, "Ah!"

As soon as Fabien stepped out of the Voodoo shop, he took to flight. As fast as lightning, he reached Laurent's mansion.

Laurent was stunned as Fabien walked through the door and shared how well the plan had gone so far.

"Well! It's all arranged!" Fabien proudly announced. "What's been done?" Laurent asked innocently.

"The trap. I met with both Stefan and Raphaella—I met Stefan at the bar Jack used to frequent. I even pretended to drink an alcoholic beverage; it made me sick to my stomach—I needed to avoid any suspicion Stefan might have about me not being Jack. Once I met with Stefan—I went by the Voodoo shop to arrange a reading tomorrow evening at eight. The plan, so far, is working brilliantly!" Fabien proclaimed triumphantly.

"I am so fortunate to have you once again! I waited so long for this moment—soon, we won't have to deal with Stefan!" Laurent said as Fabien smiled and nodded in agreement.

"There is one thing you must do before Stefan, and I arrive," "What is that, Fabien?" Laurent asked, and ceded control to Fabien.

"You must arrive before Stefan and I arrive—quietly, of course, Raphaella has never met you; therefore, she will not know who you are. You will walk in and make her believe you are a passerby simply interested in a session. She will inform you of a prior commitment— our reading. Once you have her full attention, you will take control of her mind through hypnosis. Once under your command—you will instruct her that once Stefan and I arrive and are seated, she will conjure every tortured spirit that has fallen victim to Stefan to come forth to help control Stefan. You will remain hidden until I call out for your help so that Stefan does become suspicious upon seeing you. Together with all the spirits present and Raphaella's help—you and I will be able to rid ourselves of Stefan and destroy him once he becomes subdued! I will finally avenge my destruction at the hands of this monster and help rid the true evil in this world!" Fabien said in a commanding voice.

"Brilliant!" Laurent replied with a smile revealing his two large incisors.

Fabien returned his smile, as he bared the same large incisors— which instantly revert into regular-sized teeth that vampires change at will.

"Where are you meeting Stefan?" Laurent asked.

"We agreed to meet again at The Rawhide bar, where Jack first met Stefan—He won't suspect a thing! To Stefan, it will merely be Jack getting him to try something different—to be open to a reading, or perhaps a psychic experience—not knowing that it will lead to his destruction!"

CHAPTER 18

Showdown

Quite unexpectedly, Laurent and Fabien could hear and see the crackle of thunder and brilliant display of lightning in the distance—it seemed almost as if the mighty Stefan himself must be listening and reacting to this plot unfolding.

"The skies seem angry this evening," Laurent noted with a hint of concern in his voice.

"Yes, they do," Fabien responded with a concerned look on his face as he walked over to the drawing-room window and glanced out at the mighty, majestic oak trees—some as old as the two vampires themselves.

"Do you feel a bit apprehensive about what we are about to do?" Laurent asked Fabien as he continued to face the window.

"Yes, I do; however, I can only imagine the great pleasure in seeing Stefan's destruction; it can't come too soon! He has reigned terror, death, and destruction in Europe and nowhere in America! —let's not forget, he wanted to destroy you and end our existence together. I came to your rescue and ultimately paid for that with him destroying me! —tomorrow evening, it shall end with the spilling of his blood and his destruction!" Fabien spoke these words with such intensity.

Laurent couldn't help but feel the immense anger and disgust his soul mate Fabien had for Stefan—while he certainly understood his lover's wrath—he wondered perhaps if Fabien had grown angrier as a spirit, or was avenging his own destruction at the hands of Stefan, the explanation for Fabien's anger.

Since Fabien had taken over Jack's body, it's as if his anger consumed him; where was Laurent's tender lover—and his eternal soulmate?

Everything Laurent treasured about his beloved, his gentleness, yet his immeasurable strength and strong convictions about right versus wrong and good versus evil seemed not to be present.

He wondered at times whether Fabien had changed a bit. Dare he admits that perhaps he missed Jack? The uncultured— uncouth alcohol-loving man who was Fabien's counterpart?

Was Laurent starting to have doubts about luring Jack in only to have him become the body vessel for Fabien?

It was in that moment as if Fabien could read Laurent's mind; he turned away from the window and once again faced Laurent— as he reached for his hand while smiling and said—"I love you with all my heart and all my soul," Fabien said tenderly. Upon hearing those words—all the doubts that Laurent had started to feel had vanished.

Once again, Laurent could see what had drawn him towards Fabien so long ago—the vampire who chose him to be his soulmate, giving Laurent his dark gift and someone he grew to love immeasurably.

"I love you as well, Fabien—I'm eternally yours!" Laurent said. The antique clock on the fireplace mantle struck five in the morning—and announced the impending dawn.

"It's been a very long evening, even for our kind—where time passes with a blink of an eye—it's getting late. Shall we retire upstairs?" Fabien asked. Laurent replied with a nod as they locked hands to walk up the opulent staircase, gazing periodically in each other's eyes.

After they entered the bedroom, Laurent walked over to the large window that looked out upon acres and acres of land—which looked out to the majestic live oak trees and weeping willow trees; as he looked directly up at the sky, seeing the first rays of light which struggled to break through the darkness. Laurent grabbed the heavy velour bedroom drape and pulled the drapes closed, shielding them from the daylight.

Both of them heard a rooster crowing in the distance, which announced the imminent arrival of sunrise, which was only moments away. They quickly undressed and got under the fine silk cover as they embraced each other. Soon both vampires fell into a deep undead slumber.

Once asleep, Laurent began to dream. He pictured the Voodoo shop enshrouded in a heavy fog as he entered the shop. The dense fog seemed almost to overwhelm the entire inside of the shop—as it had outside.

Raphaella was nowhere to be seen, but several figures stood there until one emerged from the fog—becoming fully recognizable; it was Jack, as he began to shout at Laurent.

Jack scolded Laurent for his part in participating in a sinister plot against him—"How could you do this to me, Laurent?—I thought you loved me? How dare you plot to have your vampire maker Fabien take over my body?"

"I'm sorry, Jack—you could never replace Fabien; that became more and more apparent each time we spent time together," Laurent answered, sounding ashamed as he avoided looking Jack directly in the eyes.

"Well, here's someone that loves me for who I am!" Jack replied—out of the dense fog, another figure emerged. It's Stefan! — as he smiled and displayed his fangs to Laurent. "That's right, Laurent, your plan failed! —now it is you, who will be destroyed, as was my original intention, this time—there will be no Fabien to save you!" Stefan said with a snarl.

Instantly Laurent awakened with a start, lying there contemplating his dream, thinking, *what was Jack doing alongside Stefan when Fabien overtook Jack's body? —This didn't make any sense! Was it just a dream? Or does Stefan have the ability to enter other's dreams?* Laurent decided he would need the help of another to help assist with Stefan's destruction.

Laurent, still shaken from his nightmare—tried to calm himself and tried to close his eyes and tightly held the hand of his beloved Fabien for the rest of the day—he had a dreamless slumber.

That evening, Laurent told Barthelme they needed to speak in private.

"What is it you want to discuss with me, Master Laurent?" Barthelme asked with a puzzled look on his face.

"Barthelme, my loyal and trusted servant for over two hundred years—I had a horrible nightmare while I was at rest. I feel it may have been a premonition of sorts."

"A what?" Barthelme asked

"Yes, I will explain that later; for now—I will need you to accompany me to the Voodoo shop shortly—before you take me into town—you will need to construct a significant, razor-sharp stake made from wood to take along with you. You will be our backup lest all else fails in destroying Stefan. Once the Voodoo queen has summoned all the dead who lost their lives to Stefan—you will be in hiding with the stake; Fabien and I, along with you—will attempt to destroy Stefan with the help of the spirits present. Should anything go wrong—you will come up behind Stefan and plunge the stake as far into Stefan as possible, is that clear?" Laurent asked with urgency in his voice.

"Yes, you can count on me—I would do anything for you, Master Laurent!" Barthelme replied, as he swore his undying loyalty.

"Good! Then go make the perfect weapon of destruction!" The clock on the fireplace mantle chimed six as a reminder of the time. "We'll leave here in half an hour—at six-thirty. It is exactly an hour's drive from here to the shop—arriving at seven-thirty. I prefer to arrive by car rather than by flight," Laurent instructed Barthelme.

"Yes, Master Laurent," Barthelme replied as he left the drawing-room and exited out the front to embark on the creation of the weapon his master instructed him to make.

Fabien walked into the drawing-room to join Laurent.

"Did you have a restful slumber today?" Fabien asked as he kissed him on the cheek.

"Not exactly; however, it was very enlightening!" Laurent replied with a grin.

"You sound mysterious—I don't understand?" Fabien asked with a confused look on his face.

"Let's say I either had a nightmare or a premonition—I'm planning accordingly," Laurent replied.

"Are you going to share that with me—as we've planned this out together?" Fabien asked sounding slightly irritated, as Laurent walked over to the window before answering Fabien; Laurent can see Barthelme in the distance as he carved a significant wooden stake.

"Don't you trust me?" Fabien asked, sounding annoyed.

"Yes, of course, I do! However—if Stefan got a hold of you and were to ask you what's planned, at the very least—you wouldn't be able to share it as you're not privy to?" Laurent explained, as he sounded apologetic.

"I guess that made sense, but I don't appreciate not knowing what's going on!—what sort of dream would place doubt in your mind about my love and loyalty to you?"

"Fabien, please!" "Don't ask; there is a reason for this; call it back up!" Laurent pleaded with Fabien.

"When do we leave for the Voodoo queen's shop?" Fabien asked coldly, ignoring Laurent's explanation, his displeasure coming through the tone of his voice.

Laurent looked over at the antique clock and said, "We leave in half an hour." Fabien was not used to Laurent taking control— nor did he appreciate the commanding tone Laurent had taken on. Suddenly, the front door opened as Barthelme entered—carrying the wooden stake as a weapon to use against Stefan.

"Why is he carrying that thing?" Fabien gasped with a concerned look on his face.

"You will find that out in due time; until then—that is between Barthelme and me" Once again, Laurent used a commanding tone.

"I'm not sure I like your tone, Laurent. Let me remind you —I devised this plan to trap and destroy Stefan, you are adding something to that plan, and you're unwilling to share that with me? Fabien appeared to be growing more and more agitated over Laurent's secrecy and display of power.

Laurent decided he needed to lower the temperature and help defuse the tension rising in the room; Laurent stepped back and softened his approach to Fabien; he chose the path of least resistance. "I'm sorry, Fabien—I guess I'm extremely anxious about what we are about to do. There are so many things that could go wrong this evening; one misstep from either of us could prove to be fatal!" Do you trust me, my love?" Fabien asked.

Laurent hesitated to answer for a moment and then looked Fabien squarely in the eyes.

"Yes, unequivocally!" Laurent answers.

"Then stop playing games and share with me what this "backup plan is? — what is Barthelme doing with a wooden stake?" Fabien pleaded.

"Alright! —if all else fails, if the spirits fail to materialize, and if together we cannot destroy Stefan—Barthelme will be in hiding and will attack Stefan from the back with a wooden stake!" Laurent revealed.

"How can Barthelme save us? He's a mere human?" Fabien replied, as he grew more and more agitated.

"Barthelme is not simply a mere mortal. Centuries ago—I had him drink some of my blood; I did not want to lose him to a mortal death.

Barthelme is and always has been my loyal and trusted servant and guardian." Laurent confided.

"But why would you need to retain him as your guardian when I have returned my love?—I have always been your protector!" Fabien continued to speak until he was interrupted by Laurent, "Until Stefan destroyed you! Then who were my protector and guardian? —I had to survive on my own and look out for myself until I arrived here and enlisted the help of this fine man—after I had inherited this mansion from my late grandfather Pierre in the late eighteenth century.

Meanwhile, you were only a spirit who only appeared to me once! —every night, I mourned my loss! Until I met Jack, which was later to become your body vessel! So, you see Fabien —without me, you would not be in a body, nor would you once again be a vampire! This time, it was I who gave you the eternal dark gift—making you my fledgling!" Laurent screamed as he stormed out of the room and up the grand staircase using his vampire speed.

"Laurent, wait!" Fabien cried out, as he ran after Laurent using his immortal speed as well appearing at their bedroom door. Inside, Laurent is preparing himself for the battle that awaits all of them. Then a knock on the door.

"Enter."

The door opened, Fabien stood there with an expression of tenderness and love on his face. "Laurent, why must we argue this way? —you and I are not enemies?" Fabien said as a single blood tear fell from his azure blue eyes and ran down his pallid cheek.

Laurent turned around slowly and took a moment before responding.

"Fabien, you mean everything to me; you are the one that took me under your wing so very long ago and transformed my very existence; I owe you everything. I love you more than you will ever realize— but you must realize I'm not the same man that fell so deeply in love with you; I was young—human, and impressionable," Laurent confessed to Fabien.

"So, what are you saying—I don't understand; I thought this is what you and I wanted?—to destroy Stefan! If you wish—we can call off this plan to destroy Stefan and allow things to return to the way they were," Fabien's mood turned from tenderness to being irritated.

"All for one thing—Jack is deep inside of you, and I will admit—there is something about Jack that I miss—dare I say I was beginning to have feelings for him?" Laurent confided. Faster than any human eye could trace—Fabien slapped Laurent across the face.

"How dare you admit that to me! I observed this man— this pathetic excuse for a human being! Arrogant and lacking intelligence— not to mention addicted to alcohol, namely a drunk!" Fabien shouted. A knock on the bedroom door interrupted their heated discussion;

"It's Barthelme."

"Master Laurent and Master Fabien—it's time to leave if we are to arrive at the Voodoo shop before Stefan's arrival!" Barthelme advised.

"Give us a moment, Barthelme; go pull the car out front; we will be down in a moment!" Laurent shouted.

"Are you committed to this plan?" Fabien asked gently. With slight hesitation, Laurent gave his answer—"Yes, I am!" Laurent looked at Fabien with a single blood tear that ran down from his blue eyes. The two men embraced and shared a brief kiss.

"Forgive me for ever doubting you! —you are my one true love— now let's go end this bastard's existence once and for all!" Laurent confided.

The two vampires left the bedroom and walked down the grand staircase hand in hand as Barthelme met them.

"The car is out front, Master Laurent," Barthelme said as all three left the estate and walked towards the rolls; once Barthelme as opened and closed the door for both, they left the driveway of Le Petit Fleur and sped off.

"We're finally on our way!" Laurent said triumphantly.

Once in the vehicle, the two immortals sat silently in the backseat while Barthelme remained equally silent. Each of them seemed to be preoccupied with their thoughts as they prepared for the showdown hoping they would end Stefan's existence.

The rolls made good timing as it drove into town. The car continued to make its way through the wide boulevards of the downtown area until it reached Royal Street, located around the corner of a Funeral gallery, directly around the Voodoo shop on St Ann.

The night air brought in the fog—which appeared to be as thick as anything London would produce.

Laurent stepped out of the vehicle and into the dense fog while Fabien and Barthelme waited in the car.

Barthelme quickly lost sight of Laurent—as Fabien's immortal eyes cut right through the fog as he saw Laurent turn the corner as he neared the shop.

Laurent rushed around the corner, and used his Vampire speed, not to waste a second as he reached the Voodoo shop's front door as he knocked on Raphaella's door.

"Just a minute!" a female's voice replied. The door swiftly opened— as a black woman who seemed to be in her early thirties, wearing a turban and a colorful African-looking vest appeared before the vampire,—he suspected from the sounds of her accented English she must be from the West Indies.

"Yes, may I help you?" Raphaella asked, she sounded annoyed by the unexpected visitor. Laurent responded, "I was walking past and looked through your window—I must admit, my curiosity got the better of me. I had to come in and see if perhaps you were available for a reading." "Why?" The Voodoo queen replied in a carefree manner.

"You see, I recently lost someone very dear to me, and I wondered if you would be able to contact them." Laurent replied as he came up with an excuse.

"Well, I have a reading at eight this evening, but we have half an hour—it will be a quick reading if that's acceptable to you?" Raphaella said—thinking about the added money she will have received for her psychic gifts—which would buy many things, including more rum.

"Right this way, I'm sorry—I didn't catch your name?" Raphaella asked respectfully; right away, Laurent could detect she had changed her attitude, from disinterested to welcoming.

He could tell immediately that her mind would offer little to no resistance to his hypnosis.

"My name is Laurent—you must be Queen Raphaella?" Laurent said; she looked at him with a puzzled look on her face "How did you know that?" She asked, sounding confused.

"By the sign on your window," Laurent replies with a half-grin on his face. "It only says Raphaella's Voodoo Shop on the window." She responded with one eyebrow raised.

As Laurent glanced at the clock on her wall and said, "Please, may we get started? It's already seven forty in the evening—we only have twenty minutes until your next appointment arrives. I don't want to be inconsiderate of your other customers and have you run late for your next appointment," while he ushered her back towards the rear of the Voodoo shop until they both reached a section of the shop separated by a curtain and a round wooden table with several chairs placed around. Each took their respective seats.

"Now, give me the name of the spirit you are trying to communicate with?" She asked, unaware at any moment she would lose the ability to control her thinking.

"Look at me, Raphaella —you will be under my control; you will not have the ability to maintain control over your thoughts—is that understood," Laurent asked as his eyes switched from their azure blue color to a deep blood-red color.

Raphaella nodded her head and answered, "I hear, and I shall obey."
"Excellent, you will receive a visit by the name of Jack Devereaux along with someone known as Stefan Vitré, in exactly twenty minutes. Once everyone is seated, you will summon all the spirits that lost their lives at the hands of Stefan—you will do this willingly and without hesitation, and you will do this quickly! Once the spirits have appeared—you will command them to attack Stefan— to hold him and prevent him from escaping! Do you understand?" Laurent asked forcefully.

"Yes, I will obey!" Raphaella responded.

"Good," Laurent said as he transformed himself into a mouse and hid under a table in the corner of the room to observe the arrival of Fabien and Stefan.

Back at the car, Barthelme reminded Fabien the time was drawing near for him to exit the vehicle so that he could appear to have arrived close to Stefan's arrival.

Fabien heeded Barthelme's advice and exited the car.

Within minutes—Barthelme left the vehicle along with his trusted wooden stake and quickly found an open window in the back of Raphaella's shop, as he looked around to make sure no one spotted him. He climbed through the window and, once inside Raphaella's shop— quickly located a place to hide before Fabien and Stefan's arrived.

Fabien, avoided his vampire speed, as he casually strolled over to the Voodoo shop, and tried to appear as human as possible. It had occurred to him that Stefan may be observing Fabien from nearby. Finally, he arrived in front of the shop as he checked his watch— previously worn by Jack; the time read seven fifty-nine, with one minute to spare as Stefan suddenly appeared out of nowhere.

"There you are, Jack! Its cold out—and the fog! Why it reminds me so much of London—you could almost hide anything out there!" Stefan said as he broke into a burst of hideous-sounding laughter.

"Hello Stefan, you're right on time. What did you mean by that? —hide what?" Fabien asked, feeling suddenly paranoid about their plan to trap Stefan.

"Jack! Can't you tell when I'm joking? —as you Americans say, lighten up!" Once again, that sinister laughter made even a vampire like Fabien cringe.

"Shall we go in?" Stefan asked.

"Gladly! This session is going to be fascinating! I know you have your doubts—but Raphaella truly is gifted; she really can see into the future; she can even conjure up spirits!" Fabien shared with Stefan as he teased him for what's to come.

"There are many that claim the ability to do that; we'll see about that," Stefan said, his tone sounded skeptical.

"I'm convinced of her abilities Stefan, you'll see!" Fabien said with a wide grin on his face.

Fabien opened the shop door and said, "Hello! It's Jack!" for a few moments—there's a deafening silence until suddenly Raphaella appeared before them from the store's backroom to greet them.

"Jack! You made it!" Raphaella said, she sounded delighted that her old friend had shown up as promised, accompanied by a stranger.

Stefan noticed Raphaella gave him the once-over and focused her attention instead on his eye patch.

"It happened as a result of an accident, didn't it, Jack?" Stefan said as he glanced first at Fabien and then at Raphaella.

"I see, follow me," she said happily, Laurent who was observing all of this was amazed at how natural she sounded, perfectly normal—nothing to indicate that she was under hypnosis.

"Please sit —make yourselves comfortable," She said as she held back the drape which separated her reading room from the rest of her shop and motioned them towards the chairs.

"What brings you here for this reading?" She asked both.

"Well, I wanted to show my friend Stefan how truly gifted you are, Raphaella," Fabien said, as he imitated the voice of Jack precisely.

"Why, thank you, Jack! I must say I'm flattered!—Stefan, is there anyone you would like to contact?" She asked the dark, brooding, mysterious stranger.

"Yes! My Mother Anne Vitré—she died quite some time ago when I was just a child," Stefan confided.

"I'm sorry to hear that, but I don't know if that's such a good idea, Stefan — the longer the dead are away from us—the angrier they are once they return, if summoned," Raphaella warned.

"If you want to know the truth, I think you're a fake and that you can't call on anything to return— much less my mother!" Stefan admitted rudely.

The Voodoo queen raised one of her eyebrows and said, "Well, Stefan, allow me to prove you completely and utterly wrong!—don't say I didn't warn you!" Instantly she heard Laurent's telepathic command from deep within her mind to call on Stefan's victims; *Raphaella, I command you to summon every spirit that lost their lives at the hands of Stefan Vitré NOW!*

CHAPTER 19

Reunited At Last

As commanded—the woman from Haiti known as Queen Raphaella calls upon all the spirits that lost their lives to Stefan Vitré.

"What is she doing Jack, is she mentally unbalanced? Stefan asked with a tone of anxiousness as he chuckled out loud nervously.

"I don't believe so!" said Fabien as he and Stefan turned around and gazed towards the front end of the shop. A sudden dense fog had found its way from the outside and slipped underneath the shop's front door—enveloping the entire inside of the shop.

Various indistinguishable figures appeared there and stood there in silence until one finally spoke out. "You monster! I died at the hands of your ruthlessness and cruelty back in Paris in the 18th century!"

"Do you remember me, you evil bastard?" Stefan looked on in horror as he recognized the twisted and contorted shape of Jacque—who was Fabien's servant at the turn of the century and died a horrible death at Stefan's hands.

"What the hell is going on?" Stefan said in a bewildered manner—his eyes grew wide in disbelief.

"What's going on is your undoing monster!" Fabien retorted. "Jack! What are you saying?" Stefan asked in utter disbelief.

Instantly—every summoned spirit appeared and stormed Stefan as they attempted to hold the almighty vampire down.

"Welcome to the end of your existence, monster!" said Jacque, the spirit of Fabien's former servant.

Stefan realized a trap had been set, a plot designed to lure him here to his destruction—so Jack and Laurent could be together; he wondered if Laurent were present and called out to him.

"Laurent, I know you're here; show yourself, you coward!" Stefan commanded.

In a fit of rage, Laurent transformed himself back and came out from behind the curtain to say, "Yes, I'm here—not only to witness your destruction but to participate in it as well!—all of us will destroy you! —and just for the record, that is not Jack who is seated across from you—but rather Fabien!" Laurent proclaimed triumphantly as Stefan looked on in disbelief and horror.

"Yes, that's correct; it's me, Fabien—as the spirits continued to hold Stefan rendering him helpless and unable to move.

It is said there are others who possess powers close to vampires; those are called spirits—the entities who died so brutally and viciously are amongst the most powerful! When called together, their rage sustained their energy—when called together, they can help defeat the evil—the one known as Stefan!

Faster than lightning Laurent displayed his Martial Arts training which he had trained so hard at—with a roundhouse kick to Stefan's face that propelled the mighty vampire backward, landing on the floor a few feet from where he had been sitting. He always knew his hand-to-hand combat would come in handy; he hadn't been wrong!

Raphaella, no longer under hypnosis, commanded, "Quickly! — go hold him down!" as the spirits and Fabien and Laurent triumphantly confronted Stefan.

"Well, Stefan, how does it feel to be the hunted?—to experience terror?" Laurent asked as he held Stefan down by the neck with his foot as Fabien drew his face near Stefan's and spat on it.

"Take that—you son of a bitch! I'm not Jack as Laurent said; I'm Fabien; do you remember me? —the one you destroyed over two hundred years ago! Well—now it's your turn! Prepare to meet your maker! May he pity your soul if you have one?" Fabien sneered as he spoke those words.

Without warning—Stefan began to morph himself into a bat, as he escaped Laurent's hold on him and from the clutches of all the vengeful spirits present.

As the bat made its way to the front of the shop, and attempted to escape—Fabien and Laurent took flight and quickly captured Stefan in the form of a bat. During this—they sensed another transformation about to take place—this time back from bat to the shape of a vampire, as they struggled to keep the mighty Stefan contained—his strength far exceeded theirs.

The ancient vampire shook off Laurent and Fabien, which sent Laurent flew through the air—as he finally landed up against a bookshelf and Fabien as he crashed through the storefront's window. Both vampires were a bit shaken but were unscathed as they instantly rose and lunged towards Stefan, each determined to continue fighting.

"Wait! There's a spirit here that I didn't call!" Raphaella shouted frantically as everyone focused their attention on her announcement.

The uninvited spirit started to take shape, its form became more and more distinguishable—it was Anne Vitré, the spirit of Stefan's mother, as he locked eyes with someone Stefan hadn't seen in over three hundred years. Anne—the one who loved and accepted him, despite his cruelty—and him being a liar and a cheat. Her son was despised and unloved by so many as a man—and continued into his immortal existence.

"Stefan! You must stop this! "Anne commanded.

"Mother, I can't help myself! I have such hatred and bitterness inside of me!—I can't control myself!" Stefan admitted.

"I am the one who was always by your side Stefan, who loved you unconditionally—when others vilified you, while you brought physical and emotional torment to others, it's what a mother does. However, I can no longer witness your continued destructive path. These two other immortals are different from you—they have managed to retain some human traits such as love, compassion, tenderness, and other emotions besides anger, blood lust, and evil! —all they want is to be together. Tell me, son, what do you love besides power and destroying everything in your sight? —are you even able to feel love at all?"

Stefan appeared to be stunned by the image of his Mother and the words she had said.

"Mother, I have longed to see you again, dreaming of this very moment—despite my many vampire powers, I could never get you to materialize in front of me as much as I wanted and tried to! You asked me if I felt love, yes—for you and one other. I've missed you for so long, until this day, as the mighty vampire broke down to cry— his cheeks became stained with the blood tears which ran down his face as he offered his confession.

"So, you do feel something?" Anne asked her son as she glided over to him—as she levitated directly in front of Stefan with a white glow that encompassed her entire figure.

"Then, for my sake—allow them to destroy you so that this part of you that is so enraged and overtaken by evil ends. You will be reunited with me; we shall exist together in perfect bliss and harmony with all of our family—in a world known as the spiritual dimension," Anne shared with her son.

"I don't understand, Mother?" he asked her softly.

"Free yourself, go in peace—for the sake of God and all of humanity, let yourself go. For once in your entire existence—do what is right, Stefan!" Anne pleaded.

"Yes, Mother, I realize what you're saying is true, but I'm fearful of laying eyes upon my maker—surely he will condemn me to the deepest pits of hell for all of my evil acts. There I dwell with the other tortured souls—with the devil himself presiding over us!" Stefan said passionately.

"My son, the fact you've admitted this—and have seen the errors of your ways and the remorse you feel—makes you different from the others that dwell in the underworld. You are different; you have a soul—unlike all those others; surely our maker will take mercy on your soul!" Anne said as she pleaded with her son to do the right thing.

"Yes, I hear what you're saying, Mother."

"Stefan, the time has come! —are you ready?" Anne asked him. Stefan stopped struggling against the other spirits and the other two vampires as he realized he must do what is right and accepted his fate.

"Yes, mother—I accept this as truth; take me away from this tortured existence. Before I leave, know this Fabien..." as Stefan abruptly stopped speaking—as Barthelme appeared before him carrying the handcrafted wooden stake by his side.

Fabien asked Stefan to continue his thought—suddenly not feeling threatened by Stefan instead sensing his sincerity based on the words and emotions which flowed out of Stefan's innermost soul.

"Fabien, I never meant to harm you—nor make your existence with me so miserable. In my way, I cared for you—when you insisted on leaving me to go back to Paris—I was heartbroken and enraged! All I wanted was us to be together—to revel in what we were, powerful vampires—writing our own rules, and existed the way we saw fit. When you swore to me that you would never make an immortal fledgling of your own, I believed you—only to be deceived by you and that you had; my love for you turned into jealousy and rage. I felt I had no choice but to avenge my feelings of betrayal—Fabien, do you recall why I came to Paris that night? It was not to destroy you—but this fledgling that you created! I had no intention of harming you; how could I destroy what I

271

had made—the one who captured my attention and my heart when we first met in that Paris café so long ago? How could I ever destroy you willingly and end your existence?" Stefan confessed.

"That's all very touching, Stefan—but you forget one essential fact. I had fallen out of love with you!— you made me do unspeakable things—by forcing me to use human beings as a food source, killing indiscriminately, which caused me to hate myself—above all else, hating you! Remember? I begged and pleaded for you to release me!—I couldn't stand to exist with you in this way!" Fabien retorted.

Stefan's display of tenderness and compassion during his confession to his Mother and Fabien quickly turned to rage.

"You ungrateful bastard!" Stefan said, he almost spitted the words out. Sensing a betrayal by the spirit of his mother, Anne, and Fabien, Stefan suddenly had a change of heart.

Barthelme rushed over to Stefan, as he prepared to lift the stake high in the air to thrust it into the evil one's heart; Anne appeared in front of Stefan to shield him from sudden destruction.

Anne commanded Barthelme to drop what he was holding. "Drop the stake!" "Allow me—the mother of this creature to rid you and the world of my son's evil presence!" As Anne lifted her arms to the sky as the shop began to rumble, and the floor started to break open—which exposed a fiery red glow from below.

"Son, take my hand!" Anna commanded Stefan.

"Are you certain, mother?" Stefan asked with a bewildered look on his face.

"It is the only thing that can make right everything you have done wrong in both your mortal and immortal existence," Anna replied as she reached for her son's hand.

Everyone remained transfixed and in utter disbelief as Stefan slowly reached out for his mother's hand.

"You are willing to do this, my son?" Anna asked Stefan tenderly.

"Yes, I have thought about all that I have done— and all that has been said. I am ready to atone for my sins and transgressions and face whatever judgment to whoever awaits me—as long as you and I can be together. I realize your undying love for me is the only thing that ever mattered to me," Stefan said as he looked at his Mother, Anne— as a single blood tear ran down his cheek.

Stefan and his Mother instantly descended downward as an agonizing scream is heard by everyone present—which is thought to be Stefan's.

For several minutes, the room remained silent; the shock of witnessing what just happened left everyone speechless. Laurent spoke first.

"Is it finally over?" Laurent asked as he reached for the hand of the one he had always loved, his beloved, Fabien.

"Yes, I believe it is. Come, let's return with Barthelme to our home so we may celebrate the demise of Stefan," Fabien suggested.

"Alright, but first give me a moment so I can thank someone who rightly deserves it," Laurent replied tenderly as he walked over to a corner of the shop where the Voodoo Queen is huddled in a corner and appeared to be trembling.

"Raphaella, I would like to thank you for all that you have done; if it had not been for you—Fabien and I would still be under threat of attack from Stefan," Laurent said tenderly.

Raphaella looked up at Laurent with wild eyes after she witnessed the spectacular series of events this evening; as she answered him— she could barely control her rage as she nearly spit out her words. "The two of you took the only friend I ever had, Jack—and used him as a vessel for your diabolical scheme to be reunited. I don't need your thanks—and I most certainly don't need vampires in my life! The only thing I wish and hope for is that someday—my friend Jack will find his way back and return!" as she broke down and cried uncontrollably.

"We did what we felt needed to be done!" Fabien said coldly. "How are the two of you so different than Stefan? You're all evil—I condemn both of you to hell as well!" Raphaella retorted as she turned away from Laurent's intense gaze, no longer concerned for her safety.

"I understand you're upset, Raphaella—but Fabien and I were destined to be together again, and nothing and no one could ever interfere with that," Laurent said, as he tried to sound sympathetic.

As he turned away from her to leave—she warned Laurent, "This isn't over," and for a brief moment, he motionlessly reflected on what she had just said as he turned around slowly to face her.

"What do you mean?" Laurent said as he felt that old feeling of anxiety building inside of him.

"You shall see vampire!" as she began to laugh.

Rarely, if ever has Laurent been shaken by mere words—especially words uttered from a human. However, Raphaella is no mere mortal, and her warning felt ominous—downright sinister.

"Are you coming, Laurent?" as Fabien returned to where he and Raphaella were speaking—prompting Laurent as he took his hand to lead him out of the Voodoo shop for the last time.

Raphaella heard the front door close and got up and walked over to the drawer where her bottle of Haitian rum was stored and gave herself a healthy pour; as she picked up the glass—she made a toast, "To my friend Jack, wherever you are—I toast the friendship we had—you are missed!" She said, as she took a large gulp of her rum—as Raphaella walked over to the round table where she had sat many times before, as she prepared to call on a spirit.

The Rolls arrived back at the estate, everyone felt the exhaustion from their battle, as they entered the mansion.

"Shall I pour you both some nourishment?" Barthelme asked. "Yes, I think that is in order, Barthelme," Laurent replied. "Right away, Master Laurent," Barthelme said as he exited the drawing-room.

"I cannot believe Stefan is gone for good!" Fabien said, finally he felt a sense of relief as he reached for Laurent's hand.

"Is he?" Laurent replied as he released his hand from Fabien's and walked over to the window—as he gazed upon the many great oak trees which lined their very long walkway, which lead to the mansion's front entry.

"What do you mean? You saw for yourself; his mother took him to the bowels of hell—the flames naturally consumed him. Didn't you hear his scream?—how can you doubt that Laurent?"

"Before we left, Raphaella said something to me that bothered me; it was almost as if she had issued me a warning that Stefan might return!" Fabien gave Laurent a puzzled look.

"Tonight, we witnessed first-hand how powerful some spirits are—what extraordinary abilities they possess, not unlike our abilities.

It appeared—the angrier the spirit, the more powers they possessed. You and I know that Stefan was filled with rage; that sort of energy doesn't vanish into thin air. What if it returned?" Laurent confided to Fabien.

"You don't think?" before Fabien completed his sentence—Barthelme returned to the drawing-room with an antique silver tray which carried two wine goblets filled with blood.

"Here we are, Master Laurent and Master Fabien," Barthelme said as he held the tray out for both vampires.

Both expressed their appreciation to their trusty servant. "Merci Barthelme" came the reply from each of his Masters. Each was seated in front of the roaring fireplace, Barthelme had prepared for them upon their return as the weather outside turned cold. The orange and yellow flames flickered before them in the fireplace as if the fire had performed some dance.

Fabien turned to Laurent and said, "I would like to make a toast,

May we never again be separated, not even for a second; here's to our union for now and all eternity!"

Laurent beamed, visibly touched by the sight of his lover's emotional toast as he answered him with a hearty "here, here!" as both drank from their goblets.

"Would you care for a refill?" Fabien asked.

"Yes, that would be delightful," Laurent answered back as he gazed longingly into his soulmate's eyes, which temporarily had turned from their azure blue color into a crimson red color. Something known to happen to a vampire's eyes whenever blood was consumed. Both immortals felt satisfied and adequately fed with the carafe of blood consumed—headed upstairs as the antique clock announced the impending daylight. The sun would be rising soon—each walked briskly up the long staircase, hand in hand, until finally they reached the master bedroom.

As they entered the bedroom, Fabien glanced at the portrait of himself as he appeared back in late eighteenth-century Paris.

"I certainly was a fine-looking man."

"You still are; you haven't changed a bit!" Laurent replied as each began to laugh.

"Come lay beside me on the bed and let me stroke your hair the way I always used to," Fabien suggested tenderly.

Meanwhile, back at the Voodoo Shop, Raphaella had done her very best to try and conjure up a spirit without any luck and had fallen asleep at the table. As she awakened, thinking, *perhaps my abilities have been weakened due to my having consumed an entire bottle of rum?* As she looked at her watch, the time read was six in the morning! She had been asleep at the table ever since the two vampires left her shop; that was nearly eight hours ago! She laid her head down on her arms and began to rest again when suddenly she was awakened by an entity enveloped in a red mist.

"You've finally come!" Raphaella greeted the spirit as it nodded, "Where are they?" The entity finally spoke, as it asked sternly.

"They went to their estate!" Raphaella replied, and as suddenly as the entity appeared—it had left.

In their bedroom, both vampires felt nourished and satisfied. Feeling Fabien's body next to his, Laurent questioned how he could be lead to believe Stefan could return. Indeed that was simply the rantings of a deranged woman—as he chuckled at the thought of it, and closed his eyes once more.

Suddenly, a red mist appeared near the bedroom window, followed by a figure's appearance! It was too faint to make out its identity from the bed even with vampiric eyesight—as his curiosity got the better of him—Laurent arose from the bed, careful not to awaken Fabien.

As he walked ever closer to the figure, some of the red mist surrounded and enveloped Laurent; almost drowning him— as if the red mist had developed tentacles that somehow pulled him ever closer to the figure until, finally, the figure's face became evident to Laurent, it was Stefan! The vampire opened his mouth to scream but couldn't. The figure in front of him became a liquid mass that entered Laurent's mouth—consuming him as the red mist disappeared entirely into Laurent's mouth.

Laurent merely stood motionless by the window; the red mist had entirely gone as he glanced back over at the bed where his beloved lay in an undead slumber.

Laurent walked over to the bed, laid back down—careful not to awaken Fabien, and closed his eyes. Shortly after the sun had set— Fabien revived and noticed the bed next to him empty. He sensed something wasn't quite right—as he left the room and used his lightning fast vampire speed and raced down the staircase and into the drawing room, where he found Laurent at Barthelme's neck, as he drained the blood of their trusted servant Barthelme.

Laurent turned his attention to Fabien to greet him in a mocking manner. Fabien merely stared at the spectacle in shock and horror.

"Good evening, my love, you've finally awakened! So sorry, but I decided I wanted some real nourishment, not just animal blood; I was in the mood for a human!" Instantly, Laurent's face transformed into Stefan's face as Fabien reacted in horror and disbelief. For a moment—Fabien was unable to utter a sound until finally he heard himself cry out, "No!"

"You thought you could rid yourself of me so easily?" Stefan said—his face had changed back to Laurent's, but spoke with the voice of Stefan.

"I don't understand?" Fabien managed to barely utter as he looked on in horror and began to tremble.

"Come now! —did you think you were the only one to perfect spirit possession?" Stefan asked sarcastically.

"No, I let you go once—but now you will never be rid of me! We were destined to be together from the very start—for all time, now come and join me as we say goodbye to Barthelme!"

From outside the stately mansion "Le Petit Fleur," another bloodcurdling scream was heard.

ABOUT THE AUTHOR

(Len Handeland)

Len Handeland has always enjoyed writing and drawn to being creative—as far back as he can remember. Back in middle school, when he and his classmates were assigned a book report, and the others groaned, Len cheered—not only being given an exciting novel to read but also composing the essay assignment. Everything had to be perfect, the spelling, grammar, and accuracy regarding the subject matter.

Later on—in his late teens, Len attended the fashion institute (FIT) in Manhattan studying fashion illustration; years later, he decided to pursue a career in the hair industry using his artistic training and creativity to excel in hair. After attending several creative writing classes and attending the San Francisco International writers' conference, he decided it was time for him to write a vampire novel of his own. Len is a big fan of Anne Rice's work (having read all of her Vampire Chronicles books) and credits her for inspiring him.

Len's afinity for horror and knowledge of the vampire genre gave him the ability to create a different story—where love is the only thing that matters and where the sexual orientation of his same-sex couples is less ambiguous.

The author is currently working on his second novel entitled "Requiem for Miriam," a murder, mystery, crime drama with a hint of paranormal added for extra intrigue, set in Manhattan and Westchester county in the 1980s. When Len isn't writing, some of his hobbies include reading and vegetarian cooking. Along with this, his other hobbies include hiking, biking, and billiards. He enjoys the performing arts and has trained in Martial Arts for over 25 years. Len lives in Palm Springs, California, with his husband, Byron, and their two tuxedo cats, Felix & Felicia (siblings). Handeland said, "I hope you enjoy reading this book and that it thrills and entertains and gives you a bit of a chill. I've had such a pleasure writing this, it truly was a labor of love!"

Printed in the United States
by Baker & Taylor Publisher Services